One Hundred Thousand Lights

A Love Song to India

Wow !

GARNETTE ARLEDGE

Garnette Arledge

Singing Stars,
Milton, New York

Drench With Splendour
On Crossing Brooklyn Ferry

Flow on, river! Flow with the floodtide with the ebb-tide!
Frolic on, crested and scallop-edg'd waves!
Gorgeous clouds of the sunset!

Drench with your splendour me,
Or the men and women of generations after me;
Cross from shore to shore, countless crowds of passengers.

Walt Whitman, From *Leaves of Grass*,

Part 11, lines 111-144

Cover and Author's Photograph: Meg Lundstrom©

Fourth Printing

ISBN-13: 978-0615652108
ISBN-10: 0615652107

DEDICATED

To

The Lotus Feet

Of All Beings

Author's Note to Her Readers about Grace and Kripa:

I love reading novels. I learn best from stories, particularly from Jane Austen. Now I can say I love writing a novel. So I have taken that love to share with you, what I hope you will find is a good story about a techie in her thirties named Grace who finds her lost treasure.

For ages grace in India, *Kripa*, has been known as the Sanskrit word for the grace of God as well as a woman's name just like in my own family here. However being age-old and Indian, the concept has many variations: Hari Kripa (grace of God), Shastra Kripa (grace of the Scriptures), Guru Kripa (grace of the Guru) and my favorite, Atma kripa (grace of the inner Self). As a human being and an author I have been blessed with all these graces through out my life – as even the horrible can be kripa, i.e. divorce, death, dearth.

Kripa fascinates me, so I have written a novel examining metaphorically how Divine Grace intervenes in one rather feckless woman's life. Even the title, which I've nicknamed *Light,* came to me by sheer grace at just the right time. Believe me, it went through several incarnations in the twenty years it took me to wrestle with the writing angels including NaNoWriMo, national novel writing month. Try that; it is fun.

As Krishna says in the final chapter of the Bhagavad Gita, *verse 18.66,* "Setting aside all meritorious deeds (Dharma), just rely completely on My will (with firm faith and loving contemplation): Do not fear." Enough theology, have a joyous time diving into the novel. May Grace be with you – and you know it. I wish to thank everyone and everything, yes even my laptop, for making this novel possible. A partial list of my gratitudes may be found in the Afterword.

Garnette Arledge, Milton, NY, 2012

CHAPTER 1, Mahashivaratri

Shivarathri is a huge opportunity for us to cleanse our minds and climb up the spiritual ladder —
Sri Sathya Sai Baba

When the playful 757 swoops circling low again and again over the Persian Gulf, Grace Avery chokes as the water bottle bangs her mouth. Furious, fearful, she mops at the overflow on her now soaked tee shirt, checks once again the seat belt tight, secure. She's still slightly airsick from the fuel odor now more so with this nonsensical spiraling. The pilot's laughter crackles over the intercom, his antics problematic five years after 9/11 when even tested passengers go into alert to unusual behavior. Still Grace enjoys adventure, long flights, faraway places, so adjusting her mobile and herself, she keys in another note to her running cyber journal.

"One hour before landing in Mumbai, flying east and low over the fabled jewel known as the Arabian Sea, an intense force seizes me, a benediction sizzling as a cleansing power hurtles itself up the innermost core of my spine. In the central channel, a red hot energy zings to my attention as it rushes by the solar plexus, through the heart and over the top of my head to the brow, then spreads out in dozens of dancing, tingling sensations throughout the body. Walt Whitman says it best, *drenched with splendor*.

Laughing, singing a childhood song inside herself: *Raindrops keep falling on my head*, she glances up. This sparkling sensation, better than champagne, has no visible cause. Something mysterious is going on inside her, settling her queasy stomach despite the high-octane fumes. Somehow, somewhere Grace Avery, former senior partner in a high tech multinational publishing firm, mislaid herself.

Now she finds to her shock that she's on her way to India with suddenly new eyes, thanks to the book on her lap. "The saints of all religions," says the author, "left a trail of faith, a power in which we can walk . . .When you get weak, and feel you could drown, go under . . . think of them and what they did, and let that power flow through your blood."

Again, Grace pulls out her mobile, "This cyber journal is better than traveling with a man, a machine won't betray me" of the gift which came along with the plane fare and the book she's reading. She supposes the non-fiction book is a guide to India, light reading, homework, for the India trip, just another going away gift especially for the journey. Yet once in the air as she reads *Saints Alive* in astonishment, she realizes something is definitely up with this author Hilda Charlton, who is she anyway? And so she dives again in her journal:

Cyber Journal
"The flight is twenty-four hours from New York via a layover in London to change planes to Gulf Air. Nothing to do but read and remember my woes, so bored with myself. After a long layover breakfast stop in Dubai, we head for Mumbai in an ancient plane where I am overcome with a deep sense of gratitude for the plane ticket and new smart phone, yet but mostly for this incredible gift, the book *Saints Alive*. It seems like a collection of teachings on various world religions.

"Yet I feel myself responding inwardly to the book, as if in answer to an ancient call from those within it: Sri Sathya Sai Baba, Ramana Maharshi, Yogi Ramsuratkumar, Swami Vivekananda, Sri Ramakrishna, Mirabai, Kabir, Poet Rabindranath Tagore, Sri Aurobindo, Mother, Mother, Mother India. Jesus Christ, Mother Mary, St. Thérèse, Jeanne d'Arc, George Washington Carver. There's an aroma of roses in the air now. Could it be coming from the book?

"The book tells of Hilda's time and spiritual adventures in the 60's in Puttaparthi, even

Bangaluru before she went back to the States, New York City. And I hear the call to come to these ancient holy sites. O, thank you, Mother India for calling me forth, for this welcome to your sacred land and for the adventures embedded in this book.

"And it is as if the very stones, the dust, the ancient site of India, sacred soil of spiritual lifetimes, bids me joy, bids welcome to a spiritual adventure.

"So now, I am to be here in Asia, in India of all places, leaving behind all the pain and grief of the double betrayal, personal and professional. I feel like I have jumped out of the safety net."

She snaps her fingers dispelling reoccurring thoughts of her previous work assignment to Singapore, then on to Tahiti with Mike McCall. They had ventured out in a catamaran on a clear evening into the gold, peach and violet sunset, only to capsize in waist deep water. Stumbling onto a handy atoll, they both laughed and fell passionately into each other's arms, swept away in the Pacific Ocean enchantment. In the moments of high union, cheeky Mike had blurted, "Marry me! What a team we make, in love and on the job." In the hours of sunrise, dawn spectacular while Grace laughed breezily, Mike campaigned for their marriage.

At last, she agreed to take small steps together once they were back in Manhattan, to see if the romance would outlast the adventure. When Grace hesitated to commit knowing she cannot love deeply now. "I'm done with all that, it's just romance."

"Nonsense." Mike, grinning, said, "We would be a great team, no messy emotions. Try it, Gracie, you might like it." Less than a month later, he maneuvered himself into her position. She was out. Now she's on her way in an effort to prove she is the best one for the job with the Hindu tech bosses.

Grace pauses, unwilling to ruin the fresh first page of her new life by deleting the last inadvertent lines. Frustrated, she grabs paper and pen from her flight bag. Then sighs, puts down the pen, sees that the high altitude flight causes the peacock blue ink to stain her left hand, her writing hand. She gropes for a wet tissue, dabbing at the mess she's made. Ink falls onto her beige travel pants, dribbling down to stain her politically inappropriate white shoes.

She grimaces and shoves the tissue away. She'll arrive wet, swamped, on assignment in India. Now shaking, sick with fear and dehydration, airsick from the wild looping of the plane, Grace weeps behind her hand. Blown away by travel and the nerve-wracking, insane circling over the Persian Gulf, Grace focuses on the coming pan-Indian festival of MahaShivarathri this year in mid-February.

Chugging on the last of her lifeline Poland Springs, she frowns at her quick mood change; she's annoyed to have thrown away the feeling of great blessing welcoming her to India. She notes the similarity of the feelings to the blessing so like those last experienced on the mid-Pacific layover in Hawaii where dancing greeters offer frangipani leis to raise the vibration of the incoming tourists. Mike said it's just quaint hospitality but something deeper was going on in Aloha, known only to the Hawaiians. What's with love anyway? Then her mind wanders further on that same trip 'Ah, Tahitian nights, white hibiscus' – no, she stops that wayward thought. As she settles herself, shakes off the distress, adds more text into the cyber journal.

"Welcome, welcome, my daughter, welcome."

She pauses, allowing hospitality to sink in. Seemingly sacred India has spoken her own words of hospitality:

"May I find the peace in my soul here that the betrayals destroyed. May I find something that will take the cork out of me so I can get on with a good life."

With this quick prayer embedded in the journal, Grace carefully tucks the smart phone back into her carry-all and slings it onto her chest for its protection: for her own heart and the machine's. Then turns her gaze out the window at the cerulean waters rushing away beneath the plane's shadow as it speeds eastward towards the white beach that means landing in Mumbai.

Swiftly on the Arabian Sea below, aircraft's shadow racing ahead, backlit by the setting sun, wooden fishing boats tilting in the water then on the horizon, come tiny islands, later modern skyscrapers necklacing the blue waters. Tears of heart's delight burst from her hazel green eyes, showering the back of the airline seat before her.

Home, home, the fabled spiritual heartland of civilization. A dream and labor with twelve years of struggle since graduating from Princeton, at last coming true. And Grace knows that the Spiritual Masters she has read about in *Saints Alive* during the long flight hold out hands in welcome. "It's been a hard time getting here.
But now is the time. I've come to dig in like the author did – perhaps. "

"And Margaret Woodrow Wilson would be pleased." Hilda stayed in India for eighteen years digging in with the Masters 'but you go direct to them' – something like that. What does she means? I'll bet I find out, Grace muses.

Seated four rows behind Grace, Mike McCall ducks his head. "What a trip she is," he laughs to himself. "It's trick or treat every time with Gracie," he sighs, wondering how the hell his PA managed to get him on the same airline, same flight, same itinerary as the floundering woman ahead. Was it a simple snafu or deliberate? She had been Grace's right hand assistant before he outmaneuvered them, to occupy the wizard's chair in the department. Or had she simply been witless? Yet another possibility occurs to him: the PA did it on Grace's suggestion. Whatever, it did not bode well. Just when he had thrown her a bone with this last assignment. "No problem, I can always outdo them. Just keep a cool head, man," he vows to stay out of Grace's sight because he thinks she's addictive. Horribly addictive. He wants no part of those warm feelings, they hurt too much – and get in the way of his intentions for his life now.

In the cacophony of the frantic airport, waiting for customs, her first sight among the mass of humanity is the very guy she wishes most to avoid. Grace waves dismissively as Mike McCall surprisingly looms up among the raucous mob scene of the arrivals and long queues. She's determined not to reopen anything with him since he stole her job so she ducks behind a tall traveler. Bad enough their Singapore meeting ends leaving them stranded in the deep water off a South Pacific atoll. His silence since their Tahitian night under the stars confirms his guilt; he betrayed her at Mystix. Well, she has one last assignment there; let no more time be wasted on him.

Immersed in her own private culture shock, she steadies herself while standing in the queue swaying with the noxious airport odors, mostly a horrid mix of airplane fuel, unwashed bodies, animal urine. A spider seems to confirm her overwhelm. The uproar dazes, bludgeons her senses. Grace stares hypnotically, immobilized, bewildered and anxiety-laden in the vast land of ancient mystery at her nemesis, a spider. She does not speak even one of the 450 surviving languages of this country, she muses trembling, deciding not to attempt alerting the unlucky man ahead in line.

A brown, furry spider working her careful way slowly and deliberately clamoring on the agent's desk before her eyes, traveling determinedly over the rubber stamp, down the ink pad, across the mountain of the uniformed coat sleeve, then slinging her web across the counter, hops onto the nylon jacket of the British passport holder in front of Grace. Seemingly Arachne has her destination firmly under control. On and on, over the navy blue jumper she scampers, heading towards the man's neck. What if she's poisonous? Malarial? A carrier of Lyme Disease? Plague? Seen as a pick-up line?

Absently she shuffles her baggage tag, visa, passport, itinerary, her thoughts more in Knoxville than Mumbai, jarred back to the present by the spider's journey on her high wire from official to passenger ahead.

Grace happens to have respect for spiders metaphorically. The vision of Arachne from inside herself spinning out ancient secrets of the universe's structural connections, encoded in her webs like neural pathways. Diamond drops of dew sunlit on fencepost. Rose planter laced with shining cobweb. Greek goddesses, destiny, mythology, PBS particle theory, tumble through Grace's travel weary mind. Spiders pull their truth from inside out to connect.

And her feelings say, remember, don't touch anything: be alert to the dangers of an unfamiliar culture. Whereas at home in New York, she would simply mention to the man before her at Zabar's that a spider heads for his neck. Here, in the land of karma, does she speak to a stranger? Her mind becomes swamped and indecisive. Suddenly the spider falls under her own momentum from the tourist's shoulder, throwing out her own lifeline from inside her belly to clamber onto the scuffed floor underfoot. Ah, good omen after all, if a spider can take care of herself, by herself, so can Grace Avery.

As she finishes the landing processes, all the pre-trip briefings come flooding into Grace's consciousness and takes over her brain: what this well-wisher and that ex-pat had warned of the dangers and necessities for survival. She packed for light traveling and a quick get-away from India.

"What do you mean, my baggage is not here?" Seeing the opaque brown eyes of the indifferent official, she shrugs, "OK, so the adventure starts with lost luggage. I'll just buy some great Indian clothes here – and leave them for the hotel staff when I check out." She takes the offered pen, writing her Parsi host's contact information on the well-thumbed Lost and Found pad. Shrugging on her knapsack with her overnight things, she turns to look for the moneychanger's booth. Smugly, she straightens her back, "I'm a corporate professional and I can do this."

Grace notes her hands are dirty again and ink-stained from the flight. Her clothes, made of wrinkle-resistant tensile are ink splotched, wrinkled and travel limp. Even her Tilley hat is too much for her. She looks foolish even to herself with her red hair tumbling out of it. She feels unwashed. She is alone among the grime, stench and roaring confusion in the luggage area, armed guards and frantically hopeful luggage carriers screaming, noise blasting. Still she feels an undercurrent of joy. 'I did it. I got to India. I am here alone. There is not one person on this planet who knows where I am at this moment.' Shouts and screams of taxi, hotel, money changing, careen through the air. And yet even through her India travel innocence comes the knowing, there is something very wrong in the air outside customs.

But what about the blessing she was promised by coming to India?

"Wow, the Mermaid," Mike himself materializes after his own entry clearing, comes up, unable to resist her after all, slipping his arm causally around her waist, "Now we can work together again, cara." He halts in mid-motion when she freezes, giving him a look of pure venom. He shrugs his gym-perfected shoulders, his jaw tightens and walks on with his Australian bounce soon lost in the melee. "There goes my lost friend," she thinks. "He's only being seductive again."

No, he's a water witch; she dismisses the longing. He lured her into exotic depths she has no intentions of exploring. Does he even remember my name is Grace Avery? *Cara*, so affected to use that lovely Italian endearment, darling. He's from Sydney. Sure, their clients had loved the piece she filed on the full moon sail to a secluded Tahitian beach known only to surfers and flying fish. She had won an award for it. Plus a bonus. Mike is winsome and a good lover, no doubt. Still. Grace watches him retreating, feeling she's made her point. "And I know he's the one who stole my job. Now he wants to cuddle? Never. I'd rather be alone than with him."

She submerges the direction of her thoughts about Mike's gentle, loving ways, "That's not a path I want to go down," she tells herself firmly, getting a solid grip on her mind. "It's a good thing I have a cool head," immersing herself into the Indian Rite of Passage, called the Mumbai International Airport.

The shrieking chaos of diverse bags, suitcases, duffels, sacks, trunks, backpacks and plastic shopping bags in myriad colors and sizes and aromas with fastenings from gold-trimmed to hemp twine. She swigs her regulated water. Giving up all Mike's sweetness that only masks trouble is no deal she concludes; partnering in a sure-fire Tennessee water-bottling venture suits her just fine. "This mad dash to India will be my last wanderlust assignment," she promises herself leaving the Knoxville airport. "And perhaps her inner response was right, telling me I'm too emotional flying around the world for a one-shot tech deal – on the hopes of restoring her position – but I can dig in one place. I do have a solid, down to earth plan. I will do it, too. I can. I will. I must."

The British tourist, the one who had NOT been bitten, no thanks to Grace, throws his luggage around nonchalantly. Yet, he's bouncing off the walls, darting here and there as if he were an old India hand, finally converting his pounds into rupees at the bank queue in front of her. He smiles at Grace as he turns, as if they are acquainted simply because in the customs line together. She decides not to mention the spider and barely nods back formally.

"Your first trip to India?"

Is it so obvious? Must be. So she decides to be truthful, choosing humility for the first time as her response. What would it help to display bravada when she feels so miniscule among the chaotic run amok? "Yes, it's a bit much right now."

"Are you booked somewhere? Do you know where you are going? Would you feel comfortable sharing a taxi with me? I'm afraid the balloon's up, as they used to say during the Blitz."

"No, no, I'm fine. Someone is meeting me. What do you mean? Is there trouble? Is that why all the Uzies out there?"

"Sadly yes, I'm afraid it's not the great entry into Holy India you might have had in mind. Seems there's been 'an incident' and the troops are called in. Landlord, tenant thing. The usual."

"Look," Grace says back, touched by his attempt to spare her concern, "If you are offering to share a taxi, maybe you are the one who needs a ride. There's a car meeting me. We could give you a lift to your hotel if you like. This seems like an extraordinarily bad time to be taking public transportation alone."

"Well then, the tables are turned. I was going to protect you," He pauses, puts out his hand to shake hers, "Niles Dashwood. Yes, I would appreciate a ride into Mumbai, not Bombay anymore."

They step out of the illusion of safety behind the Arrivals glass barrier into a human morass, a crowd of men with thin brown arms and beseeching faces and wailing

8

screams. Passing through the barrier of relative safety in the airport, into a mix of hawksters, tourist guides, money changers, taxis, tuktuks, pedicabs and bicycles: solicitors of all kinds, yearning, yearning. Pickpockets, thieves, legitimate businesspersons, hopeful family members, returning relatives and workers, she sees Mike hopping into a limo with all his luggage intact.

No lost baggage for the big shot Aussie. She frowns. The noise level is terrific as if a Greek Chorus had broken ranks to shriek out the wails of innumerable dramas. But there is a hand-lettered sign Grace Avery. And just before pick-pocketing, they whisk into a mid-range Ford Taurus to safety behind glass again. Not that window glass is all that safe, she thinks, overwhelmed and disoriented by the sensory overload.

Although Grace does not know it, her car is also considered limousine, India style, yet she's grateful for the air conditioning within minutes of disembarking. Coached that her entry into India would be a knock down, drag out culture shocking experience from airport to city. Instead being in an air-conditioned car with a driver blows her mind. She laughs. Niles Dashwood smiles, he's experienced, but they share the joy. To be in India at cow dust time.

Mumbai offers high modernity of skyscrapers and global logos in a blaze of neon amid the prevailing traffic pollution in the world's largest democracy. Yet the brief span of time passing day to night in India where only the sky remains traditional overhead. In 1947, at Independence, in village India, cow dust time would be walking down a dirt lane passing one room wattle homes, seeing tiny clay dishes filled with ghee and cloth wicks shining the holy light on the doorsill, incense burning inside at the quick change from the brief dusk to black night. "India among her thousands of odors still has her incense now on dashboards an altar of spiritual figures, artwork of the gods, whether car, bus or semi," Niles notes. "Each vehicle broadcasts in profuse spray paint the region, owner's belief system and/or popular culture. If one knows the symbols, each one is like a calling card or huge billboard of the driver's tastes."

Instead of looking for some evidence of ancient India, Grace gazes at the ghost eyelash of the moon in the faintly coral and blue sky above the high Royal Palm trees as a noisy flocks of crows settle even around the airport. A sacred cow bumps along the narrow lanes before the freeway at the side the Ford. Outside the car, seemingly millions of people press on the roadside.

"It is rush hour," the driver comments dryly as the car snakes through the mélange. "It is always rush hour in Bombay," Niles says, unconsciously using the British misnomer of Mumbai. Politely, no one corrects him in the car. Some things require getting used to.

At each traffic signal, even with the windows up for the AC, begging faces peer and press anxiously. Seeing their straining faces, the imploring crescendos rising until the green light blinks, unsettles Grace. She expects to see poverty, she's heard of the terrible poverty. It is here, even more dire than she could imagine. Niles lets down his window, handing out ballpoint pens to the begging children. "Although they want candy, it's better to bring packs of pens to give out. If they have a pen, they can go to school." Grace gags, overcome with the need, as much as the stench.

What she did not foresee are the Indian women. Kilometer after kilometer, silent women stand, shoulder to shoulder, frequently a child akimbo on hip. Standing with dignity, their posture impeccable, mostly the saris terribly worn of cheap nylon but in bright colors, faces wracked with tiredness, dirt, hunger, disease. And still, the beautiful spine and shoulders erect and at ease. She was to observe many, many, even myriads of women standing in the wreck of domestic life, with the same indomitable stance in odd contrast to the impassive khaki-clad soldiers with weapons guarding the long, narrow road. Traffic is practically at a standstill, creeping bumper to bumper through gasoline-polluted air. India's ancient fabric of life overwhelmingly packed with people, animals, and all on the roads.

They drive warily through the city, sensing something terribly wrong in the air. "I wonder if this desperate feeling is part of the India vibration? There is a tremendous amount of fear in the air. Is it mine, or contiguous to the city?"

"The news is bad. You will see a full report on the news tonight," Niles says. "Here we are, at the five star Taj Mahal Hotel. I'm staying here. Thank you for the ride, I hope sometime I will be able to return the favor. See ya," grabbing his bag, he leaps out of the car and waves the car on. He did not offer to tip the driver.

"Humph, that's odd; to leave so abruptly, well, please drive on. Are we almost there?"

Shortly this is true; adding another layer of Grace's culture shocks, the Ford turns into a circular drive, past a private guard, into the spacious landscaped grounds of her host's high-rise apartment complex. Mr. Arvind opens the penthouse's front door with hospitality to the large, luxurious flat overlooking a jogging track and the Back Bay then further out the Arabian Sea, close by the Queen's Necklace Promenade, on what was once called the Marine Drive and has been since renamed as the Netaji Subhashchandra Bose Road. The shore of Back Bay includes the famed Chowpatty Beach of Mumbai, now unswimmable with pollution. Her hosts point out the joggers and swimmers despite the postings. On the balcony, above the tall tree canopy, Grace is offered a cool golden fruit drink in a frosted glass.

As they become acquainted, Grace bringing news of the mutual friend who had arranged the gracious opportunity, Joan Zul, the co-worker who gave Grace the Hilda book. The talk centers around Hilda, who had known the wife's parents in the late 1940's. The family befriends Hilda when she and her dance troupe first came to India, performing charity benefits for education and medical centers. "She would meditate day and night, then be bright and powerful in the performances. What a fierce spiritual being, what a laugh, what warmth. We honor her memory. You are blessed to have her book to guide you. She always pointed to other masters, yogis. But it takes a master of the universes to recognize one truly."

Afterwards, gratefully Grace surveys her suite, ecstatic herself at showering. The shower room turns out to be a large cement square with a curb-high division in the center. On one wall is a portable showerhead with a long coiled arm. A white plastic stool. A white plastic bucket. Soap on a rope. On the other side of the curb are rows of generous towels and fluffy terrycloth robes and the water closet. Grace gratefully savors her first cold shower in India during 110-degree weather, rubbing herself as dry as the humidity permits. She expects cold showers so that is what she receives. Only to have her Parsi hosts laugh with delight when they find this out, over the delectable light salad dinner. Later, they show her how to turn on the hot water geyser, a welcome lesson.

By 1:30 a.m., traffic far below has slowed to a murmur. The silence seems to be uneasy, only a moment from uproar again. Grace wakes, mulls over the news of violence from the people protesting landlords against rising rents. "We know we are on a tinderbox in India, so many passionate believers. In Gandhiji's time, even as his followers practiced non-violence, it was a bloodbath at any moment.

"The technological revolution has tempered those passions somewhat as more and more geeks come from all levels of society – even women practice this computer to-do" – he smiles unaware Grace was just such a tech practitioner. He goes on to explain that his religion is Zoroastrian, the family tracing their ancestry to Persia – "although we did not come with Alexander the Great, but with the active trading during the time of your St.

Paul. We are called Parsi in India now. Farsi in the Mid-East.'"
"But this subcontinent, you will find millions, billions if you can visualize that, people who are still without any real subsistence. And they get excited, very emotional. So we must have order. You will be fine in ashrams. Do not worry. Our troops know how to handle the crowd."

As she reviews her host's assessment of the front-page news and the riots, her fears rumble. He seems fatalistic, remote in this penthouse distanced from the lines of women along the highway. She listens to the overhead fan, deliberately calming herself. She is still on New York time, it takes a long clock watching before going back to sleep at dawn, but as she drifts off, she hears a voice laughing, "Welcome home, daughter."

And tomorrow she will board her plane to Bangaluru, the Silicon Valley of India. Grace thinking, I wouldn't want to be alone in a striking mob . . .

Mike

From the Mystix company car sent to pick him up at the Mumbai International Airport, Mike spies Grace getting into a Ford with a clearly British tourist. He groans with jet-fatigue and something more than the blanketing humidity that the brief encounter with his former colleague and lover sparks. "I thought I was done with her; she's poison. Makes me feel all sorts of things I've left behind. Emotions – and I suppose some guilt, fear, lust of course. But I really am the better man for her job. I don't let feelings get in my way – well, that is for long."

As the thoughts jam one on another, Mike suddenly notices that the bumper-to-bumper traffic crawling through a massive troop of men in olive green tunics and knee-high red socks. Men at attention, carrying heavy weapons. Men with trouble on their minds that has nothing to do with a failed romance. "What's going on here?" he says to the hunched shoulder of the driver, who despite the air conditioning is sweating heavily.

"Nothing, nothing," the man begins, catches Mike's glare in the rearview mirror, "Ah, sir, just another strike against the slumlords. It will go nowhere. Soon be under control – as usual people will gain nothing."

Mike pressed his lips against a quick retort. This man may be in one of the thousands of sects in India: he did not come to get involved in politics just to do business. Maybe a holiday afterwards.

12

"I see, so the women lined up facing the armed soldiers are tenants?"

"No, sir, they are standing in sympathy, hoping to forestall violence."

"Well, that's good for me to know. Thank you."

The car inches along the wide commercial boulevards into the quick dark. Vaporous street lights flicker on as the driver steers the big car onto broader, Acacia-lined streets.

High stucco walls, ancient walls line the avenue. Occasional ornate gates, carved wood or new stainless steel show driveways curving through lush gardens. Tall Coconut Palms, Cassia, even an ancient Banyan hang over perimeter walls giving the panorama an atmosphere of privilege and history as they cruise through a placid area of the city.

"Here, sir.

The driver pulls sedately into a wide cobbled driveway, the gates opening automatically as the car noses inside the walls. They glide slowly deeper into the compound, a terraced hive of private quarters inside landscaped gardens with as center stage a mighty Kailaspati tree sheltering the multilevel complex. Mike's tough veneer loosens as he inhales gardenia and oleander so beloved by his grandmother in Australia.

His host Sushil Patel, dressed in the custom-made all whites of the upper crust Indian at home, waits on the colonnaded verandah along side a white-haired butler dressed in perfectly laundered kurta (shirt) and dhoti (wrapped traditional male wear), who bowing, opens the limo door. "My friend, welcome," Sushil bows, palms folded to heart.

"Phil, glad to see you – it's been too long, buddy," Mike bounces out of the vehicle, clasping his college roommate by the shoulders. "Now I see you in your habitat, I understand where you get your calm."

"Oh, Mike. Good to welcome you here. Not so much like Sydney after all – but you are here now. Come, let me give you a drink. Smooth flight?"

"Crazy loon pilot dipping and diving the Gulf out of Dubai then running into a lost love who cut me dead in the airport just now, otherwise it was fine."

"Tell me more, or better wait until dinner. Do you wish to dine here or sample some

Mumbai nightlife?"

"Definitely stay in. I'm expecting jet lag soon. But I must say this is quite the place, Phil, I thought you were just a regular bloke like me."

"No, no, no, this is not mine. I am only the youngest grandson as my father is also. That's why I am a working stiff like you."

"You wish, buddy. But actually I am here on a job – I've had a promotion thing, got to check in with the techies in Bangalore in a couple of days. And, that former girlfriend to avoid. She's someone who cannot stand me – anymore."

"Not another one? No, kidding aside. Sorry. What did you do to earn her enmity."

"Oh, not so much. Took her job – for one thing. My new job. Then I decided not to follow up after our try-out honeymoon in Tahiti."

"Mike, you better watch your back. India has a way of settling old scores. Besides it's bad timing, buckaroo, my airline is going out on sympathy strike with the Tenants Protest tomorrow. You won't be able to get a plane out of the city after dawn."

"All right then, I go tonight. Can you get me on a flight? You flying it preferably."

"No can do, not a strikebreaker myself, kiddo, but I will see if I can get you a seat. Here, go into my apartment, take a shower, shave, why don't you, while I make some calls to see what can be arranged."

When Mike emerges freshly groomed with a bit of the travel weariness sluiced off in the state of the art shower, he's dressed in clean travel jeans, tee shirt and blazer. He finds Phil chatting with a stately, sari-clad beauty. "Ah, Mother, this is Mike. My mother Sharada Devi. You remember meeting her in Sydney. You took her out to your grandmother's studio to see the gardens. She's willing to meet you again even after hearing some of our Aussie hi-jinks."

"None true," Mike says bowing over her delicate hand, "He's a charmer your boy but not to be believed when he's spinning stories."

She laughs, "I have five sons, Mike, I know this one through and through. I don't rely on your blarney either."

"So will you be my mother then too?" Mike responds.

She turns with a graceful trail of her silk sari, laughing kindly, "Come now, we will at least feed you before you get back in the air. This way, please."

They cross the central garden, winding among the rose blooms, and up five low steps onto a broad veranda, with low Indian dining table, candlelit, among potted ferns.

Sushil excuses himself to check on a flight for Mike as well as to monitor the strike. Sharada Devi gestures to Mike to sit, and spreading her silk serviette, says, "I remember well that you have the disconcerting habit of blurting out important questions, as if they were a joke, Mike. But if you need a mother who will tell you the truth, I can do that."

Mike ducks his head, confused by her directness. "Mrs. Patel, I am not the same happy-go-lucky college roommate you remember from Sydney. Things happened, unspeakable things, I've changed – I hope for the better. I'm a tough guy now. Hard. A new man and proud of it. Dog eat dog."

"Well, we loved you then just as you were. You cannot have lost your soft heart – entirely. Nothing too awful . . .

Blindsided by her compassion and directness, he had forgotten she is a psychiatrist able to go directly to the emotional core.

Tears glaze his blue eyes but do not fall. With the serviette, he pretends to wipe his mouth after a cooling sip of mango juice, to forestall the flood he was trying, had been trying so desperately to dam for a decade.

Like the mother of sons she is, Sharada Devi quietly places her hand on the back of his. "Your grandmother?"

"Yes." Long pause as he harshly controls himself. Deep breath, sigh. "Ok, I will tell you . . . German-hating thugs broke into her studio – she was ninety for God's sake. Beat her – horrible things, sprayed hateful slogans on the walls and then . . . "

"She died."

The atrocity looms like Ayers Rock, as Mike once again uncovers the buried memory of the day he dropped in on his grandmother, minutes after the violence. "She was still alive when I got there, she died in my arms, saying "Forgive them, they know not what they do."

"Ahh, quoting the Christian Bible. Thinking of you even as she lay dying. Incredible woman." Silence falls.

"Well, that's my story."

"And you are still working on the forgiveness part?"

Mike squirms, "Nope, it didn't work. I tried, Ma, I cannot. I needed her to stay with me. She changed the world with her love."

Silence.

"Yes, Mike, I will be your mother. Don't worry. You have come to the right place at the right time. You have a family now."

"What's this? You kidnapping my mom?" Sushil enters the portico, joking.

"Hush, son. Mike is now more than your college roommate; I have just officially made him your brother. So be good boys and have your dinner nicely."

Sushil at 36, used to his mother's ways, seats himself, winks at Mike and says, "OK, Ma whatever you say. BTW, Mike, I have a sunrise flight for you to Trivandramnapuram, it's the only thing leaving."

"How far is that from Bangalore?"

"About five-hour flight."

"So I could drive it if necessary."

"Not at all. It would take several days. A train 17 hours. No, what I recommend is that you do go to Trivandrum, then get yourself down to Kovalam Beach for MahaShivaratri, the great all-Hindu festival. You could come with us to Puttaparthi except the place will be mobbed. Not a great time to experience Bhavagan Sathya Sai Baba for first darshan.

His mother says, "After the crowd leaves, we will stay on there for some time, so then you come join us. Sushil will arrange a flight and I will introduce you at the ashram."

"And in the meantime, you will enjoy the beach, the surf, the fresh fish and the bathing beauties," Sushil says, "wait out the strike, experience the Arabian Sea surf."

"I have to entrench my position in Bangalore by Monday."

"Not to worry; it will happen in the right way. There's a negotiation going on now for some strikebreakers from Russia or Bulgaria, I'll keep you posted."

"And what's so enticing about Kovalam Beach that you want me there?"

The mother says: "I have a feeling. You must go there."

Grace

Grace arrives back at the Mumbai Airport before dawn on MahaShivaratri, the most holy and festive occasion in all of India. She heads blindly through the interior terminal for her Air India flight south. Or it should have been Air India, but there are soldiers with weapons on alert in the street of Mumbai quelling the anti-landlord uprising now with a sympathy airline strike. So Bulgarians have agreed, for a price, to supply planes and Russians the crews as her host predicted. Her first Subcontinent experience is chaotic, Grace, confused by the turmoil in the terminal, is directed to another gate across the field.

Are the planes B-52's like her grandfather built in World War II? Can those old birds still get off the ground? He had handed on his fierce love of the United States to her. But now, she must be mistaken; hopefully these are newer models. Hopes dampen, for when seated and in the air, barely it seems, water starts trickling from the overhead bulkheads in her row. A woman in Duchesse silk satin sari trimmed with 24 karat gold designs pulls out her Burberry raincoat, demanding from the unshaven stewards a change of seat. Grace hums "Raindrops keep falling on my head" to self-soothe. Then Grace hunkers down damp and discouraged. An Indian airlines pilot slips in close-by, because he cannot be legally working, tells her "no more room" settling into the now vacant but soggy seat. They join in singing "Raindrops keep falling." They laugh together nicely, yet Grace surprised at the repeat of her thoughts.

He is all charm and charisma, pulling out a miniature banana, peeling it, and offering the pale fruit. Forewarned not to eat any fruit in India, except that with heavy peel, leaving only coconuts and bananas and mangoes and papayas, she accepts it timidly to find it unimaginably sweet and comforting. Realizing his kindness is ingrained; Grace thanks him. Polite, but keeping her distance. Formal. She does remember not to talk to strangers on planes or in hotels, even in ashrams, but that seems impossible in a subcontinent with such sweet people.

'Your first time in India?' he says conversationally.

Grace nods. Clearly.

'And you find Mumbai under siege, I am so sorry. It is a beautiful city. I hope you had a chance to see Bose Road and the view of the Arabian Sea?" She melts her pretended reserve, dissolving at his gracious manner, and such a considerate welcome to India.

"O, yes, I did as a matter of fact, I stayed on Bose last night, someone in New York arranged for one of her business associates to befriend me when she found out I was planning on coming to Bangalore, um Bangalorum, Bengaluru I mean."

"There, now, I have said too much," she says. And instantly wishes she hadn't said that either.

He beams. "Bangaluru, so near to Sri Sathya Sai Baba of Puttaparthi. My parents are devotees. I attended his schools for the youth of India. Education in Human Values programs. Massive water projects. Feeding the hungry population. Free hospitals, operations for children that restore sight, repair hearts, legs to walk and run. You have heard of the SuperSpeciality Hospitals, where even for the most complicated of procedures there is no charge? Lives saved, eyesight restored, diseases cured . . ."

Grace nods, put at ease by his manner and his knowledge of the traditional holy man whom millions in India and around the world acknowledge as a true teacher whose absolute consistency of bliss, giving service (seva) and divine love proves his truth (Sathya). When she first read of his mission in *Saints Alive* on the plane over the Atlantic, her heart strangely warmed:

In a letter to his older brother when Sathya Sai was twenty, he wrote: "I have a task to foster all mankind to ensure all lives full of bliss. I will not give up my mission or my determination. I know I will carry them out."

The pilot folds his hands in the traditional Hindu greeting of heart to heart (Namascar), bowing from the wholeness in him to the wholeness in her.

"Yet you are traveling alone?"

Hmm, must she give everything away to strangers? He senses Grace's reserve and immediately backtracks.

"Do you know how to get to Swami?" Grace shakes her head, saying: "No idea. Just going to Bangaluru. But you must, of course, know how and I would be glad to accept your advice there. All I know is that this plane goes to Bangaluru and it's about five hours by taxi to his ashram."

"Well, yes. And there are planes now directly to Puttaparthi you could have taken. But you are on a flight to Thiruvananthapuram. Yet you think you are going to Bangaluru."

"Oh no, where is that? Far from Swami? How will I get a hostel? I was given the name of one by some friends in New York.

"But you cannot stay there clearly tonight. You will be at least 17 hours from Bangaluru. Anyway, a hostel is not for you. I will guide you to the hotel we use in the airlines."

So here's a dilemma after all the warnings she had received on caution about the legendary con-persons in Asia. "You are a tender morsel ripe for plucking," Her brother Christopher used to say, "do not give yourself away. Be firm, take care of yourself."

But this man knows Baba; his parents are devotees. He is genuinely appalled at the name of the hostel. And she is on the wrong plane due to the strike.

There's a silence, for Grace does not know how to respond. The awkwardness is, however, all on her part, although that does not reassure her as the handsome stranger reaches into his breast pocket. "Here's my calling card," he says, scribbling something on the back. "This is a fine Bangalore hotel, not too costly but appropriate for you."

"However, first you will need to stay somewhere until the strike is resolved. So for now, when we land, you must go to Kovalam Beach Resort, on the very tip of Southern India. The beach is glorious, rest, recover from your flight, and then go see Baba. All India will be celebrating Shiva, the oldest living God in the world still worshipped. You will hear Sanskrit chanted, our sacred language, which predates any other living tongue by millennia. You came in time for MahaShivaratri. All will be celebrating. Join us, you clearly have been invited to the party."

Grace, stunned, looks at him. The pilot adds: "Be sure to take a taxi from the airport. You will find your Baba. No worries. Baba says 'I call my own to me.'"

And with that, he tips his white flight hat, with its gold braid, and moves away up the aisle without lurching. The plane is bouncing awry; people responding to the flashing fasten your seat belt signs.

He turns, waves, mouthing, "Call on me if you need anything." And disappears into the front cockpit area. The plane stabilizes as she reads: Sathya Sai Baba in red ink on the front, with a scribble, "The Ashreya" on the over side.

Chapter 2, Alone in Asia

Meditation is a first class cure for the illness of worldly existence; anyone who follows this rigorously will achieve quick results in removing defects in character –

Sri Sathya Sai Baba - Dhyana Vahini

Unaware that she tracking Mike McCall south, by journey's end to the southernmost tip of India, Grace is running a fever, coughing harshly and longing for cleaneth. Clean sheets, clean water, clean air, clean hair, clean clothes. For she flies on the damp Air Creepie Crawlie, with harried, overworked strikebreakers, still unshaven. And now knows she heads not for Bangaluru but the furthermost tip of the huge subcontinent.

Less than two days in India, again she's lost and into another strike. In the open-air riksha she selects by herself despite advice to take a taxi, Grace believes she is now completely alone. No contacts in Kerala State, no plans, no meetings, no gurus she knew of from *Saints Alive*, seemingly no reason to be here. She's going in the opposite direction she intended. Except for the mix-up due to the strike and the one alluring take charge moment upon landing in Kerala State when she confirms her agenda, changes the itinerary, and books at the Kovalam Resort Hotel at the travel agent's web site all through her smart phone. Wide white beach curving along the confluence of the Indian Ocean and the Arabian Sea. Five Star resort hotel, kayaking, rolling surf, artifact fishing boats, ocean-side restaurants serving fresh catch of the day – literally what the fisherfolk just pulled out of the pure aquamarine water.

"OK, so I'll start at the southern tip of India and work my way back up but first I am going to do some ocean kayaking," she tells the travel agent online. "I am serious about India. So first I will taste the Indian Ocean."

Settling into the back of a three-wheel vehicle powered by the energy of the pedaling driver, unable to shake off the obsession of being a great lady of the Raj, her wide brimmed Tilley hat, sunblock for her red head's skin, hidden waist wallet full of her entire India expense money, some *pice* coins in her right hand to dispense to the outstretched hands as the open air vehicle stops at red lights. "But I'm not Raj of 1880, even tho' my hair's a mess. I'm not some sheltered maiden in E. M. Forester's *Passage to India*. I know the caves are sacred, that holy meditators have been chanting sacred sounds, meditating and building up the energy for thousands of years in India and that's experience bound to touch visitors. I want those experiences even if Miss Adela Quested didn't."

As the riksha skitters through the packed broad thoroughfare, Grace bounces back to her twelfth grade English literature class and the group book report on the famous novel indicting the Raj, by one of England's stellar novelists. The teacher, earnest Mrs. Fennel just out of Yale, assigned them to a panel. Each student had to defend one character's point of view, English, Hindu, male, female, ex-pat or just off the boat, solider, physician. Grace drew Mrs.Turton, an openly racism matron of the Raj, experienced only in British India not INDIA, with all the prejudices and stereotypes of her role the author could bestow. Yes, teenage Grace, untried and spoiled, had connected with India then. Through, first, Forster's critique of the authoritarian, racist Raj.

But more so later through Margaret Woodrow Wilson, eldest daughter of the President, who, like Grace, came to South India. Margaret Wilson changed Grace's point of view to honoring Spiritual India. Grace had studied Margaret's letters when she was at Princeton, researching the Presidential papers in the Wilson Library. She came to think of the long departed Margaret as a spiritual way shower because she led her directly to Sri Aurobindo who was definitely on her list of ashrams to explore, added now to those from *Saints Alive*.

But now, like other aspects of her own family's bigotry, she shudders with shame that somewhere in her bones she could find a bit of the Raj in herself. She knew she had M.M. Kaye's *Jewel in the Crown* in her lost luggage but she hoped somehow that her focus had widened with her Margaret Wilson experiences. It had been barely acceptable in high school to defend the Raj, and how the panel had beaten her up for those sympathies, and how right they were to do so. Her eyes perhaps opened a slit or two, enough so that that panel was one of the memories that made her cringe at her family and its narrowness. Then at Princeton some classmates mocked her for her Margaret Wilson-Hindu interest being 'mystical' as if it were a nasty word.

The pedicab continues along Mahatma Gandhi Avenue, lined with British government buildings, now sensibly recycled by the State government of Kerala. As the vehicle weaves in and out of heavy traffic, sides open to the toxic fuel odors and combustion of frantically busy India; Grace notes the jammed sidewalks. With people, of course. But not walking, running, talking, gesturing, shopping, selling, sauntering people. Instead men in white lying head to toe, on the broad sidewalks. Thousands of men, lying in orderly rows, under makeshift canopies of green and white striped plastic. Lying quietly, resting, perhaps sleeping, with not one inch of personal space between the wiry bodies.

Her curiosity reaches fever pitch at the mysterious sight of row upon row, block upon block, of prone men in white pajamas. At least she knows that *pyjama* is an Indian word, from her Margaret Woodrow Wilson fixation. Grace blushes, noting that somehow she is attempting to retrace Margaret's spiritual journey.

How was it, she asked the Wilson scholars, that the daughter of a pacifist President of the United States, came to die in India as the obituary in the 1944 *New York Times*, stated: "having found perfect peace." "What does she mean found peace? What does she mean by perfect peace?" For how could Margaret have possibly found peace in roiling India?

The riksha darts rapidly to the right, pulling into a cobbled circular driveway. Grace feels caught by astonishment first, then bewilderment. She believes the beach resort is only an hour away.

"You go here," the driver says, pointing to the hotel entrance. Grace digs in her heels, "I certainly will not!"

She scrambles in her shoulder bag for her smart phone, then waves it at the grimacing driver. "See, it says here, Kovalam Beach, 13 kilometers, just as I told you at the airport." The driver shrugs. Clearly he does not or will not understand. Grace feels tears starting. One of her Indian nightmares. That she would just puddle up, weep helplessly, sitting on her luggage in a bus station where no one speaks anything she can understand and no one helps.

But this is a five star hotel with the doorman saluting her, reaching in to take her knapsack and holding out his right hand to escort her from the riksha. Inevitably it seems, Grace is going into at least the lobby of a grand colonial mansion, now Astok Hotel, gorgeous with white portico and lush plantings of Royal Palms and bright red Canna lilies. She surrenders, "might as well be graceful about this. Surely inside, I will find my way."

Grudgingly, she pays the driver, even giving him a tip because after all it is Asia, as everywhere the worker is worthy of pay. Grace wanders into the three-story lobby, noting the black and white marble floors, grand interior columns and rich mahogany furnishings. Like in the Metropolitan Museum of Art, a floral display of rare but local flowers dominates the grand lobby. A white dinner jacketed pianist is playing in an alcove, "It had to be you. Wonderful you."

At the shiny desk, Grace is met with suave deference and English spoken immaculately. "Welcome, Madame." With accompanying bow.

"There's been a mistake; I did not want to come here. The riksha driver agreed to take me directly to Kovalam Resort."

Bowing again, "Ahhh. But Madame does not like our hotel?"

"Yes, I do, of course I like it. It's magnificent. But I do not have reservations here. I have reservations at Kovalam. And that's where I asked to go."

"But surely, madam, you would wish to safely spend MahaShivaratri here?"

Grace, feeling the jet lag and culture shock seize her, sighs and lies. "I am sure this is a beautiful place to spend the most sacred night of the Indian year, but I did so want to swim under the stars in the ocean tonight. Can't you help me get there?"

The clerk, his wide deep eyes moisten to Grace's surprise. Men can cry in India with dignity? He unbends: "You know our holy days?"

"I have been doing my homework, longing to be in India for this one night. To swim in the Indian Ocean, at the southern tip of India."

"I will see what I can do to assist you, Madame," he responds warmly. "But in the meantime, it is not a good time to be traveling in Thiruvananthapuram right now. If you will register for a room, just sign right here, oh, only for the afternoon. I think it will be resolved by then." He is immoveable in his determination she will be staying.

Resolved. What 'it' will be resolved? But Grace receives no answer as she reluctantly turns over her passport, 'regulations, Madame,' and fills in the form.

Naturally, the room is lovely, highly polished furniture and floors, matching chintz coverings and a private balcony overlooking an English garden of roses and shaded in one corner by the ever-present purple flowers of the jacaranda, plane tree. She tips into the bed and is instantly asleep, still nursing jet lag.

In late afternoon as she awakes, the quick dusk of twilight cascades, mingling into shadows in the garden outside. A gentle tap on the door, English tea arrives. Grace fills a cup, pours a real bath, sprinkling in the hotel blend salts. Soaking, relishing being clean again, Grace ponders whether she could leave this luxury. Yet her determination to fulfill her itinerary, her plan, is stronger than the allurement of comfort and class. At least she is no longer feverish.

Fortifying herself with a last cup of now very strong black tea and milk, Grace once again tries to get to the ocean resort. This time, another clerk at the desk checks her out without a hindrance directing the doorman to secure a taxi.

Night falls swiftly; soon drops the sudden Indian pitch dark, except for the electric vaporous lamps streaming yellow in the enormous and crowded city. But eerily, no taxis are on the road, so she is back in a human-powered riksha again. This time she hopes for someone who will actually take her to her desired destination.

"Do you speak English?"

"Yes, auntie."

"Good, then we will go to the Kovalam Hotel Resort."

"Tonight? Perhaps another time would be better."

"I want to go tonight," she notices his fatalistic shrug.

"Yes, auntie."

The fragile vessel pushes off from the seemingly safe harbor of the English style hotel into total darkness. The driver's dashboard is decorated with a single photo of a slight form clad in scarlet. The eyes filled with compassion under an enormous puff of hair. Grace keeps glancing at it as they zoom back onto the main thoroughfare. She notices that the traffic is packed, heel to toe but only on one side of Mahatma Gandhi Boulevard. Their lane is nearly empty of traffic while bumper-to-bumper in the opposite direction.

From the open sides of the yellow pedicab, Grace gazes with a professional traveler's eye at the massive and ancient city, impressive civic buildings, technology mixed with

British colonialism lining the broad avenues. Circling a roundabout in a pedicab flimsy among the whirling cars, mini-trucks and painting deity-bedecked semis and buses with Xmas lights, frankly terrifies Grace. The paintings — often coupled with lines of poetry, religious and/or popular sayings — represent the driver. The images on the trucks are mainly religious yet to her mind, garish. The landscapes, celebrities, mythical creatures, and national heroes astound Grace. She holds onto her Tilley tourist hat with one hand, her sunglasses protecting her eyes from the road dust and gas fumes swirling into the doorless vehicle. Grace sighs. Her beige tensile pants screaming foreigner as blue jean or sari-clad women stroll in butterfly colors on what seems to be the major shopping street lined with rows of jacarandas, scattering thick purple blossom carpets.

There is a weird feeling in the thick, hot air now. The sight of the ghostly dark moon, crescent white in the brief dusk, pleases. Grace shuts down in the intense dark subtropical night. The pedicab creeps by huge blocks of the famous Thiruvananthapuram textile factories whose fabrics will travel the globe as a major source of income from top to bottom of India's economic ladder. Until becoming a technological center, gorgeous silks, rayons, nylons-viscose, cottons, from textiles factories were the backbone of Thiruvananthapuram economy. Grace ponders the eerie and unexpectedly silent smokestacks.

Abruptly, the jogging pace of the pedicab slows, so Grace calls 'faster' to the driver. Turning a corner, he cuts his eyes to her over his sweat-stained shoulder, the whites stark against his brown-black eyes. The tendons on his arms and legs like wet steel in the unrelenting heat. The driver shrugs. Grace thinks again: Either he does not know, isn't telling or does not understand American English as he claims.

She gives up, wilting, pushing back against the hairy seat, hoping to make her tall self small and invisible in the riksha. Grace in one breath shifts from tourist to uneasy stranger in a now pitch-dark night, suddenly recognizing all is not well here.

Recognizing she is more alone in this culture than she had ever been before, she wilts. Even marooned in the Pacific Ocean off Tahiti, she had been with handsome Mike. The stars closer, friendly then. She quivers. "No one really knows where I am," she says aloud to no one. The driver again looks at her and looks back at the stalled cars in the other lane. "I could end up just another statistic. Why did I bounce into this vehicle where I am so vulnerable to the street," forgetting the driver said he spoke English. The ever-lurking fear that seems to live just below the surface of all her thoughts, blasts forth, gripping her throat. Instantly she feels she will drown in the danger, as suddenly, flames ignite on all sides in the dank, humid air. The sidewalk men mass around her. Panicking as she witnesses first ten, then hundreds, leaping to thousands of torches, as the once inert men who had been face up on the sidewalks rise in waves, grab burning flames, massing on the side of the wide empty lane. Empty except for Grace's pedicab. Torches magnificent in the dark, yet terrifying. Grace garbles into her mobile at the same time scrambling in her knapsack for her knife. Grace pulls out her nylon cosmetic bag to find her red plastic Chinese fish boning knife. She slips off the cover surreptitiously in her lap, as from a distance the sound of shouts, screams and loud Indian music blasts through the air.

What with her lost luggage fiasco, the knife had merely raised the eyebrows of the customs inspector. "I write cookbooks," she lies to his amusement. "I carry it with me as standard gear wherever I go." He sends her on, muttering *women*. Grace does not perceive her grace.

Holding the knife now close to her chest, she wishes to be back in the Blue Ridge Mountains. But she isn't there now, just a lone female caught in a seeming frenzy of a mob on a volatile night of the Hindu calendar. She grabs for the driver's shoulder, with the knife in her hand. "FASTER," she screams.

The driver stiffens, frantically jerking the frail bike-vehicle to the left. Grace glances at the knife in her fist, a pitiful defense that seems to contagiously spark panic in the driver. She hardly notices the beauty of the torchlights swaying in orderly rows in the dark boulevard under the protective jacaranda leaves. She does not recognize the chants as holy mantras. She spouts hysterically into the mobile, "India, land of frenzy juxtaposed with fascinating beauty."

Rows and rows of running khaki-uniformed policemen, bare knees pumping above long red knee socks, armed with batons, scream, whistle at the snarling traffic in the other lane. Into the smartphone, her running commentary (at least she would leave her murder on record.) "How far am I from that hotel? Why are these men marching with torches?" Then "Where are you taking me?" Grace demands, clutching the hanging strap. Why is everyone so unwilling she get to Kovalam?

The driver looks briefly over his shoulder, his white shirt drenched in the sweat also streaming down his face. His knees pump the petals. He touches the dashboard photo in a prayer for help.

Cruising jerkily past the stalled traffic, the riksha driver takes a sharp left turn into an alley. Again, he twists the whites of his eyes back at her, terrified. Suddenly more strongly, it comes home to Grace that she is in a foreign country, no one knows her or who she is. She is a stranger, completely lost and at risk. What was she thinking, coming to Asia by herself? If only she had not rebuffed Mike in Mumbai. The driver speeds on through the night pedaling fiercely, the sounds of yelling seemingly pursuing them. The streets are rough now; tenements lean over the narrow ill-repaired roads amid the odor of sewage.

Grace's hand cramps around the knife. It's pitiful, really, she knows. What would Madame Chang's Fish Knife do to protect her from a mob? Just cause more danger perhaps, infuriate the kidnapper driving the cab. But why would a riksha driver want to imperil her? Surely she does not look like real money.

Once, he turns, stares at her with intense fright, the whites of his eyes showing. But pumps on; breaking any speed laws. After awhile, sounds of shrieking nipping at them, the driver turns left, then right, then left again until Grace is totally disoriented.

"Or is it worth his life if an American woman is in the vehicle? Why is this driver so terrified even in his own city? O my God, is he afraid of me, of my knife, my little chopping knife?" The streets narrow, housing close together. She flinches from the odors of debris in the gutters. Something is very wrong. It is now much darker. Recognizing her own contribution to the driver's panic, as the orderly thump, thump, thump of the marching men pass by, Grace decides to reason with him about slowing down so taps his shoulder. He shouts with terror.

He stops short, tipping the pedicab over just before ejecting her into a back alley in an about-to-erupt Asian city. He screams Baba. She screams as a hand reaches through the open sides, grabs her, pulling Grace into the garbage-strewn alley.

"Mike! What are you doing here?"

Mike laughs loud and long, shaking the hand of the riksha driver. Grace stands up, wobbling and amazed. Grace leans, still sick and trembling against Mike's outback shoulder. He grips her upper arm tightly, steadying her while she fights to get her pounding heart under control. "I saw you from my taxi," he says, wanting to reassure her that she has nothing to fear. Then bends, and gives her a long, slow, steady kiss. Grace, appalled, still shaking, starts to wrench away but the tenderness of the kiss deepens. She means to break it off but her body nestles closer into his familiar frame; she still fits perfectly into its planes and hardness. Responding to the embrace as if still on the silly sandbar island off Tahiti, she answers kiss in kind. Mike's arms tighten around her as she starts to feel safe in his arms. He widens his stance and pulls her towards the wall to deepen the union.

But the roar of chanting devotees, the eerie torch shadows on the open alley's clay walls are too close for such intimacy for Grace even if it were her style. She slaps him. He pulls away, laughs delightedly again. "O, Gracie, Grace, I've missed you. Here, help me with my luggage, will you?" he says nonchalantly, seeking to rouse her ire. "What happened to yours? I saw you berating this kind driver who was trying to get out of the festivities. My cab is stuck in the stalled lane. So I thought I would 'rescue' you. And hitch a ride to Kovalam."

Grace tightens her jaw. "Festivities? Oh no, I thought it was a riot, part of the airplane strike." Grace lifts her head, gazes at him astounded at his 'nothing to fear' platitudes, for here they were hiding from a riotous religious rally. But there was no going back. He had rescued her. Again. She adjusts her knapsack and says coldly, standing tall, "Well, thank you for that. You did show up at a convenient time. And no, I won't help you with your luggage. You're tall and strong. Carry it yourself."

"C'mon Grace, you are the only riot here. He's trying to earn rent."

She shakes her hair free of the tourist hat, as if willing the kiss into nonexistence: takes a deep breath while the driver and Mike steady the vehicle as she climbs in with great dignity. "I guess you could come along – for the ride," she says, mumbling. So through the night they speed, like Ichabod Crane riding from the unknown chasing him. The countryside is completely dark. The darkest dark Grace ever in for they are out of the city now, rushing through the black night, only the billion stars overhead and the feeble headlights to light their way. Mike hunkers down and goes into deep sleep, swaying with the rhythm of the ride.

Later, the driver stops, says "Chai?" and at her negative nod, hops out, hands her one anyway, quaffs something from his tiny metal cup and resumes the race. Mike sleeps on, totally at ease. "What, or who, are we racing from?" Grace wonders as she throws out the liquid amoebas. Her other hand curls around the red plastic fish handle, but now hidden in her lap in case Mike spots it, and laughs at her again. "Or is it towards something?"

Then suddenly below, there it is, a half moon of Christmas lights, sparkling like Rockefeller Center for the holidays, around a crescent of white sand at the bottom of a sheer cliff. Kovalam and the Indian Ocean lie far below. The driver turns hairpins, down, down, down the steep cobbled street. One-story cement buildings in sea resort colors, coral, blue, lime, pink festooned with lights of all colors. Gayety fills the air, crowds' rush down to the water's edge. At the bottom in safe Lighthouse Harbor, her hotel nestles on the beach. The driver swings around, jumps out with a shout! "Sai Ram Ki Jai!"

"We made it, auntie. We made it through the holy procession of the Dance of Lord Shiva. Put away your little knife. We are here. Welcome to India! It is the night of MahaShivaratri. May he dance with you!"

Grace steps ankle deep in the powdery beige sand. Nearby a small group of Tibetan people gathers around a swirl of tiny, red clay handmade bowls, each cup holding what smells like some kind of liquid, melted butter. From the hotel, the doorman carries out a tray with two coconuts each with a sipping straw and frangipani blossom to the new arrivals. Mike gestures, "What's going on over there?"

"The fishing people and Tibetans refugees are laying out a mandala for MahaShivaratri celebration this night. It is a Tibetan tradition to make these designs with butter lamps. One hundred thousand lights as offerings prayers for auspicious year of World Peace."

Grace says, "Why are they called butter lamps?"

"Each little cup has the ghee in it, and a handmade cotton wick. In the dark of the night, they will light all the lamps and the oil of the ghee, what you know as purified butter, which will burn until all the oil is consumed."

With Mike looking on, whatever the fare, Grace pays the driver much more than he asks, his big white-toothed smile tells her, but she does not care as she is wrung out from her baseless fears. She actually arrives in time for the party. Mike strolls off, to find somewhere to bunk after Grace rejects his suggestion they share a bed.

In the Kovalam Resort Hotel, reception signs her in taking his time, then escorts her to a large ocean view room with a wide piazza sheltered on one end by flaming bougainvilleas, the orange trumpet vine so redolent with sweetness. Beyond, the ocean is dark under the carpet of stars. A text message comes in:

"Meet me downstairs. You will know which beachfront restaurant. Wear something Indian. Mike"

Grace deletes the text, gazes around the simple yet spacious room. Queen bed, rosy bedside lamps on tables either side, rattan chest, coconut woven mat on the floor with generous balcony, set up with a square table plus two chairs and a rattan chaise lounge covered in green and white silk.

Kovalam JOURNAL
"This is perfect, like a beach resort room should be, the vines, the ocean and night sky with stars and ghost moon the décor. A ceiling fan, bathing room, pegs for clothes. Nothing fussy or overdone about this room, yet the aroma intoxicating.

"Let the beauty of India shine and nourish me. For I do not know what vision quest I have been through to get here, but it was hellacious. As if demons were trying to keep me from this refuge. No, no that's imagination, but I did have to go through some initiation within, an initiation on mythic lines, battling my own fears, only a determined driver and my inadequate weapon, that mincing knife. All the rest was the will to get here despite the temptations. Like that bathtub in the fancy hotel.

"Well, India is mythopoetic Mike always spins. And what in heaven's name is his note about? Why would he presume I would be willing to dine with him – on a beach – again?"

Grace lies back on the silken pillows, does a quick wiki search: *"It is believed that the whole world was once facing destruction so the Goddess Parvati gave her worship to her husband Lord Shiva, who had brought about the danger, to now save it. She prayed for the living souls who remained close to the Earth in space after death – who are like particles of gold dust in a lump of wax – that during the long period of the Pralaya (deluge) night, should, upon their becoming born again, have his blessings, but only if they worshipped him just as Parvati did. Her prayer was granted. Parvati named the night for the worship by mortals MahaShivaratri, or the great night of Shiva. All India Tibet (when possible), Nepal celebrates MahaShivaratri. In evening a grand procession in Thiruvananthapuram starts from thousand-year-old main temple with side parades joining into a huge surge of dancing marchers. Decorated floats, richly caparisoned elephants and folk art forms attracts thousands of devotees and tourists. The music is a magical effect of Indian percussion and wind instruments making the MahaShivaratri Procession the most thunderous, spectacular and dazzling of sound and colour, followed by*

31

fireworks."

"I should have done my homework earlier," Grace grounds her teeth, forgetting she had not planned on being in this city but in Bangaluru. There must be another plan unfolding, she supposes she'll find out just what that plan is. Pondering to herself the richness of the Hindu celebration whose sounds had so panicked her as the driver sought to avoid the ecstasy in Thiruvananthapuram, Grace quickly makes up her mind to meet Mike later. But only one person at Mystix-New York had known she had a contract job in India, much less Mike. How did he find her here at the resort, where she had not expected to be, anyway? Grabbing her waist purse, she leaves her room for the gaily-lighted beach shop adjacent to the hotel. She wants festive clothes for tonight.

Leaving the hotel in the dark, Grace is drawn to the Tibetans focused on the elaborate mandala of butter lights. With a bright and welcoming smile, a woman whose coral and turquoise earrings and necklace attract Grace's appreciation, gestures, holding out a tiny cup. Grace, because of the warmth of the gesture, crouches in the sand, accepting. Her guide smiles, gently laying down a cup, Grace models it, knowing somehow she had been invited to add her energy to the 100,000 prayers. Both women rise. The Tibetan's hands folded together, she bows, says: 'most auspicious.' And goes back to the ritual.

When Grace enters, the shopkeeper also greets her with folded palms, "You are a queen! Thank you for coming into my shop."

Taken aback by the effulgent welcome, Grace shakes herself with surprise and says, "Since tonight is a festival for all of India, I wish for the proper attire."

"Madam, my name is Abdul, I am Muslim. I am not Hindu or from here, but from the beautiful Kashmir, Dal Lake in Srinagar, home of floating islands of rare flowers bordered by snow-tipped Himalayas. However I have many luxurious sari and salwar chemis for your selection. This way please. Please sit and my girls will show you what I believe must only enhance your beauty."

Completely unprepared for the fulsome sub-continent sales pitch, Grace sinks to a silk hand-woven Kashmiri carpet. Before her eyes come a parade of silks and duchesse satin, brightly colored, trimmed with gold and silver, brilliant florals in scarlet, vermilion, cerise, emerald and sapphire, all vivid jewel colors.

"No, no, something simple, please, these are too grand for me."

"Umm, a queen must display her splendors on MahaShivaratri to honor the deity."

Grace, rising, "Perhaps another time."

"Ah," deep bow, "You girl, bring out the culottes now."

Grace, attention sparked, turns to see a rapturous sheer cotton gauze long skirt, actually swirling full pants cunningly made to appear like a gown with a design of hibiscus blooms in purple and cerise on a white background. Strikingly elegant, the bright colors more a Georgia O'Keefe painting than discernable flowers. She gasps.

"Yes," says Abdul.

To complement the outfit, he adds long earrings of tiny gold bells, a hand-woven pashmina in translucent white shot with thin gold thread, golden chappals (sandals) and a lavender sari blouse. The bill is one hundred rupees – less than the ride out.

"Now go to the beach and celebrate on this new moon your new life. And remember, somewhere in South India, by the ocean, someone will be always praying for you."

Abdul places his right hand mid-chest, and bows. She hears him as she walks away from the shop – "And that is how you treat an American customer."

MahaShivarathri

Grace dons her new clothes just before midnight, the next afternoon in New York City, twirling with a deep, unexplainable satisfaction. She never cared particularly about clothes, beige twill pants, tee shirts, maybe a cream over-shirt, sometimes a Prada black velvet blazer, or a safari jacket. Running shoes, minimalist wear. Non-alluring casual business wear. She laughs to see her reflection in those most feminine yet confining yards and yards of seductive material, which both hides from, yet beckons the eye of the beholder with its supple revealing yet complete swathing. "This is fun, I'm glad I'm not just observing the big party. It's a good thing to lose luggage."

The sari blouse, lavender shantung shot with gold fiber, exposes her taut midriff in ways no tee shirt ever did. But her privacy comes with the long wraparound pashmina shawl. "All I need is some kohl outlining my eyes and perhaps jasmine in my hair," she muses, laughing her way down the stairs, to come out upon the festivities of the Night of Shiva.

Ahead the ocean with her cumulative soft waves, gently undulating on the pure white sands that form the bowl of the harbor. The sea smells like old wood and salt, mystery and the deep, satisfyingly real. Above the unknown stars of the Southern Hemisphere frolic, light years away. The merest sliver of moon hangs seemingly like beneficence. To poetic Hindus, this sliver is an eyelash of the consort of Shiva, Parvati, patroness of the All India party, MahaShivarathri.

In as many temples and ashrams as the stars overhead, continuous clanging of bells, drums, horns and voices rise in ritual chants in a veritable mart of joy. "Mart of Joy," where does that phrase come from, asks Grace, ah, yes . . .*The Gospel of Sri Ramakrishna* quoted in *Saints Alive* . . . His evocative phrase for the true delight of ecstatic celebration. A mart of joy, surely this electric air, the stars, wind, evocative music, and the sounds of ancient sea swirling among the revelers ignite the night. Grace turns left. The refugee Tibetans' one hundred thousand butter lights are glowing prayers, a ring of musicians and local residents chanting and drumming with ancient hand instruments. The clamor is deafening yet thrillingly joyous. She heads away from the cliff where the beach ends abruptly, heading for the alluring dance music, strings of lights and ocean-side tables. Celebration is the word, tourists and residents reveling in the energy of a nation en fete.

Looking from one improvised cafe to another playing Mike's game, she churns through the white sand, ankle deep, passing roped off gatherings. These restaurants and bars without walls, at the mercy of the tides, with ropes and lines of lights marking separate entities. French, or German or South American, clientele staked out for the festivities. Perched mid-way between the sea and video stalls, jewelry and clothing shops, open to the night, goods hanging from widely opened doors, she spots their meeting point with the sign Australian Indian Rest. Only that betrayer Mike, her Mike, would choose such a place.

As she enters, still wobbling in the deep sand, a young man with the Kerala State look, thick curly blue-black hair, large dark eyes, pencil slim, dressed in sparkling whites the same color as his teeth, intercepts Grace.

"You look so India," he exclaims, spreading his arms out wide, rejoicing in her appearance. "Jai Jai, MahaShivarathri. Om Namah Shivaya." Basking in his delight at her respect for the sub-continent-wide frenzy of joy, Grace laughs back at him as she re-flings the shawl over her shoulder like the women of Kerala. It was verily liberating to be in these colors, these fabrics, and deluged by the wild music. "This way," he says, leading her to a rough-hewn low table on the outer edge of the restaurant, the gentle waves leaving white foam no more than five feet beyond. Mike McCall half rises, laughs, sweeps his bush hat off in a mock-bow. "Devi herself, I presume." The waiter pulls a low-slung woven-seat chair out of the sand, and holds its balance while she pauses as if maneuvering for stability.

"Jasmine, for the lady's hair?" queries a wandering vendor, a tiny ancient woman. Ruefully, with a half smile, Mike purchases, oddly enough without bargaining, and drops the strand into Grace's hands. Immediately the graceful intensity of jasmine fills the air. Grace's eyes sparkle. Shiva even provides the final touch to her attire.

She fastens the sprig to the back of her hair as millions of Indian women were doing that night. Night blooming jasmine, all the intricacy of Asia caught in the heady aroma – and on Shiva's night. Even Grace, the independent woman, is under its magic net.

"How did you know I would come after our wild ride?" she says, still standing, her voice a challenge.

"And thank you, Mike, for the pretty flowers," he replies.

She half-laughs. What was this guy up to? They had parted barely civil to each other not two hours ago, both viewing the parting with relief and pleasure. Co-workers in the editorial department at Mystix neither had time for the other, in fact had not seen each other somehow since Tahiti until MahaShivaratri. He avoided her deliberately while he plotted getting her job. The wretch!

"Thiruvananthapuram has eighty percent of Kerala's IT. Isn't that why we're both here?" he responds to her silence. She shakes her head 'no', loathe to tell him her assignment lest he swipe it.

"Isn't that why you're here too?"

"Thank you for the flowers, Mike," Grace says in mechanical doll voice. "We are hardly about to tell each other what we're up to, since you pushed me out of my job. Now isn't that right?"

"Listen, Grace, all India is celebrating. I invited you to dinner, to this sacred night, because I want to make up to you for what I had to do. It was either you or me, you know that, maybe you think the days of chivalry are not over, but that was business," he shot back.

Mike: "I saw an opportunity and took it."

"You trampled in, making the opportunity happen."

He shrugs, "You left an opening. I took it."

"So, it's my fault that you took my job. Must you blame me? Don't you take any responsibility for your actions?"

"In the corporate world, that's what we do, advance."

"I know, it's a legal name for cheating. No, there's no 'we' about it. It's not how I operate; you know that. I care. I care for my writers. I respect them. Provide opportunities for them. Where is your heart, Mike? It's not just a job, we were team mates."

Silence, Mike looks out at the ocean. "Well, perhaps I could have done it a better way. No reason to hold it against me."

Grace, one moment ago, with half a mind to join him for dinner, looks at him, a red flush rising to her cheeks. Anger. "Poor choice of phrase, wouldn't you say?"

The square jaw Mike clenched after his explanation tightens further. "You never indicated you remembered that first night, the only night. I thought you were into sex, seemed like you liked it. Listen, Grace, can't we make amends. You walked out on me without a word when we got back to the city. OK, I did go after your position, I thought you liked a good fight."

"Between equals," he adds to her silence.

Grace's head hides her face as she settles into the swing style chair. What could she say? He was right. She had been a competitive tiger, turning her heart over.

"That was then," she says slowly. "A lot has changed. Everything has changed. In fact, although I wouldn't admit it in New York, but here, the music, under the dark night of the moon, the sound of the Indian Ocean, the aroma of jasmine, these clothes, I'll just say, perhaps what you did was the best thing that could have happened to me."

"Could have happened?"

"Well, ok you demanding bastard, the best thing AT THAT TIME," she suddenly laughs. "Ok, ok, truce, all right?"

"No, I don't like the short-term implication of the word. What about we write a peace treaty tonight?"

"First, how did you find me? Know I would be in India?"

"You know it's odd. I was on a nightmare plane from Mumbai when I overheard a charming steward chatting up an American babe. I was in the seat behind, non-dripping, you never saw me, did you?"

"Am I to believe this, this, this barefaced lie? You hacked my itinerary."

He spread his hands as innocent as the blue baby Krishna, "Only after overhearing your conversation on the plane today."

She stares in amazement at him, had he really been on the same plane, at the same gate, waiting in the same terminal and she hadn't seen him?

"Listen, kid, it was only a fluke. As it happens I was on the same flight from New York keeping behind you all the way. I didn't relish your lashing tongue. Then with the strike, I had no idea you would be continuing on. But I couldn't help myself from watching you. I got a big kick out of you and that spider btw," he chuckled. "I think it was that spider and your struggle that changed my mind. You were so cute. I could see the wheels turning. And that pilot was so charming, wasn't he? He happens to be my college room-mate."

His eyes avoid her open mouth.

"And then it was no problem to tap into your schedule – you know that. But I am curious. I thought you would have arrived this morning at the hotel, what kept you? Business in town?"

Grace sits as straight as the lounge chair allows, struggling with her wild thoughts, debating between hot and laughter. Over the karaoke Fred Astaire croons, *It Had To Be You*. Rowdy laughter rises from the surrounding tables, she could choose either to run or stay. Clearly her choice entirely.

"It's not often one has a chance to rewrite history," she begins.

Mike picks up his champagne glass, saluting her. "I'm waiting."

"Mike, you are the most exasperating person I've ever known," she says as the waiter, sensing the change in atmosphere, darts up to fill the glass before her. His eagerness palpable, hoping to soothe the rough water between the couple.

"What do you say on MahaShivarathri, sir?" Grace says to the blue-black man who welcomed her so fulsomely to the restaurant as he pours the intoxicating, enchanting drink. "Om Namah Shivaya." He says triumphantly. "It's all the Mother's play."

Swirling around them stars come down to embrace the ocean's long *Aum*. The crescent moon winks in the clear night sky; 1930's dance music and the laughing eyes of the clever Australian smiling across the table at the shift of something in Grace.

"Oh, ok, let's be friends then, tonight."

CHAPTER 3, Lost Friend

Your Friend stands on the other shore, but you never think in your mind how you may meet with
Him – Kabir

Surprisingly Mike is good company. As the hilarity around them swells with the
diminishing hours of the dark night of Shiva, the southern stars radiate overhead.
Around them, holiday makers, whose Euro-month long, or two, vacations allow
extended partying. They treat Indian sacred ashrams like house parties, Mike tells her:
"It's a difficult time for your quest, what you see tonight at this resort village is not
typical – in fact you cannot say anything in India is typical because of the vast variety of
experiences available."

Around their quiet pocket of intimacy, the revelers dance, sing, wine and smoke an
endless variety of the addictions of choice. Everything is available in India, every
pleasure, every depth of despair, every experience, he says. Again Grace knows what
she finds will be her choice, as seen through her personal lens. Yet tonight, for Grace and
Mike it is not about dissolution as it is for some at Shivarathri, but the loving path of
repairing a relationship in a world of their own by the dark blue sea, the gentle rocking
reflecting the waving slip of the crescent moon.

When the waiter comes with their order, Grace invites him to pause in his busyness,
taking a moment to look over the murmuring water. Curls of foam call them to dive in.

"Yes, lady," he says, "You see the swirling dissolution, the frolic of destruction led by
Nataraja, the dancing form of Lord Shiva, in the cosmic dance all around you," he
hunkers down in the sand with his elbows on their table, deboning the fresh fish. "You
are interested, I believe, in the mystical significance of the dance of Shiva. The poetical
beauty of the awesome Shiva in his Nataraja form is said by the poet Ananda
Coomaraswamy to be the synthesis of religion, science and art. Like the symbolic trident
Lord Shiva holds, displaying the three-fold philosopher, lover and artist. Yet no Hindu
deity can be put in theological categories alone, for the opposite is also there in each."
He pauses, looking earnestly at Grace's bemused eyes. "You understand with your
heart, do you not?"

Grace suddenly realizes this waiter has revealed to her something she had not known, but in a moment of synthesis, knows to be true. She has spent many years fine-tuning her intellect but it was the spiritual heart that awakened with *Saints Alive,* and perhaps her fascination with Margaret Wilson that led her to spiritual India. Not the high tech writing assignment or getting her job back after all. In her own duality, its opposite also true.

"Who are you?" she gasps.

"Just a beggar, your waiter, nobody you know," he replied his eyes shining while he parses the large grilled fish delicately. "I am Indian. This complex land is my home. It is nothing I know but what you draw from me." He wipes his knife on the napkin, tucks it in his sash, unfolds from his knees up as if doing an intricate Hatha yoga asana. Bows, and dances off to serve the German table now raucously singing their own bawdy words to Josef Strauss' *Off to Holiday.*

Grace gazes at the flickering candle in the clay butter dish between her place and Mike. She has tears in her eyes. Mike, with tact perhaps heightened by the waiter's humility, focuses on his own plate, giving her space to collect herself.

Grace says softly out loud: "So the dance of Shiva, stirring up the fierce destructive force, is a metaphor for how one could understand any activity: each act is threefold. Each act: creation, preservation, destruction. And each act, any one of the three, contains all three, thus unveiling a blessing. How we use our will to choose how to live. You want to make amends for our destructive relationship. I need to create a new life but am unsure what lies behind the veil of this seemingly solid society, what we call the world. I know with all my being there has to be more than one broken relationship even a reconciled one. There's still work, friends, mates, family, arts, play to experience. But my question is how to get to blessing?"

"Aww, honey, why go down that theological hole? You are talking heavy introspection. You are asking to understand the one great mystery. Why not just enjoy the night and each other, Gracie cara mia?"

"But Mike, I think that must be part of it too, Every Thing I do mean, is a piece of the mystery. I just don't know how to get to the inner truth. I want to dive into the ocean that Shiva is churning and find out . . ."

"Yes, find out?"

"I don't even know what to call it. Sri Ramakrishna would merge into the deep ecstatic wordless state as soon as he would even start to say the enormity of the truth of life. And he was, is rather, the real thing," She ducks her head, toying with the food. Her yearning powerful.

"Grace, don't go all mystical on me, now that we've found each other again. We have a chance now."

Her eyes again swimming with tears, "Mike, I just can't. I have to solve this mystery. I have to find, I HAVE to find the way in. I have to! How can something destructive be a blessing?"

"Well, couldn't you eat your dinner first? Start with that," he put on his thickest Aussie drawl for her amusement. "Then tomorrow solve the secret of the universe. Tonight, all India is lit up with celebration he told us. Let's enjoy what the gods have been kind enough to spread before us." He held out his fork, a tender morsel of firm white fish with the aroma of ginger, garlic, cumin, touching her emotions with his gesture. She was not even tempted but for the sake of his evening, accepts the offering.

"It's amazing, Mike."

"Stick with me, buckaroo, and I will show you the truly astonishing."

Grace laughs, choosing her response. "OK, Mike, what's the most astonishing thing you have for tonight?" She's filled with light, balmy, delicious, laughter at his sudden change. What had happened to Mike? It's as if he's a different person from the New Yorker she worked with just days ago.

Amidst all the ambient chatter, shouts of laughter and cutlery pinging on china, Mike reaches past the soft illumination from the candle to take her hand and sings in a mellow baritone: *Some Enchanted Evening, You Will Meet a Stranger.*

"Now let's go for a swim in that big drink out there, melt like salt dolls in the sea," he says when they finish dining.

"Ah, Ramakrishna, you quote him to me? Tonight."

"You're not the only one who can read, doll face." And Mike recites ode to Lord Shiva:

> *Om Tryambakam Yaja Mahe*
>
> *Sugandhim Pushtivardhanam*
>
> *Urvarukamiva Bandhanaan*
>
> *Mrityor Mukshiya Mamritat*
>
>
> We hail the fragrant Three-eyed One
>
> Who nourishes and increases the sweet
> fullness of life.
>
> As the ripe cucumber plucked from its vine,
>
> May we be liberated from death.

Walking bemused along the beach towards the One Hundred Thousand Lights, bare feet in gentle surf, Grace holding up her skirts from the salt water, they see a bookstall and wander over to it. Excited by English language books, most likely discards from tourists, Mike finds a gem. *Kabir* translated by Rabindranath Tagore, 1956 paperback, worn but readable, three rupees.

Mike turns to her: "Here, sweet one, take this with you on your mystery quest. Tagore opened the world to the poetry of the Indian soul, and btw was awarded the Nobel Prize for Literature in 1913. Let the mystic poet Kabir be your Agatha Christie."

> Kabir says:
>
> O my heart! You have not known all the secrets
>
> Of this city of love: in ignorance you came,
>
> And in ignorance you return.
>
> O my friend, what have you done with this life?
>
> You have taken on your head
>
> The burden with heavy stones,
>
> And who is to lighten it for you?
>
> Your Friend stands on the other shore, but
>
> You never think in your mind how you may meet
> with Him:
>
> The boat is broken, and yet you sit ever upon
>
> The bank; and thus you are beaten to no
>
> purpose on the waves.
>
> The servant Kabir asks you to consider; who
>
> Is there that shall befriend you at the last?
>
> You are alone, you have no companion: you will
>
> Suffer the consequences of your own deeds.

* New Day

Grace cuddles deeper into the generous hotel bed as the clearing mists of rose, gold and plum reveal sunrise. She is alone now, thankfully; Mike who knows where. After her too brief sleep of the jet-lagged still on NYC time, Grace rises finally to accept a tea tray from room service, carrying the thin china cup out to her balcony, for now she recognizes the sound of Mike showering inside. It was her first view of Kovalam fishing village in the sunlight. Down the beach to the left, all signs of the impromptu cafes and their strings of

Christmas lights now swept away by customers and crews as the 4 a.m. high tide sends them scrambling back to higher ground, butter lamps dissolved. To her right, from the hotel, fifty yards of pure white sand, a rising steep rock face.

Straight ahead, rocking gently, the shining aquamarine sea, with a carmine path to the sun. She longs to dance across the waters as the blood red sun rises from the true East. Because of the naturally curving harbor both sunrise and sunset will be spectacular she notes. "I am in Asia, at sunrise, surrounded by scarlet trumpet vines in profusion, sipping Jasmine tea, in India, India, India, watching 2000-year-old descendants of carved wooden fishing boats putting out to trawl for fish which I could eat for lunch if I like. The men chanting what sounds like Jaya, Jaya," Grace shivers with delight. The sky is blue; the air gold.

"I am free. I can do anything I want next. INDIA! Not what my position rules."

She breathes out, savoring the concept of freedom. However, the joy lasts for only a moment as then the circling thoughts start. One by one, she pays attention to the serial narratives each tells, watches the thoughts float one after another across the screen of her mind.

But here's the change after MahaShivaratri: Grace does not hop on any one thought, merely observes it passing through. "As long as I don't get on the train, as Margaret Wilson said referring to the Advaita teachings of Swami Vivekananda's when she and Joseph Campbell were editing a Vedanta book, I am a not passenger tied to that journey. I can hop on and off the story at will. How glad I am to suddenly understand here what I only read back in Princeton, in the not so good days."

Having learned this new way of watching her thoughts, Grace thinks she has anchored it. But, no. That's why it's called 'spiritual practice' -- now she will need to strengthen her ability to focus. Thus as the thoughts march by, in the silence of the dawn, Grace begins to notice an undercurrent, a refrain that she recognizes like an underground river she lives with all the time. She's going deeper into levels of her history. Suddenly in the clearing is a negative voice, whispering words of despair. Old words she knows too well, words that forecast unhappiness, pain, grief, intense sorrow. But in the new day of Shiva's dance, the next day of creation, the day after the fire, after the destruction, the day of the new dawn, Grace looks closely at her thinking process. Rather than getting involved with it, she watches the words, begins to hear a pattern, begins to hear – yes, a voice. A familiar voice, a woman's voice, a German voice.

Grace opens to her cyber journal the monologue. Paying closer attention than previously to something annoying like a noisy fly on the wall, she starts recording the words.

"You vill never succeed, not with your arrogance. You think you are a queen and so great. You act like you own the world, like the world owes you homage. You walk around with a crown on your head, like you so beautiful and so giving, but you are cold, hard and evil. You are worthless. You are the one who is causing all this trouble. You vill pay for it. You are a filthy, a liar, a dirty killer of God. You expect everyone to vait on you. You are nothing but ugliness."

Grace sobs, puts down the gadget. She's engulfed, forgetting her 'practice' now enmeshed in the words whose hideousness terrify her. "How could this voice belong to me? Why would I ever say those nasty things to myself? I need a shrink, Am I going mad, hearing voices, letting ugly thoughts rule and affect me? Follow me from the US?"

That shopkeeper said to me last night: "You are a queen." What did he see? What does he know? I suppose he's a fakir? There are people in India, fortunetellers, seers, people with what my mother called 'second sight.' We had a nerd at Mystix who was prescient; she could always put her finger on the missing clink in the article before anyone else. She's someone I may look up in Bangaluru.

Meanwhile the rough voice wails on in Grace's head. She dashes down the mobile, hurriedly pulls on her bikini, down the stairs and streaks out to the beach, diving into the waves which are no longer gentle but breakers now. Sputtering and frantic, Grace falls down helplessly again and again, each time she tries to get to her feet another powerful deluge washes her down. Crying, confused, at the mercy of the water, Grace thrashes about now on her knees, now crouching trying to brace against the avalanche of the seemingly hostile water all serene, placid beauty at dawn. Creation, preservation, destruction from moment to moment, yet seemingly the entire ocean attacks her. Once down again, her mouth opens and salt water gags her as she flounders in the rough waves. Heavy wet sand fills the bikini top, stretching the cups in exaggerated mounds.

Suddenly a tanned hand wrenches her upright facing the hotel. "Gracie, are you out of your mind?"

Once again, Mike shakes her, clearing her eyes and ears. "Come on out, now. And don't go in the water again until you know how."

Grace, now that she's safe enough, starts pummeling his wet chest. "I will do what I want!"

And both collapse at the edge of the surf in astonished laughter. Blowing her lips, sputtering off droplets of water streaming from her eyes and hair, "tears are salty too" she manages to get out. Mike whoops with more laughter, grabbing her.

"Honey, what possessed you to . . . ?"

"Possessed? Why did you say possessed, Mike?" she clutches his wrist, "Tell me, do you think I am possessed?"

"For God's Sake, Grace, what is this? I just wanted to know why you would jump into unfamiliar water when you obviously don't know how to ride the waves, that's all."

"Ah."

Mike looks at her with familiar exasperation déjà vu of their working together at Mystix. She is so stubborn.

"Trying my patience here, Grace. It looked like you were running away from something nasty in the woodshed. That's all. If you can, tell me what's up?"

"Cold Comfort Farm indeed. I was just meditating on that lovely lanai, journaling, when I, I, I."

"You?"

"When I heard an ugly voice."

"And that scared you who has fired more men than Donald Trump before breakfast."

"Mike, I didn't."

Mike lifts an eyebrow, spreads his arms wide, "If the shoe fits . . ."

"OK, I am a responsible manager. And I did get stressed at Mystix. Until you maneuvered me out."

"Oh? It's my fault you are hearing voices, my queen?"

"Don't say that. I'm not anything like that, really."

"What, what did I say?" Mike pauses taking his concerned eyes off Grace, suddenly noticing a long single line of fisher folk, thin, sun-blue black men actually, walking very slowly along the shoreline, heads down, eyes riveted left, on her, on Grace.

"Grace, you have a bikini on! OMG, filled with sand, let's get out of here. Don't you have any sense about India? I wish that voice had told you to wear a cover-up. Bikinis, especially that little bit of lime green nylon are red flags. Next you will have a long line of 'suitors' outside your room. Especially with the sand expansions."

"What on earth are you talking about, I got this at Bloomingdale's."

"I'll bet you did. But didn't you read about the dress code for women in India? No body parts, except the face and hair-do, showing."

Grace ducking under his arm is already running for the hotel. "Don't just stand there, come on." She yells over her shoulder, disappearing into the lobby.

"Sorry, fellas, show's over. American you know," using an exaggerated Aussie accent.

General laughter at Grace's expense follows Mike into the hotel.

Running up the hotel stairs to her second floor quarters, grinding sand into the cement and her soft city soles, Grace nearly dies of embarrassment. And as usual her first thought is "Cursed."

Mike is right behind her, laughing, pushing her forward, but she manages to slip in the room slamming the door in his face. "Come on, Grace, let me in. It's nothing."

She flings herself onto the bed beyond caring about protecting her bed as her clean refuge at night. Her wailing intensifies as she kicks her legs neatly depositing all the remaining sand into the sheets. She is between chagrin and a full-fledged adolescent temper tantrum. Mike snickers but has the sense to cool it realizing some nerve now exposed.

"This happens in India all the time," he begins wanting to tell her it's the culture gap between old world values and the US life style. "If we were in Goa, no problem," he says through the door. "They've seen everything there."

All this emotion, he realizes, this crying fit is about more than what met the eyes of the village folk. "Gracie, what's the matter – really?" But the weeping of deep despair continues, muffled somewhat by her pillow.

"If you let me cross the threshold, I'll give your job back," he wheedles; hoping to make her so mad she will open the door to hit him.

Grace sits up in the messy bedclothes. "Go away. It's not about the stupid job, you ass. Just go away. I'm having a nervous breakdown."

"I am not going away and people don't have nervous breakdowns over bikinis."

"A lot you know about women," she sniffles.

"Let me in and I will show you what I know about comforting a crying woman."

Wails intensify.

"Ok, ok, I take that back. Just let me in and tell old Mikey what the problem is."

"Mike, I do better alone when this kind of thing happens."

"Nope, you don't, nobody does. And what do you mean – happens? You make a habit of this? Be careful, you gotta stop, I hear it's bad for your skin – not that I know all that much about women's skin."

Grace giggles. "Mike, you are impossible. Give me some space to take a shower. I give in. I will meet you at the restaurant behind the hotel for breakfast. Twenty minutes tops."

"That's more like it: deal."

Bamboo Village

In a grove of tall palm trees, real palms trees Mike points out, nestles a Kerala-style beach house. In contrast to the cement box hotels with added Indian touches, Bamboo Village handcrafted replicas of traditional teak shelters. Luxuriant color spectrum hibiscus in planters line the borders of the sandy dining patio. Again low tables and chairs like they occupied on Shivarathri, each set with South Indian batik fabric and colorful napkins.

The same waiter comes forth to seat Grace, grinning broadly but with a quick side gesture of Mike's, bows discreetly, saying, "Welcome, we meet again thanks to Lord Shiva's *leela*."

Handing out the menus, he murmurs, "You know leela? The simple translation is the Divine Play, the laugh of the Lord, his tricks and frolics to awaken and shake up mortals. You know, life's a game, enjoy it."

Grace smiles, still somewhat watery. She knows exactly what he means. Practically drowning in the neon bikini according to Hindu teaching was God laughing AT her, but says nothing to the two men.

Mike says, "Say, you following us?"

The waiter bows again, "No such thing. We set up our restaurant on the beach last night to celebrate, but this is our Swami's place where we regularly are." He wobbles his head side to side in the graceful Indian manner of acknowledging 'yes' which to up and down nodders from the US looks like 'no.'

"Hey, great," Mike waves with a gesture of introduction, "This is Grace, a friend of mine, and I'm Mike." He half rises offering to shake hands, while the waiter at the same time bows again." They laugh, two different customs of courtesy.

"I am Anil," he says with dignity, his hand on his chest. As last night his clothes are the sparkling clean, pressed cotton white shirt and long pants. "How may I serve you today?"

Grace smiles: "I have a list of things I want to do. Massage, shop for a . . . umm clothes, " she pauses, swallows hard determined not to say bathing dress, "and find more bookstores. You know places you can recommend?"

"The place you found your Shivarathri outfit is good. But perhaps you would care to pay less?"

"Yes, that would be great."

"After your breakfast I will show you some places. Not relatives."

Mike says, "Oh buddy, we would be glad to go to your relatives. No problem."

"Very nice of you, Mike. Would you like to start with a Kerala-style breakfast then?"

Anil sweeps into the latticed main building. Soon, classical Indian music comes into the secluded garden. Other tables start to fill up with travelers; many of the women in sarong style wraps, men in Hawaiian flowered over-shirts and shorts. Grace recognizes some of the German diners from the loud table the previous night. Their conversation is subdued, coffee immediately ordered amid groans.

As Anil serves Grace and Mike, he inquires if they like the music, placing fresh squeezed orange juice, slices of local papaya and mango dotted with chunks of pineapple arranged in a mandala. He squeezes fresh limejuice over the fruit, holds out a sugar bowl, but both decline the extra sweetener. He pours Chai lattes for both into delicate cups.

Mike says, "Oh boy, this is great. Tell us, what is that music?

"It is our swami playing the sitar with the morning ragas. You know Ravi Shankar?"

"We know of him," Grace says.

"Every time of day has its own appropriate sound, just as every part of the human body has a sound that is right for it at certain times of the day and night. My swami plays for you this morning, Madam."

"Grace."

"Yes, Mrs. Grace."

"Grace. Just Grace . . ."

Mike interjects, "Anil, this is the most stubborn woman you will ever meet. She wouldn't marry me even if I asked her, right, Gracie?"

Grace her mouth full of the succulent richness of a recently plucked papaya, emphatically shakes her head in the American NO! Anin smiles widely, "Oh, so you accept, Ms. Grace, the delightful Australian has won your heart?" He is enjoying the intricacies of the head gestures.

"The delightful Australian had forgotten my name until I told it to you," Grace starts . . . as Mike, sputtering, emphatically starts to deny it.

"You gentlemen have nothing better to do today," inquires a gentle voice over Anil's shoulder, "But to tease the New Yorker, who is our guest in ancient India?"

Anil bows, touches the chappals of the orange robed monk, "Swamiji, just playing."

"Hmmm, if you have a grievance, just let it go," he says to them. "Cruel jokes and teasing are harmful to the whole being."

Mike, rising, holds out his hand offering to shake in the hearty male way. The Swami, like Anil, bows, yet then takes the hand hanging in the air. "It is not our custom to touch each other on first meeting. But I have been to Canberra, so, of course."

"Will you sit with us, will you take some fruit?"

"Nothing, I thank you. I have some massages scheduled this morning. Perhaps," turning to Grace, "you would enjoy an ayurvedic massage this afternoon? I make a blend of 250 flower and herbs in my oil."

"Definitely, yes, you name the time, I'm here."

"Good, I will see you at 1 p.m., then you can go back to your hotel for afternoon rest."

* Pride and Prejudice

Anil slips a list of shops on the table after they have dined. The Germans are now consuming great quantities of bacon, ham, eggs and white bread toast with grape jelly and drinking more coffee. With the calories, the noise level rises.

"Ugh," Grace protests, "Let's get out of here. It was so serene before those brutes came."

They go back to the beach, find where it meets the road at the foot of the cliff. Anil had directed them to a bookstall. It is alongside Abdul's shop. "Say," Mike says, "Do you have a thing against Germans? It's been a long time since the forties."

"None of your business, Mike, it's something I was born with. I hate them so much. I despise them, nothing I can do about it, and my whole family's the same. So I just avoid them. But I wouldn't do anything to a German."

"Say again, are you Jewish then?" His voice rises in intensity.

"No, Christian."

"Doesn't sound like the Christianity I know. But what do I know, I'm just a heathen a-theist."

"Well, then, you really don't know what I am, do you now?"

Grace pushes past him abruptly to slip between two tightly packed clothing racks in lieu of the bookstore. It reminds her of her favorite discount stores of years past: Loehmann's, Klein's on the Square, A&S basement. Racks of shrieking loud colors, patterns with huge flowers, swirls, abstracts, in silk, gauze, acetate, polyester. Grace wants cotton, modest color, one garden variety or solid color. She sweeps item after item by, the familiar sound of hangers clicking on clothes rods orientating her to herself.

Finally she chooses a blue and rose Indian-style playsuit, long skirted, ample material, to wear swimming. Several salwar chemis, the long sheath and close fitting trousers underneath, one in muted navy blue with matching embroidery; a pastel peach and another in turquoise. Shawls to go with. A white cotton nightie and a white Indian sweater-jacket with pockets as she has observed the majority of women favor. And a woven basket purse to carry them all – she paid more to avoid the plastic one.

The shopkeeper is thrilled. She is his favorite customer, he says. "Please accept this shawl, madam, as a token of my appreciation." He is happy with his 1000 rupees. So she purchases Mike a dressy Nehru shirt to make up for their discussion about Nazis as she calls all Germans. She comes out of the stall looking for Mike.

But Mike has evaporated. "And I don't care anyway," she tells herself going back into Abdul's shop next.

He was glad to see her, so she buys some silver rings, opal, moonstone and then a deep red garnet for good luck, he told her. "Now, come, you will like some books? Do you know our Kabir?

Since Mike had given her Tagore's translation of Kabir on MahaShivaratri, Grace is interested in Abdul's introductory talk:

"Kabir is one of our most respected ancient poets. A weaver, he possibly was born in Varanesi in the 15th Century. And brave, a knower of the One Ultimate God, he challenged the caste system, declaring the equality of all human beings.
His poems, like Rumi, call the seeker to know God within. The foundation of the poems is Truth or *Sat*, an all-encompassing Love, Humility, Compassion and Unity, no matter what one's religion or other personal preferences. The poems are for avoiding lust, anger, greed, attachment to perishable things, and ego. Remember God by repeating *Sat Nam*. Kabir's devotees are both Moslem and Hindu, like those who loved Shirdi Sai Baba, who believe in simplicity of food, clothing and belongings. That one should only acquire what is needed for sustenance. They are vegetarians and avoid the use of alcohol, tobacco and other intoxicants. There are many of his followers in North India. His teachings are beyond boundaries, no system fits either one of them."

When Abdul completes his lecture, Grace realizes he is a school teacher displaced by the recent troubles in Kashmir, Grace is even more delighted with Mike's gift, so she dives deeper Kabir teachings.

She opens to Evelyn Underhill, the Anglican mystic's introduction: "Beauty makes no demands on you, as you move into the power in the word, wrestling with your angel."

She thanks Abdul for the teaching, then selects three dog-eared paperbacks that catch her attention: *Grace and Grit* by Ken Wilbur on the life and death of his wife Treya; *Flight to Freedom* by Findhorn's Eileen Cady on recovering from life's hard knocks, and Gloria Steinem's *Revolution from Within*, on building self-esteem. Some light reading for the trip to Bangaluru to accompany her copy of *Saints Alive*.

Kabir says:

The jewel is lost in the mud, and all are
seeking for it;

Some look for it in the east, and some in the
west;

Some in the water and some amongst stones.

But the servant Kabir has appraised it at its
true value;

And has wrapped it with care in the end of the
mantle of his heart.

CHAPTER 4, Bangaluru Trips

The pages are still blank, but there is a miraculous feeling of the words being there, written in invisible ink and clamoring to become visible. – Vladimir Nabokov, novelist

When Grace returns to the beach resort hotel, reception hands her a note. "You better read this one upstairs, Ms Grace," the amiable boy behind the desk tells her. At 4 a.m., his rising sleepily from the grass rug before the desk when Mike walked with her back to her resort room signaled that his job comes with the floor to sleep on as well. By a blazing white-toothed smile, he made it known that he approved of their coming in and going up stairs together.

Last night Mike joked her as they walked down the passageway, "Now reception thinks, and so will the whole beach by tomorrow morning that we are a couple – thanks to the Cosmic Dance of Lord Shiva. By the way, would you consider being my Queen of Hearts?"

When he pulled her to him gently, giving her time to absorb his meaning, he bent down for a kiss. Grace's body responded just enough for him to take the kiss, then extend it. They melted into each other outside her door. His body pressing hers back against the carved wood. It was a soft kiss at first, exploring each other in gentleness, yet increasingly passionate. Mike pulled her arms up so they slide around his shoulders, Grace responding with a mixture of surprise and delight. The kiss persisted, tenderness gaining intensity until both lock into one.

Finally Mike murmured, 'Your bed or mine?' Grace bestowed her key willingly.

Now, after her shopping spree, it's the same key the desk clerk hands back to her with Mike's note.

Gone to B'lore on business. Nice time last night. BTW, I'm German; the oma immigrated out to Sydney before the second war. See ya if I see ya, M

"Twice! Twice this guy betrays me! First he steals my job at Mystix, now when he, he, he . . . " Grace slams her basket full of the new Indian clothing on the table, where it bounces off, hits the floor spilling the pretty clothes, so she kicks them for good measure. "That rat. He let me think he was a happy-go-lucky Australian bloke with a talent for spatial numbers and great sex."

She stamps over to the sheer curtains, rips them back, stalking onto the balcony where she throws her body down in the rattan chaise, gazing moodily at the Indian Ocean. It is glassy, midmorning tropical hot, the fishing boats on the distant horizon heading far out the Persian Gulf. A couple kayaking just off shore heads west towards the lighthouse. Their laughter floats over the still air.

"Well, I did not come here to feel sorry for myself, nor for a one-night stand. I came to decompress from the States, the city, and the mess at work, former work and to get it back. I took the assignment in Bangaluru to get away, learn new ways of living this one life I've been dealt. So far, I lose the game, set and match."

Wafts of laughter again. A spirited breeze brushes the jasmine garland she placed so lovingly on the table last night. The scent reminding her of the night of passion, of the MahaShivaratri, they shared. The growing excitement, the wonder of each other's bodies, found again no longer lost, then playing with touch, coming and going, into the deepest shared intimacy either of them claimed to ever know.

"I gotta get out of here."

Then she remembers the ayurvedic session set for one o'clock. "Maybe I will go for a swim first, light lunch, massage, nap. Then I'll see what to do about this."

She surprises herself into the idea of trying swimming again at the beach of her bikini humiliation, but still it seems like a good alternative to the rat hole of continuing to focus on Mike's surprise news. What did the author of *Saints Alive* say? Keep Your Mind on Your Own Business, KYMOYOB.

Accordingly, she fishes up the new cotton floor length playsuit from the floor, gathers and stores the other purchases. Then frees her red hair hanging down loosely as she had seen in Sanjit Ray art films of Indian women bathing in rivers. By the time she gets herself together and down to the sand, the light-hearted breeze rises to sulky wind, stirring up waves. To Grace the waves are huge; crashing noisily on the white sands yet she figures it's only her fear magnifying the situation. She lets her ankles be pounded, flounders, rethinking her choice. But such her state of angst; she forgets to panic just pressing forth into the seething water.

Without a thought, she plunges into a big one just before it breaks. To her surprise the force twists her body and carries her over the wave, which she then rides gracefully inland. In that split second, something inside her mind shifts.

"Riding the wave, oh, that's what they all mean, to just hop in it, don't tangle with the crash, turn and flow with it. It's not about efforting; it is more about my facing the force, catching it, and letting it go by me. To see the attack coming, because I've invited it somehow by being right here at this time and place, but not to stand there and get swamped but to turn just in time with it and use the energy of the action. Keeping Your Mind On Your Own Business. KYMOYOB."

Grace has discovered the theory of Aikido, the gentle if robustly acrobatic Japanese martial art.

"'Take the force that's rushing towards you because you have provoked it.' I suppose that means just be willing to engage, in this instance, with the ocean. Then still minding my own business, not engaged in fear or attack, turn to join it as it rushes by. O wow. I think I've stumbled on a metaphor I can apply. No more wild rides like the riksha. What would that ride have been like if I had not drawn my knife but instead supported the driver in my mind in his effort to arrive safely. Well, he had been sensitive enough to feel the terror in me, so he would feel the support too, a shift inside me. I know I would have been more relaxed and confident about the whole thing."

She stays in the wild water, playing with the wind and the waves until her fingers crinkle into a whiteness. Each ride sweet and gentle on the wild horse of the ocean. "Mother," she calls out, "just like a wild free mother carrying me home." She is reluctant to leave the buoyant sea. No one stares or laughs at her. She feels rocked by the sea as if it were the great mother she loves. The ocean supports her but she is not yet one with it, still separate and alone on the vast living water of life. She has yet to merge with the elements, supposing she's a fragile craft on the ocean. On not one – yet.

"I believe my life could be like this from now on – as long as I remember the wisdom of bravely facing then turning my mind to ride out the fear – towards handling gracefully with the spirit of non-reaction. Using the mind to go beyond the situation."
Then Grace remembers reading from the book Mike bought for her. A confirmation:

Kabir says:

When at last you come to the ocean of happiness,

do not go back thirsty.

Wake, foolish one! For death stalks you.

Here is pure water before you; drink it at every breath.

Do not follow the mirage on foot, but thirst for the nectar;

Shruva, Prahlad, and Skukadeva have drunk of it,

And also Raidas has tasted it:

The saints are drunk with love; their thirst is for love.

Kabir says: 'Listen to me, my kin!

The nest of fear is broken.

'Not for a moment have you come

face to face with the world:

Your are weaving your bondage of falsehood,

Your words are full of deception:

With the load of desires which you hold in your head,

How can you be light?

Kabir says: Keep within you truth, detachment, and love.

The Little Flower

Grace leaves the Mother Ocean, and goes back upstairs, no longer chased by ugly thoughts. She notices the cleaning staff placed her copy of *Saints Alive* on the pillows that she shared with Mike only this morning. On board the overseas plane, Grace had looked at the author on the cover, noting she seemed to be about eighty, wearing a sari, yet not Hindu. Hilda Charlton, the strength of the gaze holds Grace in an embrace of fascination. She read for hours on the flight, barely understanding what she was reading of the esoteric concepts but laughing at the humor and the stories of Hilda's adventures with real people, Spiritual Masters, across all boundaries of religions. Since then, Grace has taken to opening the book at random for guidance.

This morning, before breakfast, she had said, 'Go ahead, Mike, pick a page and see who you get."

In a lazy postcoital way, he took the book, half laughing, opening seeming at random, to Sathya Sai Baba, read a bit, and determinedly handed the book back. "He's near Bangaluru, maybe I will find out something about him from friends I know who are devotees. She sounds like a real trip. Careful of this book, it's not to mess around with."

Grace laughs lightly, in delightful pleasure, "Oh, I'm enjoying it, she's makes me laugh." Then she opens at random to the photo of St. Thérèse of Liseaux, called the Little Flower. 'Call her name and from her heaven world, she will send you a flower as a sign she's giving you grace. Watch today for the flower and the kripa she will give you. It will come.' See, Hilda's playing with my name. I know she knows I'm loving her book."

In the shower room, after pouring bucket after bucket of water to wash off the sea salt, Grace with her wet hair tied into a chignon, wearing the peach outfit, goes to the hotel's patio dining area on the sand. No Mike, not that she expected him, kicking herself she even looks around for him. So she seats herself at a low table, eventually ordering the Anglo-Indian invention, Mulligatawny soup combining tamarind concentrate, lemon juice, coconut milk, red lentils, just because she read of it in Kipling, deciding against the smashed potatoes even though the name's cute because she's going onto the massage.

While she's waiting, absently playing with a red hibiscus blossom the waiter hands her after she places her solo order, he comes back up to the table.

"Yes?"

"Ms Grace, you wait for Mike?"

"No, not at all."

"You like some company?" his liquid brown eyes tear at the idea of the missing Mike. "Nice lady, American she says from CALIFORNIA! Just check in. She doesn't have anybody either. Shall I ask her to join you?"

Something sharp forms on her tongue as she is about to deny interest but instead, minding her own business plus the triumph and relaxation from the swim, changes her course and replies: "Oh, that would be fine, thanks."

A tall, deeply suntanned, blond slips into the lounge across the table, "Hi, the waiter tells me you're from the States too. Mind if I join you? I'm Kathleen. I'm just here on holiday as the British say, just arrived. Still jet-lagged. You like swimming??"

Grace, a bit breathless from the chatter, nods. "Yes, the waves are fabulous. Will you go in?"

"I grew up surfing off Santa Monica, I saw you in the water just now from my balcony. Looks like you must have grown up body surfing too. Where did you learn it? Ever try Hawaii? Malibu? I've been at Goa, what a blast that place is. All the pot you can ever dream of, practically just lying around."

Grace deletes needless gigabytes from the chattering, "No, actually, I just ran in and got the hang of it, just now."

"Cool."

Grace, pleased she turns off the faucet of words adroitly, nods. But Kathleen chatters again,

"Why are you here? How long will you stay, what are you doing this afternoon?"

"As a matter of fact once I've finished the soup, I am going for an ayurvedic massage." "Cool. Let me know how it goes. I love massage, you know? Is the guy cute?"

"He's a swami." Afterward as she is getting up, Grace says the usual polite partings, to which Kathleen replies, "Do you know anybody else here, spot any interesting men? Want to have dinner tonight then go down to the video stalls?"

"I tell you what, when I get back from the massage, I'm going to rest, but I will meet you here for dinner. Say 8? That's early for India, have to watch the sunset first you know."

"Oh, ok, fine. Guess I will find something to do. And don't forget to take your flower. In California we say, beauty is a state of consciousness."

"Oh, thanks. You'll find plenty of shopping, books, ocean kayaking. Just don't wear a bikini, I've already found that out. Bye now." Grace walks away, just now noticing at last that she holds Sister Thérèse's gift:

"My flower, a red hibiscus!"

Mike

At sunset the pilot walks across the Curzon Court lobby on Brigade Road in Bangaluru, he's wrung out. Criss-crossing India by air to get to the chanting all night at Puttaparthi's MahaShivaratri then monitoring the agitated strike confabs for settling the now India-wide sympathy strikes stemming from the Mumbai slumlord protest, he appears undone. Yet within his central core the blaze of truth sustains him as he hops into his car heading for his mother's town apartment.

Coming upon her, stately, fresh, serene, cool, simply welcoming him onto the garden terrace overlooking the city, he settles restored because of his mother's vibration, into the lounge chair. And he knows she also sat straight and cross-legged on the marble floor all night, singing the sacred chants note for note in harmony with Baba leading the gathering. Baba faithfully there as he had always been for all of Sushil's life. Seemly a tiny dot on a dais in the vast hall, a divine glow on his face illuminated on giant screens so each participant sees his smile. India's sounds of ecstasy: drums, gongs, stringed and percussion musical instruments, thousands of people with metal hand clackers playing with emotional frenzy in the unending gale of sacred bhajans, lead singers alternating male and female. The energy had an intensity and power as thousands of people, not all Hindu by any means. Moslems, Christians, Buddhists, and foreigners from around the global, welcome at the Abode of Peace, the city of souls. For as the founder said,

"Everyone who comes here comes because I call them – Sathya Sai Baba."

When she was born, Baba held her, blessed her. Her whole life was Dharmic – all the milestones in a person's life marked by the kripa and blessings the Sathya Sai Baba spiritual heritage provides.

One of the early fifty families to be Sai Baba devotees since the early nineteen forties when he declared his mission to the world, who acknowledged and known the fourteen year old boy as reincarnated holy Avatar, known to Hindus tradition as God come on Earth. Sharada's parents and grandparents petitioned Sai Baba for a daughter – a girl to love and serve the Divine as they did. She was named after Sri Ramakrishna's devoted consort, Sharada Devi. The whole course of the extended family's life centered around Sai Baba across four generations.

In the honored Hindu tradition, Baba gave her first food, initiated her in writing and studies at schools, preformed marriage and blessed the next generations. In the sixties, after undergraduate years in India, she and her husband who became a heart surgeon, lived and worked in Los Angeles, where they raised their five sons. Sharada did her medical and psychiatry training there, while continuing with the active global Sai Baba community.

At last returning to India in the 1990's to the multigenerational family home in Mumbai, with her husband, S.R. Patel, they donated their skills freely to the Sai SuperSpeciality Hospital. Now with four sons married, professionals, solid good citizens giving back to India through the service projects of the Sathya Sai Trust.

Yet the youngest son, Sushil choosing Australia for undergraduate studies, not married, is an adventuresome airlines pilot – and her secret favorite. She loves and respects them all, their wives, grand and great grandchildren. The immediate family a *satsanga* in itself for Thursdays and Sundays, although not all lived in the ancestral compound, or for that matter in Mumbai. At present she and the father, her husband, divide their times to be in, Puttaparthi or Bangaluru to be close to Swami, as they still call him, and to the hospital.

To Sharada, Sushil was the golden boy, even-tempered, equal-faced to all, generous and wide-spirited. She knew the airlines position suited him: there he is required to be grounded to the details yet free of the Earth's allurements. Even during his time in Sydney, amidst the sports and parties, he had kept to the Five Principles of Swami's human values program:

1. Truth, including honesty
2. Love, including compassion
3. Peace, includes contentment
4. Right Conduct/Action, therefore courage

5. Non-violence, appreciating other cultures

Ancient as the Bhagavad-Gita, universal as the stars' orbits, a personal code of conduct in mundane activities.

Yet as Sharada listens to Sushil's account, considering his request that he bring Mike to her and thus to Baba, she pauses. This Australian man, only, like her son, in his mid-thirties, yet with his face lined as most meat-eaters, with a tenseness around his mouth and emptiness in his eyes – Mike McCall for all his humor and courtesy, she says to Sushil, is suffering from anomie.

"Mataji, what is that word 'AN-uh-mee' you are labeling my Mike with?"

"It's an old word from a French philosopher Emile Durkheim meaning social instability and alienation caused by the erosion of norms and values. But it has its Indo-European roots in India as do so many global words. When it's applied to society as a whole it means lawless. You could say nomad, nemesis, numb as easily. Not able to love, to connect, to trust God or anyone else. He thinks he's alone on the planet."

"But, Mata, Mike's a good guy. He's great, really. You know how he loved his grandmother."

"I am not judging him, nor labeling him with a diagnosis. Son, he's a modern man, he is only odd to those of us who know the human norm of lovingkindness, joy, devotion, mindfulness. He's depressed, the media might say. His emotions are bleak. He's isolated, urban, feels cold and hollow inside, perhaps even with a touch of paranoia. What's considered smart or normal overseas."

"And your point is . . .?"

Sharada laughs gently. "Yes, of course, you are right. If he is interested at all, you must arrange for him to go to Baba."

"Mataji, you could make that happen."

"No, we told him in Mumbai about Baba. No persuading, no recruiting, no allurement. It is not up to us to bring, it is all God's holy play. Baba invites, calls."

As if to change the heavy subject, she says: "Tell, Sushil, how was Mike's MahaShivaratri in Kovalam?" She knew the resort was a gift from Swamiji, a chance for Mike to de-stress, ease into India in terms a foreigner could grasp. What India offers so many who come for the breezes, ocean, music, stars, festivals. Still if away from commercialization, life on simpler terms where perhaps they may meet themselves. "Did he relax, enjoy and accept grace."

"Mataji, that's just it. Grace. Mike's having a double whammie with a woman named Grace."

Her laugh tinkles, carries on the warm breeze over the flowering jasmine vines edging the terrace. "So Sai leela. Not only is grace Swami's gift to humanity, well, all incarnations, but that's a woman's name. The Lord at play in the fields of life."

Sushil says ruefully, "And this Grace or Gracie as he calls her, over her objections . . ."

"I'll bet so."

"She seems to be just what the doctor ordered for him. He loves her, I am sure – and yet he left her. He wouldn't say more than that they met by chance, had known each other in New York, had dinner and a swim in the ocean at Kovalam on MahaShivaratri – and then he left. Washing his hands of her forever. He says she hears voices."

"Voices, hmm."

She pauses, her technical training alerting her to a possible diagnosis of schizophrenia. Yet knowing full well that within the mystical traditions of the world's religions, not only India, that direct perception of the Divine may well include not only seeing the form but hearing as well. The catch is that the line is thin between diagnosis and genuine mystical experience.

"Jeanne d'Arc heard voices," Sushil proposes.

"And so do some serial killers. NO, it's not the hearing that's pathological. It's the content. Does the voice, or voices, have Divine Love in the words? But even that's complicated. Still we don't know her; we don't know the whole situation. We are talking about Mike. I'm sure he has wandered away from his True Self."

"Ma, he's not the same guy I roomed with at Sydney. Then he was fun loving, warm, whimsical, kind. A kindness so deeply ingrained. Sweetness, something so sweet in his eyes – otherwise I wouldn't have issued the invitation to meet you again in Mumbai."

Sushil flung his hands out and brought them back hard scissor-like, "But now he's hard, like rocks our women pound for the TransIndia Highway."

He pauses, "He told me he had maneuvered this woman Grace out of her job in New York. And then when he saw she was in trouble in a cab in Trivandrum, he rescued her – from the Mardi Gras parade he called it – then slept with her after that, surprising himself by proposing, only to find out she's crazy, hears voices. Hates German. Says a German woman is shouting insults at her. Thinks she's cursed."

"Hates Germans? Where'd that come from?"

"Mike didn't ask. His grandmother, you met her remember, was German."

"Yes, vividly, I know how he loves his grandmother – as do I. But I do not understand why he threw Grace away. We did meet his *oma*, we went to her studio. I still prize the woven shawl, display it as the fiber art treasure it is. She had the bluest eyes. Mike has those eyes from her, so clear, so kind. And Grace hates her?"

"Well, no, she doesn't know her – she just hates and fears Germans."

Sharada Devi looks out over the jasmine to the treed neighborhood. Bangaluru has been compared in the past to Paris for its wide boulevards and gracious trees. Now pollution fills the sky with the technology boom. In the distance, sounds of continuous traffic but on the high terrace, peace prevails.

"Must be past life then."

"Mataji, Mike – or Grace either I imagine – doesn't accept reincarnation."

"No problem. The Dalai Lama says reincarnation is just a theory. No one can prove it one way or the other. But it's a theory he accepts – and if someone can scientifically prove reincarnation is not so, or so, even His Holiness will abide with the science. But until then . . ."

"Ma, we know. We don't just believe in reincarnation. It's not an article of article of faith or theology. We know."

"Yes," she smiles, caressing the back of his hand where he suddenly places it on her arm," Yes, we know, my darling son, but let them have their 'theories' if it comforts them."
A green lizard scampers across the path through the potted ferns just then. They laugh. "Details, mere theology, belief systems. Why did the lizard run across the path, my son, just now? Is it a sign he is reincarnated?"

"It's his nature to run – all else is speculation. From the mind."

"Exactly."

They continue together on the terrace. Arms linked, calm and peaceful now, their bodies, minds and souls at peace in the air liquid with Divine Kripa and smoothness. When they rise, Sharada Devi says: "So now Baba brings them to him from New York. Did they travel together on the same plane?"

Sushil laughs, "Yes, but they didn't plan to - something Baba arranged no doubt."

They enjoy the divine play, laughing and go into the wide living room as the sun sets quickly.

"How beautiful. From the US an unhappy woman. From Australia a lost friend. My son, may we ever be blessed with astonishment at our Baba's love."

Kovalam Beach
For the massage, Grace circles behind the hotel to the Bamboo Village guest area, carrying the towel the Swami told her to bring, her gait free and easy. It had in fact been nice to have a chatty companion at lunch, and dinner plans too. "I am fine, just fine on my own. I prefer it. Buckaroo Michael, who's that?"

She walks through the deeply shaded garden, passing the patio dining area and down a sandy path through heavy vegetation following the gold-lettered signs to a grass roofed teak building with lattice and mesh screening open to the soft breezes. The orange-robed man watches her walk through the sand path.

"You walk on the balls of your feet with each step you take. Not good, you must train yourself to put your weight on your heels as you put your foot down. Too much strain on the foot mis-aligns the spine. The heel is stronger, will protect you from hip and knee problems later – which even now you are developing since wearing too many high-heeled shoes. Wear shoes that breathe. And barefoot in the house. Or slippers."

Grace, amazed at his hectoring tone, wonders what she's signed up for? What kind of swami is he anyway? Don't they have to go through ordination like a priest? Don't they have a head swami overseeing them?

He gestures for her to enter, indicating a stall. "I am a Hatha yoga master, you may call me swami. There are many kinds of swami, the word's meaning may include teacher, guru, master, a term of high respect. Now take everything off, and wrap the towel around yourself. Lie down on the table. I will come back then."

She obeys and lies on the wooden table noting that the floor is sloping to a drainage grate in the corner. "What have I signed up for?"

Swami enters, telling her to close her eyes and imagine being in a garden of peace. "I will begin with my special oil, a secret blend of flowers and herbs. The main flower is Ashok, which heals and purifies, a healing you desperately need. Your body is in bad shape because your mind is full of turmoil. I will help you. Do not move and keep your eyes closed please."

For more than an hour, the Swami's strong and oiled hands knead and smooth the muscular system of her body. He spreads the aromatic oil copiously, spattering the walls, until it oozes in a stream to the drain. She feels like an Alex Grey illustration of the anatomical workings of body. The massage goes very deep between the fascia, the band of fibrous connective tissue enveloping, separating, or binding together muscles, organs, and bones. It is very deep tissue work he is doing but with a heavenly light touch. His long, slim fingers delicately incising the body painfully, but abundantly oiled, while her mind floats on the fragrance of the aromatherapy oils.

Grace feels years and yards of personal history coming off her as her mind quietens and slowly rests as in a peaceful garden. Yes, he was right, there is a place inside me of peace. She also notes there is now seemingly an enormous distance from her corporate New York life and the badminton bird she had been – batted back and forth by her emotions, ups and downs, highs of triumph and lows of despair. It's as if she has found a quiet center where there is a priceless pearl of peace; everything is working together for good.

Where had she read that, all things working together for good? *Saints Alive*. Yet, it never seems in her life that anything works out well after all – especially recently – like last night with Mike. So what's so good about then suddenly being dropped? It must be the cursed German that made him leave.

The Hatha swami gently murmurs into her reverie as he finishes the massage, holding the soles of Grace's feet with the palms of his hands. She seems to be in some kind of relaxed trance state from the flower oil dripping drop by drop onto the middle of her forehead.

He murmurs, in a quiet voice bringing her back from the reverie, "I had a dream last night for you. The Mother gave me a white flower to give to you."

Grace opens her eyes in surprise. Flowers keep falling on her. Could it be that Hilda is right, about St. Thérèse giving her flowers? Would the Little Flower make other things happen for good too?

"The true test will be when I go into Bangaluru on the job and have to see Mike again, of course."

India by Train

As the sound of the waves caress her, Grace wakes from a night dream with a jolt, making up her mind she will leave immediately for Bangaluru from Trivandrum rail station. The dream makes her uneasy; what had she gotten herself into in India? Was she losing herself to lotus eating like Odysseus? She questions her decision to travel alone in a completely unknown country. Yet was she alone. Dutifully she pulls her journal out and inscribes the dream:

Journal
"I am at a banquet where a stranger sits next to me. The waiter, or a cop, comes up, saying something in a language I don't understand. I figure he is messing with me, so rather than figuring out why he is asking for my passport, I just give it to him, as he seems to want it so strongly. He comes back shortly. Giving me another, smaller, aqua covered passport – for Jordan. I am horrified and rebel. No matter how lovely Queen

Noor is, or the art treasures there, or opportunities to hear Rumi, I do not want to go there. My banquet neighbor explains I have willingly given up my US citizenship by handing over my passport in response to the waiter asking me if I wished to do so. He says I will be happy living in Jordan. The men will like my body type exceedingly. I am horrified and rebel. Sad to be losing my women's rights, to vote, belong to US. So he says I can still visit New York but Jordan will be my home from now on. Get used to it, he says, nothing you can do. I then see the passport is to Yemen. Even worse. Not so much Rumi, more suffocating clothes, no rights, kept behind bars. As I go to get on the plane I think, well, I will have to marry a US citizen and get back home that way."

Grace shivers with fear at the nightmare. "I don't have any idea what I am doing here, I will go to Bangaluru, fulfill my contract, and fly right back to New York. Then she remembers she has promised Kathleen they would definitely go ocean kayaking today. Perhaps she is not so alone as she imagines. She's glad now of the 'so-called' nightmare because it gives her good feedback not to let fears runaway with her adventure. She decides the dream, by giving her worst imaginings, is a signal to reframe and change her minds. All of them.

After dressing in her long sun suit for swimming in case the kayak overturns, tossing on the new gauzy Indian cotton cover-up, Grace goes to reception desk and arranges a train ticket for the next day. When the receptionist demurs that it is a twenty hour ride, what had taken a few hour by plane down from Mumbai, Grace pauses, collects her inner strength, then says, "Oh, ok, this way I can see some of the country."

"Not good idea," the Swami says when she tells him at breakfast on the Bamboo Village patio. "You have no idea what you have done. It's a long ride, very slow, many stops, thieves, dirt, and it's not wise for a white woman to travel alone. Another thing, did you book first class?"

"Of course."

"Then at least go back and change it to second class, with sleeping benches. Con artists go after tourists in first class sleeping compartments. You will lose everything, all your money, all those many things you bought from Abdul."

And Abdul says essentially the same thing, "Not a good idea, my queen, you should not travel on the railway alone."

Her stubbornness rises. "But I can. I will be just fine."

Abdul shrugs, rolling his sparkling brown eyes, "Ok, do it your way, my queen," he puts his right hand to his heart, "But know that someone in South India will always be praying for you. Your journey will be a night of faith." He bows, tears come to both their eyes, and so she buys another ring.

The kayaking is glorious, with an amazing sunset of lavenders, carmine and peach in layers with rays of the setting sun under-lighting the edges of the clouds. Just before she goes to sleep, after having packed for the early morning departure, Grace thinks about Mother Theresa of Calcutta and her words from a pamphlet she and Kathleen while exploring, had picked up in the small Roman Catholic Church inland from the beach, well back behind the Hatha Swami's. Kathleen had insisted on taking her photo there.

"Love is not love until it is love in action" — *Mother Theresa*

She dedicated her life to helping, unwanted people. But wait, what had Mother Theresa said about that: "There are no unwanted people. All have God. God wants them." Grace decides to discard yet another prejudice, a projection, this time of Moslems as so clearly pointed out in the dream. She takes the Hatha Swami's teaching: "so you have an obstacle – let it go." All in all, It's been a good Valentine's, even with no fine romance. Despite Mike. She adds another layer towards loving, just loving for love's own sake.

Kabir says: 'Whether I am in temple or the balcony in the coup or in the flower garden, I tell you truly that every moment my Lord is taking his delight in me.'

When Grace wakes up in the pre-dawn in Kovalam, she feels as if a big pink rose of love is surrounding her. Just before launching the rail saga, she quickly throws on her beach suit and runs down to the ocean, opalescent in the tip of the rising sun. One last embrace in the loving waves of the sea. And in the dawn of sunrise, Grace, perhaps for the first time ever in her life, thinks 'I am beautiful. I am beloved. I am love.' Her thoughts drift on a haze of self-acceptance as she floats in the ocean, buoyant in the salty waves.

"My soul mate is my true self." With that sudden realization, she loses her balance with a start, flips over, sputters and dog paddles until she is upright again. Again, despite her splashing, comes a thought, "I am a light filled being whose presence brings an instant deepening of awareness to all I come in contact with." And it's not a voice outside but deep inner knowing.

Grace, in shock at the thoughts she had never entertained, nevertheless tucks these words into her heart to ponder later. "My soul mate is my own True Self." What on earth could this mean? "I thought soul-mate meant someone who totally understands, loves, forgives, even blesses, just by being together. I will have to think about this more. There are three tests of discrimination if something is true in writing code: is it eternal or temporary; true or false; vitally important or is it unimportant? And in *Saints Alive*, Hilda says, "Does it have love in it?" These are tools to help me discern, but only I will be able to say if, for me, my soul mate is my own truth."

Kabir says:

How could the Love between Thee and me sever?

As the leaf of the lotus abides on the water: so thou are my Lord,

And I am the servant.

From the beginning to the ending of time,

There is love between Thee and me; and

How shall such love be extinguished?

Kabir says: 'As the river runs into the ocean,

So my heart touches Thee.

On India's Rails

Before Grace checks out of the resort, packed and ready for her next adventure of the twenty hour rail ride, she checks herself in the mirror: "Navy blue salwar chemise to avoid travel stains, light weight for coolness, paisley shawl folded over left shoulder for shelter, basket of clothes, the knap-sack with cosmetics, smart phone, water bottles and the other books. Abdul's jewelry (do not display any of this on the train, please I beg of you, he pled) with rupees and American money belt tied around her waist under the clothing. A simple bag with the *Kabir*, coins and ticket, five hundred rupees for travel expenses belted outside around her waist." Thus her hands are free, although she feels like a pack animal carrying all her worldly goods. And she notices her jaw relaxing, tightened from the working years. She leaves the bathing dress for the resort housekeeper.

One last trip to Abdul's shop to say good-by and board the taxi he has ordered for her. "And don't talk to strangers, especially men who are charming. None. Absolutely none. Do not look at them, do not let them catch your eyes and start talking. And be careful of women too, those who are too friendly and helpful. Don't let anyone stare into your eyes – black magicians out there. And don't be afraid either. Do not show fear if you have any left! Absolutely."

"I thank you for your kindness. O Abdul, I will be all right."

"Asia is vast, chimerical, many layers. Maybe so. Maybe not. Whatever is; it's opposite also is. No one can 'know' India."

"I promise to pay attention. And I still have my cooking knife."

"Give it to me. You must not carry that. I thought I had convinced you to discard it."

"Ok, if I keep it for fruit? Now are you satisfied I am going to be safe?"

"My queen, Allah protect you," he says, not conceding an inch. He gestures to the taxi driver. "Make sure she gets on the right train. I am giving her money for your tip. The 9:30 a.m. train to Bangaluru, second-class, window seat, facing the engine. Right! On you go, my queen. Safe home."

On the uneventful ride into Trivandrum, Grace muses over her conversations with Abdul, how he was so emotional about her life as she revealed bits of it to him, the death of her parents when she was in her twenties, both by cancer, (O Allah preserve them in their garden), the divorce before she was thirty, and when she said no children, his palpable pain that she had no children to love her and take care of and they her. Grace feels her lack through him, while at the same time having no experience with such diametrically opposite values to hers. It is sad not to have family but only mostly at the holidays, while before she felt free of obligations and thought that is worth the loss. Still she firmly believes it's a strange world to bring children into after all. Like other women in their thirties, she would remain on her own because now she could. And live better, free of some fears. Abdul wanted to know all about the divorce, urged her to try for reconciliation. She said only: Not possible. And he put his hand on his heart and cried.

"But I felt such happiness when you first came into my store, my Queen; I have much hope and faith in you. I know your life will work out. Send me a picture of you and your husband in front of your house, please."

Grace is deeply touched and yet, remembering his words in the taxi, knows he presumed Mike her husband. 'Que sera, sera,' ran through her mind, which flitted briefly on Mike. She left out the backstabbing way he out-maneuvered her position at work, even losing a crucial report to make her look incompetent. No, there certainly would be no picture sent to Kovalam Beach of Mr. Mike McCall or whatever his German name really was. Irish indeed. German grandmother . . . 'I'm gonna wash that man right out of my mind.' As for her former husband, she never thought of him – deliberately.

So the taxi suitably reaches the outskirts of the huge city, Grace sees that the roads are peaceful, over for now are the religious processions or riots or strikes or protests. However the main thoroughfare is still as clotted with traffic and its pollution. The driver weaves skillfully through the deluge of all sorts of people, cars, trucks, buses, motor scooters, bike and auto-rickshaws, plus the passively wandering white Brahma bulls.

She remembers Abdul's parting words: "Peace be with you and your God. He is the only thing you have, otherwise you are alone in the world."

And his last words, waving goodbye outside his shop and home: "Ask Him to come."

> Kabir says:
>
> The Lord is in me.
>
> The Lord is in you, as life is in every seed.
>
> O servant! Put false pride away and seek for Him within you.

The ticket from Trivandrum to Bangaluru costs 1035 rupees. Grace shocked, forgets that a rupee, the most common currency, is not equal to a dollar but more nearly twenty cents. She is shocked at the cheapness of around twenty five dollars when she finally translates the sum, and even more shocked at the price the taxi driver directs her to pay for two liters of bottled water, seals unbroken not waxed because that would indicate re-bottled with amoeba-filled local water, a bag of Kerala cashews, five two-inch bananas and a packet of turmeric-flavored hard pretzels.

"Madam, you must have more. Some curd rice, curry potatoes, pudding, pickle perhaps."

Grace shakes her head, she just couldn't bear anything unwrapped, prepared at street stalls, thinking dysentery and hepatitis thoughts.

"I'll be fine," she says not hearing her stubbornness or comprehending the saga of the journey. "Don't worry."

"What will Abdul say? He told me to get you food."

"Tell him I did not let you."

He shrugs, stubborn woman was the opinion written all over his face, and took her things to the railway car. "Take good care of this lady," he tells the conductor, giving him an envelope Abdul slipped him.

"You!" the conductor says. "Of course, of course. This way, Madame," and Grace waves good-by to the last person in India who knows where she is. Grace is alone again as the train leaves the station.

He shows her the compartment, while saying 'I saw you on MahaShivaratri, dressed like an elegant Indian.' His wide smile reassures her, not so alone after all. How had he remembered her? Still it was comforting. She taps in her cyber journal: "Surprisingly clean if you don't look at the floor. The window a bit dusty on the outside, two green leatherette benches. Each could hold three US citizens, or twelve Indians, facing each other. Drab industrial colored walls. But daily life passing by is well worth the long ride ahead."

She watches eagerly as the train weaves through the city, then hours with only deep vegetation in a thousand shades of green notched by small crossroad settlements, backwaters, houseboats, until the drone of the tracks, ka-clack, ka-clack, ka-clack puts her to sleep. Fully dressed, with her carryall as pillow, her feet on her basket, she stretches out and sleeps deeply. Saying, 'this is a blast,' as she surrenders to the swaying rhythm of the slow train, perhaps 40 mph. "No wonder it takes a full day and night."

At one stop, a young couple Bollywood-like in Gap jeans and tee shirts, Nike running shoes and ear plugged IPods enter the compartment. The girl finger-snapping to the buzz in her ear. Grace sits up; takes out a book Kathleen had asked her to pass on to a friend at the Ramana Ashrama. It's by Dr. Paul Brunton, who having first visited Sri Ramana in January 1931 published *A Search in Secret India*. Grace is astounded, and determining to go to the east from Bangaluru to that ashram in Tiruvanamalai. She emails ahead immediately for a reservation. "I'll go there first," she decides completely by impulse. Or is it intuition, she wonders?

Clearly the couple longs to be alone, Grace deduces, and so not surprised when the husband slips out after an hour, popping back in to beckon his bride. The friendly conductor looks in, "Another compartment. Honeymoon." Grace smiles, glad they could find their privacy elsewhere. As the train rocks along its tracks, Grace slips into a reverie bemused that riding the train is like riding the wave. "But now I am the wave also."

Seven long, slow hours later the trains puffs amid its diesel fumes into the large city of Cochin at about four in the afternoon. They had only gone an inch on Grace's map, checking her device. She has been drowsing again, in a sweet siesta with the rhythm of the train. Her water consumed, only two bananas left, half a bag of cashews. Vendors race by, hawking aromatic if greasy food which as hungry as her stomach shrieks, she just cannot bring herself to buy. Maybe some Chai? It's boiled. But when she sees the vessels with their scratches in the metal, and who knows what lurking in each crevice, she waves the provider on. "I don't have to eat. I can go without food easily."

She picks up another book, the Gloria Steinem, as four businessmen dressed in suits, come into the compartment. They are educated and prosperous. Grace keeps her eyes on the page where Steinem describes her post-college stay in Mumbai as they discuss something in Malayalam. But at one point she stretches, and the older one who seems charmingly courteous, evidently waiting for the chance catches her eye. As if he had been waiting for the moment for conversation.

"You are from the US?"

"Yes, New York."

"Oh, too bad, California is better." (Again!)

"So I heard in Kovalam Beach."

They question her rather politely . . . Knowing they would be expressing sorrow like Abdul to find she is not married; she makes up a story to stall the tears in their eyes and their compassion. So tender their hearts.

"Engaged. Going to meet my fiancé in Tiruvanamalai."

Yes! Good. What does he do?"

"Ummm, a banker."

Stony silence. Evidently, banking is not respectable here either.

"But is he a good man?"

Grace sighs; it never pays to lie, her father said, because you have to remember what you said.

"Yes, he is a very good man. Spiritual."

"Yes, of course. Has he been to see Sai Baba?"

There it is again, that name from Hilda's book, it seems to be on everyone's lips. "Later, maybe."

"You can not come to India without seeing Sathya Sai Baba," they say.

"Are you going there yourselves now?"

"Oh no, we are going to the World Cup in Bangaluru. England and India playing. We have tickets. Very hard to get tickets for the World Cup. You could not get in; there are no more tickets. The stadium is completely booked. But you can watch on television. Everyone will be watching. You must watch the match."

The quick Indian dusk descends, complete darkness coming upon them. The boss pulls out a Styrofoam hamper, opens it, looks at her, and quickly says something to the fourth man. He leaves the compartment.

"Will you join us for dinner, please? My wife has made it for us."

Grace is terrifically embarrassed at his kindness after all the warnings about 'cons.' As she surmises the lowest on the totem pole sent out to forage for himself. It is his dinner she is being offered. She hesitates.

"No, thank you. I have my dinner."

"What do you have?"

"My driver purchased what I asked for."

"What is that?" There was no getting away with a social lie.

Feeling like a fool, she shows her remains, half bag of Kerala cashews, two tiny bananas and the packet of hard turmeric pretzels. She's learning she cannot out-polite an Indian.

"You have snacks. You must eat. Otherwise we would be insulted. You must, no option," he says like the executive, father and Indian head of household he is. Grace puts down the Steinem book.

So she accepts the folded banana leaf bundle to find inside chilled perfectly prepared curd rice (yoghurt) with whole cardamom, curried potatoes, spicy green beans and yellow squash, chapattis and the always chutney, which Kerala call 'pickle.' Again Grace is amazed. Someone is certainly taking good care of her. She *pranaams* with gratitude and the men continue to enjoy their conversation with her telling her things about the States she never knew, for in fact, their information is askew but she does not think it proper, or kind, to correct it as their guest. She does not know as much about India, herself. There must be layers and layers she never could know in the vast ancient land. However she feels grateful for her 'piece of the elephant' as the teaching story goes.

A few hours later, the light dim, the conductor enters pulls open the top bunks, spreads out the men's bedrolls of pressed white sheets and light blankets. Grace is astounded. She did not know about this custom nor had Abdul thought to provide the information.

When they see she is going to sleep under her shawl, the leader will not accept it, snapping for the conductor, pressing rupees on him, so her bedroll like theirs is spread out for her. The men leave the compartment, she guesses so she could change but she was not about to do that. What she was now in desperate need of is the washroom and a toilet, for talking to her urgently were two liters of bottled water, five bananas, snacks and a full course Indian feast, minus blistering hot 'pickle.'

Then, as if planned, the leader comes back in, beckons to her, and has the conductor conduct her to the ladies room. A true ladies room, with sign saying so, except the toilet is an open hole on the floor to the tracks but her mission gratefully and with relief, accomplished. What would she have done without her kind guides? Something was clearly up.

Lights off except for the pale greenish running lights of the train rushing mightily forth if slowly through the dark Indian landscape, passing villages shrouded in night blackness, small towns with swinging bare bulbs strung in front of an occasional clay Chai and toddy bar building. Rocking along, miles and miles and miles of unremitting night, remote stars and the waxing moon overhead, Grace sleeps like an innocent unbothered by the men's snoring. In the waxing moon after MahaShivaratri barely any ambient light streams from the sky.

Approaching dawn, the train pulls into the outskirts of Bangaluru the guardians say as they wake her very politely, giving her time to straighten her clothes, comb her hair and organize her bags. Grace forgets to use the facilities in the general rush of departure from the train.

"Where are you going now? In what hotel do you have a reservation? I will tell you if it is good for you."

Everyone she meets has opinions about her choice of hotels it seems. "Oh, I am not going to a hotel, I am going to catch a bus to Tiruvanamalai right away."

"No, you are not," he commands.

"Yes, I am. I have friends expecting me," she plays her winning ace.

"Strange friends to let you take the bus. Only the, ummm, tribals, the village people take the bus. You must take a taxi."

"How far is it?"

"Four hours."

"Four hours," Grace surmises that will cost a fortune to take a taxi for four hours thinking in NY terms. "I will take the bus."

"You remind me of my daughter, she is stubborn too. You may take the bus if you allow me to get you a porter to carry your things, someone who will not run off with them and who will take you to the correct bus."

> Kabir says:
>
> Why so impatient, my heart?
>
> He who watches over birds, beasts, and insects,
>
> He who cares for you whilst you were yet in your mother's womb,
>
> Shall he not care for you now that you are come forth?
>
> O my heart, how could you turn from the smile
>
> Of your Lord and wander so far from Him?

Then the Good Samaritan says: "And get some food to eat, please." She smiles at him, why were the men in this country so worried about a woman traveling alone? She had been fine. Tennessee Williams was right, the kindness of strangers. She is unaware that India has one of the world's highest statistics for rape, especially of widows and unprotected women. But as an innocent, God somehow actively intervening in her day-to-day life. Some theologians have convinced themselves that divine intervention is a myth, not possible. Grace is starting to doubt their doubts, aka opinions.

So seemingly alone again in a vast mass of humanity and traffic, she takes the bus east, yet placed by the porter next to a tiny village woman whose sole possession is the South Indian plastic basket-purse with only an empty woven rice sack at the bottom. Her right nostril has a hole for a ring but it's empty. Next to her, Grace feels like a giant stuffed white bear, surrounded with tiny, thin and beautiful people who stare and stare and stare at her, smiling broadly at her with gleaming white teeth. Grace shares her last cashews and pretzels with her seatmate, slipping unseen a hundred-rupee note under the empty sack in the basket.

The bus stops periodically at Chai stalls in villages and everyone pushes off, pees openly on the side of the road, drinks scalding tea despite the scalding hot weather and packs back into the bus. Except Grace, who couldn't think of peeing on the side of the road with a hundred eyes watching to see how the white woman would manage what to them was entirely natural and usual. She gets off, buys some rose water and a string of jasmine. She gives the jasmine to her seatmate, who tucks it into her hair. "Evidently one of us has no money and the other a full but disciplined bladder." Grace contents herself with spraying rose water on her face when the heat is about to annihilate her. Everyone watches that. When the oven they call a bus passes field upon field of marigolds, or at least deep orange flowers, the shy seatmate plucks Grace's sleeve and points. They have no common language. It is a beautiful cross-cultural moment between just two women in a brief stillpoint, called the language of flowers.

Further along commotion arises in a village as six young men carry overhead a prone woman toward the bus. With lots of yelling between villagers and bus driver, a thin girl is laid on the floor in the front near the gears. The bus bumps along some kilometers, until the husband screams aloud. The bus stops short amid wailing and the now dead woman removed. Grace surmises this bus was the only way to get to medical help, but alas, too late. She's seen more than her share of death and dying in her short life, but now wonders at her equanimity. Something inside her changed, transformed, she believes this comes from the Ocean. With this newly uncovered, sense of her Self, she breathes her first prayer since childhood for them all her kin, this village family. In that moment in the face of tragic death, her grandmother's night-time prayer comes to her lips: "Lord Jesus Christ, have mercy on us."

Finally, aching with the stretched balloon inside full of urine, she sees an arrow signpost for Tiruvanamalai, the home of the sacred mountain Arunachala believed to be the form of Shiva on Earth, with a thousand year old Shiva temple, Ramana Maharshi Ashrama and Yogi Ramsuratkumar. He is the immediate goal in sight because she read the chapter in *Saints Alive* about his remarkable life and spiritual journey. There is no husband there for her, of course, as she lied boldly to the mannerly train passengers. She dozes, blessing the Bruton book *A Search for Secret India*, for like *Saints Alive*, written in easily understood language for reader comprehension. Between them, ineffably leading Grace on her journey to this, her first ashram.

But then to her, shockingly, the men passengers yell. Those who stared unremittingly at her the entire journey when not laughing and calling to women on the side of the road, scream out in a roar-as-one at the driver to stop. The bus is passing by the well-known Ashram, which some call the most beautiful ashram in India, fluffy Kathleen had told her. The occupants surmise this is where American Grace had to be going.

The driver reluctantly stops and lets her out; her basket is passed along to her. Then she stands on the side of the road in the dust, walking very deliberately so she does not pee in a gush on the front steps of the Abode of Peace before a watching busload of curious men.

Kabir Says
O Kin! When I was forgetful, my true Guru showed me the Way.

Then I left all rites and ceremonies, I bathed no more in holy water:

Then I learned that it was I alone who was mad,

and the whole world beside me was sane;

and I had disturbed these wise people.

From that time forth I knew no more how to roll in the dust in obeisance:

I do not ring the temple bell:

I do not set the idol on its throne:

I do not worship the image with flowers.

It is not the austerities that mortify the flesh

Which is pleasing to the Lord,

When you leave off your clothes and kill your senses,

You do not please the Lord:

The one who is kind and practices righteousness,

Who remains passive amidst the affairs of the world,

Who considers all creatures as one's own self.

That one attains the Immortal Being, the true God is ever within.

CHAPTER 5, B'lore Mike

One attains the true Name whose words are pure, and who is free from pride and conceit – Kabir

Mike struggles up the fourth floor stairs to a tiny, vermin and fly flecked room in a pension in Bangaluru. His trip from Trivandrum to Bangaluru, the flight of hell over at last. Only to arrive at his North American style hotel dog-tired to find his booking nonexistent, and no room at the Inn. Sushil's iPhone does not respond to his calls, so he shoulders his flight bag, walks out on the massively crowded street to wander through Bangaluru.

Only to find that without a reservation none of the high-ranking hotels along Mahatma Gandhi Avenue will take him, dirty and unshaven. Dazed, he continues to wander through international logos until he sights an Indian area down narrow Commercial Street bursting with Indian shops, a real, non-touristy market in Asia, with clothes hanging from awnings, brass and plastic cooking vessels, electronics, DVD's, videos, perfumes, spices, saris, shawls, and green, red and yellow ugly fruit, as he calls the myriad exotic foods displayed. Street vendors plague his steps, soliciting with various horrors they desperately hope will appeal to the dazed foreigner

He comes to a side alley, staggers down to the Krishna Hotel, a blue mirrored, narrow, steep building and negotiates a room. Four stories up thin grimy stairs, he's panting when he unlocks the door. And gags. "This will never do, I cannot stay here."

But he does, flopping exhausted on the thin mat less than six inches from the concrete floor. Instantly he passes out from the exhaustion of his flight from Grace. The nightmare of the Trivandrum airport, after a sickening flight (must have been the same crazy pilot out of Dubai) he groans, passing out with fatigue.

Ramanashrama

When the yelling on the bus startles Grace awake she realizes the bus driver is being hectored into stopping directly across the road from Sri Ramanashrama instead at the bus depot in the hectic town center. She sighs, grateful for the bus passengers demands. They know this stranger is heading for the ashram all the time she thinks she is alone. India's is like that Gracie thinks.

On the north side of the road, tangible serenity emanates from the low airy buildings surrounded with gardens, broad piazza steps leading up the gate. Shaking her damp and crumpled navy salwar chemis after its two-day wear, Grace struggles to walk nicely through the arch into the large courtyard, noting the 400-year-old Iluppai tree she read about on their website, yet burdened with the pressing need for relief. An ancient guard yells at her, shouting and pointing to her chappals. She leans over to release the sandals to their fate on the busy road, until he expresses satisfaction and allows her to enter. She does not realize he is there to guard the shoes as ferociously.

Not an auspicious beginning for her first ashram living, she thinks wrongly, following the signs to the office. Overhead fans move the intense hot air as a white clothed, mid-age man writes behind his desk. Because it's now so urgent she looks around for a restroom then is forced to say to the dignified man:

"May I please use the toilet, sir, " she says, overcoming all other forms of courtesy. He rises, opens a polished wooden door and gestures courteously to enter.

Later, he rises again, "Did you email for a reservation?"

"Yes, from Trivandrum, about two days ago. Grace Avery."

"Good, we do not accept guests unless they reserve," Grace thanks their web site silently for the guidance advance reservations are required.

"You are traveling alone? How did you travel?"

"On the bus from Bangaluru."

"Oh my, you did take a risk, didn't you?"

"Everyone was very kind. I wanted to see India up close," shuddering slightly remembering the tragic death.

"And I will bet you did see that. Well, welcome, here is your key, meals are served on time, there is Aarthi and reading of the Scriptures at dusk followed by the evening meal."

He points to a garden path, which meanders west of the Pali Thirtham, or tank that looks like a venerable swimming pool. "You walk that way. The peacocks will not hurt you. Do not try to touch them. The canny monkeys will bite with sharp teeth, so stay away from them. They like to tease ladies, do not respond, or try to touch them either. They want fruit."

Grace shrugs on her knap-sack and takes up the basket heavier each phase of the journey, and walks barefoot along a sandy path towards a two-story yellow building with a long balcony, passing units of low single rooms. Deeper then into a wondrous garden of large shade trees and palms, stately clumps of cultivated grass, flower borders and trellises of climbing roses. The second floor room has, thankfully she rejoices, screens on the window, soft lavender walls, a simple bare bed, a desk and hooks for clothes. The bathing room is near, along the open balcony that runs across the front of the second floor.

On the bed Grace spreads out her cotton sheet combo towel recommended by Abdul, she lays her warm shawl at the foot, sets out her cyber journal and ink pen for sketching, these with her books under the loving gaze of the founder's photograph. Her mind is repeating thank you, thank you, thank you for the pristine room yet she is extremely, desperately thirsty in the steamy tropical heat.

She slowly nibbles on the last hard pretzel to evoke maximum saliva, and falls into a grateful nap. Some time later Grace gently wakens to the sounding of temple bells and chanting. In the cement-gray bathing room, she quickly pours buckets of water (undrinkable signage warns) over her, air dries instantly in the hot air, changes into a fresh salwar chemise, the pale turquoise, and walks slowly through the garden following the beckoning sounds. She notes her red hair is now sun-streaked and her Celtic pallor changed to golden from the intense sun. She's never before been able to tan, despite teenage trying, going immediately into lobster. Somehow the Indian sun, while searing and intense, gifts her with a golden glow. Or is that wondrous happiness from inside, coming out?

The temple is immaculate. A life-size statue sits upon what she was to find out is Ramana's tomb, next to a room older, dark and cool with a full size sacred cow statue, a *nandi*, she recognizes from the buses and stores as relating to Krishna, the cowherd boy, one aspect of the Triune One uber God, with Lords Shiva and Vishnu. There she follows the melodious chanting into a large marble hall, spacious in height and breath. Women in saris sit around the perimeter of the hall against the walls. When the *pujari*, celebrant priest, waves the camphor lights in a circle around the altar while ringing a bell, all stand, so Grace does. Then she sits, like the women; partially leaning against the wall, with her legs folded akimbo copying them in meditative posture. A meditation flows over her; the golden mood is infectious with the sacred. She closes her eyes in the good peaceful ambiance. Ananda means bliss. She learns by experiencing it. This is to be Grace's first conscious meditation. She knows it's a gift; nothing she did herself to attain, just sitting. A gift from the charged air permeating, soothing and stilling her life's accumulations of woe.

After awhile, she knows not how long but the sun is far towards the horizon casting those mystical long shadows through the plants, Grace stirs, moves her legs gingerly. It is sunset.

The chanting grows too loud and ecstatic for her ears, so Grace leaves the temple. She finds an enclosed patio with potted plants. Inside an intimate room with a couch towards which a packed group of meditators face Ramana's couch. All is just as he left it after his final *mahasamadhi*, discarding the body in high meditation. Over the couch a clarity emanates from the large photo taken very near the end of his body's life. The room is another meditation opportunity. She ponders Bruton's words describing his enlightenment there: "*I find myself outside the rim of world consciousness. The planet which has so far harboured me disappears. I am in the midst of an ocean of blazing light. The latter, I feel rather than think, is the primeval stuff out of which worlds are created, the first state of matter. It stretches away into untellable infinite space, incredibly alive.*"

Grace stays focussed by force of will until the 7:30 p.m. mealtime. She has a circulating idea in her head she had already meditated in the large hall so why do it again? But she stays still, loath to leave the ambiance of deep peace and comfort, simply there. Outside, she affirms, "I really must learn how to meditate, wonder what those people are doing in there. I don't think I'm supposed to just sit there absorbing peace? Don't I have to do something esoteric? Special breathing, say a mantra, see visions?" She knows not Emptiness is meditation. When one is Self alone, awareness abounds. Love fills the air when one lets go, Hilda wrote. And Ramana said: "At the end of grasping, peace comes."

As the gong sounds, people move leisurely towards the dining area, she follows. Hoping for drinking water. A woman, who looked similar to a friend in New York, gives her silent directions to sit on the floor joining long rows of travelers, with room for 800 people, then silently guides her through dinner. Grace finds the food quite good, mild naturally sweet carrot curry with the usual cold curd rice but served on the concrete floor with a large banana leaf as the plate. Like the guide, she uses her fingers but not very successfully. Afterwards, a banana and fresh cool buttermilk for dessert. No water. Yet she is completely nourished.

After dinner, which was an easy clean up, Grace acknowledges, tossing the banana leaf into a compost bin, rinsing her face and hands. Outside her guide introduces herself as Christi from Toronto. Christi takes Grace, both walking barefoot along the sandy paths to the small ashram store where she purchases a dozen bottles of clean mineral water. She feels excited and luxurious, just like shopping for precious items at Tiffany's again.

"I've spent several months in the jungle, living in rural communities," Christi says in shock at Grace's extravagant urge for expensive water. "We have to find better ways of life than our monster energy consuming cities, don't you agree? Perhaps we can learn sustainable measures from village India."

Grace, while she considers herself an environmentalist, for after all she believed Al Gore, does not have an opinion about sustainability. But a fear comes up in her, which she expresses, to Christi who responds, "Why not destroy our current way of living? It's excessive and dangerous to your health. Your fears are only your mind nattering on, according to the teachings of Ramana."

Christi then gives Grace a short course about the Hindu spiritual journey. "Sri Ramana became relatively well known in and out of India only after 1934 when *A Search in Secret India* came out, which became very popular."

"I read it on the train yesterday. But does modern India have people like that? Alive today?

Christi, shocked at Grace's spiritual illiteracy, said, "Yes, there are many hidden saints – and some not so saintly, beware of the imposters. There are saints alive today."

"What else do you know about Ramana's history?"

"Here's a quick course: Check out books by visitors here that include Paramahamsa Yogananda (*Autobiography of a Yogi*), Somerset Maugham (whose 1944 novel *The Razor's Edge* models its spiritual guru after Sri Ramana), and Arthur Osborne's writings. Sri Ramana's name spread throughout the 1940s.

Even as word spread, Sri Ramana was noted for his belief in the power of silence and his disinterest in fame or debate. His lifestyle remained that of a renunciate from age nineteen when he experienced for three days of what appeared to be death, but is known to yogis as deep *mahasamadhi* (unresponsive, immobile state of consciousness).

Later, at a devotee's request for songs to sing while wandering for alms, Sri Ramana composed *The Five Hymns to Arunachala*, devotional lyric poetry in Tamil. In glowing symbolism, the hymns tell of the love and union between the human soul and God, expressing the attitude of a soul that still aspires. His teaching became simply: Who Am I? To ask only this question at each thought. You can do this with deep feeling while here, see what happens. Just focus your thoughts on *"Who Am I?"*

Sri Ramana was noted for his belief in the power of silence. Naturally, he led a modest life."

"Oh, my goodness, similar theme runs in the poetry of Rumi and Kabir," Grace exclaims thinking of the verse she read before leaving her room.

Kabir says:

One who is meek and contented, one who has equal vision,

whose mind is filled with the fullness of acceptance Work and rest are filled with music:

And the radiance of love is shed abroad.

Kabir says: 'Touch those feet, of one is who is one and indivisible, immutable

And peaceful; who fills all vessels to the brim with joy, and whose form is love.

Christi says, "Yes, you have been gifted reading the deep mystical strain throughout all poetry. But here's a story that will tell you about real world spirituality. I assume you know that death of the body is a sacred event to Hindus?"

Grace didn't, but was willing to learn, as she had just experienced close up a tragic death on the incoming bus. Noting that the other passengers merely accepted it as an everyday normal event while still grieving at the loss. She had once heard US Poet Laureate Billy Collins say he spent his high school years practicing to be a poet by repeating, 'death, death, death' through the hallways.

"On the day of his mother's death, in the morning, Sri Ramana sat beside her. Throughout the day, he had his right hand on her heart, on the right side of the chest, and his left hand on the top of her head, until death around that night, when Sri Ramana pronounced her liberated, literally, *Adangi Vittadu, Addakam'* ('absorbed'). Later Sri Ramana said of this *moksha* (liberation): "You see, birth experiences are mental. Thinking is also like that, depending on *samskaras* (tendencies). Mother was made to undergo all her future births in a comparatively short time."

Another time, a student asked Sri Ramana: "This thing called *moksha* (liberation), can you give it to me?" – to which Ramana Maharshi purportedly replied, "I can give it, but can you take it?"

Christi continues: "When cancer in his body was diagnosed, many medical systems were urged by the worldwide devotees; all proved fruitless until the end of March 1950 when his devotees gave up hope; we know now that hope is another trick of the mind. During all this, Sri Ramana reportedly remained peaceful and unconcerned. As his condition worsened, Sri Ramana remained available for the thousands of visitors who came to see him, even when his attendants urged him to rest. Reportedly, his attitude towards death was serene. To devotees who begged him to cure himself for their sake, Sri Ramana is said to have replied, "'Why are you so attached to this body? Let it go.'" And also:

"'Where can I go? I am here.'"

Grace is floundering; all this theology about dying is outside of her understanding. So Christi tries again, asking if she's heard of Henri Cartier-Bresson, the French photographer?

"Of course."

"Well, he was staying near the ashram for some weeks before Sri Ramana's death. He took some of the last photos. Cartier-Bresson reportedly said: 'it is a most astonishing experience. I was in the open space in front of my house, when my friends drew my attention to the sky, where I saw a vividly-luminous shooting star with a luminous tail, unlike any shooting star I had before seen, coming from the South, moving slowly across the sky and, reaching the top of (the holy mountain) Arunachala, disappeared behind it. Because of its singularity we all guessed its import and immediately looked at our watches – it was 8:47 – and then raced to the Ashram only to find that our premonition had been only too sadly true: the Master had passed into nirvana at that very minute.'"

Cartier-Bresson was allowed to take pictures of the mahasamadhi (here meaning final rituals) preparations. Reportedly, millions in India mourned his death. Christi says "Here, read this: I have a copy of long article about it in the New York Times:

> "Here in India, where thousands of so-called holy men claim to be in close tune with the infinite, it is said that the most remarkable thing about Ramana Maharshi was that he never claimed anything remarkable for himself, yet became one of the most loved and respected of all. Sri Ramana's teachings are all about self-enquiry, the practice he is most widely associated with, yet Sri Ramana gave his approval to a variety of paths and practices from various religions.
>
> "Sri Ramana warned against considering self-enquiry as an intellectual exercise. Properly done, it involves fixing the attention firmly and intensely on the feeling of 'I', without thinking. It is perhaps more helpful to see it as 'Self-attention' or 'Self-abiding'. The clue to this is in Sri Ramana's own death experience when he was 16 [sic]. After raising the question 'Who am I?' he "turned his attention very keenly towards himself." Attention must be fixed on the 'I' until the feeling of duality disappears.
>
> "Although he advocated self-enquiry as the fastest means to realization, he also recommended the path of *bhakti* (devotion) and self-surrender (to one's Deity or Guru) either concurrently or as an adequate alternative, which would ultimately converge with the path of self-enquiry."

Kabir says:

The light of the sun, the moon and the stars shines bright:

The melody of love swells forth, and the

Rhythm of love's detachment beats the time.

Day and night, the chorus of music fills the heavens.

'Kabir says, My Beloved One gleams like the lightning flash in the sky.'

Yogi Ram

The strong hitch to accepting what Christi tells her about Sri Ramana's teaching to start by stilling the distracting, enticing thoughts is that Grace believes something is different about her mind. "Others might be able, with practice to stop the flow of chatter, but I am dealing with a real problem." She often says she feels haunted. As her plans for marriage, children, family, beautiful home, gardening, travel even her partnership in the firm, fall away with Grace convinced she is cursed not yet understanding that in each life, things just happen.

She goes to sleep that night, wondering if cleansing the mind is possible for her. "If Ramana is here, perhaps others are also. Could that German voice be embedded in my subconscious? Or outside me like a horrible ghost? But the really important question is about how to find release, washing those thoughts away. How does that happen? It would take something powerful to free me."

She awakes to sounds of monkeys and crows and other fauna busy raising the sun into dawn. She sits up dutifully as the Kovalam Swami had directed, closes her eyes, as thoughts of Jesus Christ skitter across her mind. She feels a great peace changing into colors she sees with her eyes closed on the screen of her mind. Peach, gold, white, lavender, sweetness, calm. Christi's lessons on the Ramana teachings to watch the mind, add no thoughts or go on detours following the thoughts, are reaping immediate benefits. Could this meditating be a blessing from Ramana Maharshi? Is he still here as he said?

According to Christi, and interestingly enough her guidebook *Saints Alive*. "Do this every morning and evening for an hour and soon you will have good old-fashioned meditations. No fancy visions or channeling voices or world-shaking directions to save humanity. You will settle into the deepest inner core of yourself and find, perhaps, gratitude in the silence. You will find something greater than you can name – and it shall be nameless."

But then a thought did come amidst all that pink and gold, go to Yogi Ramsuratkumar this morning.

Simply, Grace notes she feels fear. "It's different," she will tap in her journal: "to observe the mind and emotions feeling fear and actually to be afraid. When observing, I don't own that fear, it's part of me but not me. Interesting. I find I can rebuke this feeling of fear, and it diminishes getting weaker and weaker with each stern rebuke until it disappears completely. So happy."

Grace puts down the mobile, to reflect. "Should I go to see the yogi now?"

She picks up Hilda's *Saints Alive*, where there is a chapter devoted to him, and opens it to read:

(p. 262): "So do you understand what he is doing? What these silent ones, these people who are never known to you, do?   . . . There are invisible ones at work, and I've always said it's these people along with the other great ones who keep the world in balance.

"He takes a stone and puts it there. He has a reason. He puts a thought behind it. And he hides behind his craziness; he hides behind his laughter. But he is stern, stern; so stern you have to do it right. And people don't understand – why can't you just do it sloppy?

"Why not? Because when he puts a stone there, he's placing it for the universe; he's placing it for the world. He's changing the world with his thoughts, with his power. I tell you, I had a letter from that man, and he calls himself with every other word, 'this old sinner, this old beggar.' Well, if he's a sinner and a beggar, he's the most beautiful sinner and beggar in this universe. He's powerful! If he puts a stone down, he changes the world!

". . . These hidden angels, these great ones, help hold the world in balance. Perhaps they appear mystical to some, foolish to others, insane in the minds of the earthly sick ones who are tied to customs . . . Well, these great ones work sacredly for their brothers and sisters unnoticed."

Still Grace just does not have the gumption to call on Yogi Ramsuratkumar after reading those stirring words. Needing encouragement, she opens *Saints Alive* once again randomly. This time to the Joan of Arc chapter, where she reads, "Take up her banner in hand and go forth." So Grace does go forth, she knows a prime directive when she reads one. Despite her fear, the call is more compelling. "Can he banish those voices?"

The next riksha pulls up as Grace comes out of the Ramanasrama. She steps up and is halfway in when she notices the driver has leprosy but the strength of The Maid carries her on. She arrives at 9:15 having been told at the Ashram the yogi's doors open at 10. She wants to be early only pausing to buy as an offering a plastic sack of blood oranges, fully prepared to wait. Then as if the path is suddenly mysteriously cleared, the iron gate opens as she approaches. A young man in white looks out, smiles the brilliant South Indian way, gesturing her into a tiny front porch, and before she can comprehend what is going on in the shaded room, she kneels in front of the Swami. He is older and a bit thicker than the photo in *Saints Alive* with Hilda but with the same fulsome white hair and beatific skin and smile and eyes. Pure Love. She shows Hilda's book with her bookmark, an early photo cut from a magazine.

"Who is this?" he says in schoolmaster's clear English, tapping it.

"Swami Paramahamsa Yogananda."

He then touches it reverently, awaking the energy, then raising the photo to the top of his head to receive its blessing. Then hands Grace a lime as prasad, indicating genially she sit across from him. He sits completely relaxed, kind, and extremely acute, aware with piercingly sharp eyes, yet mellow and after Grace's heart stops beating wildly, she becomes very calm and comfortable in his company. It's true his clothes are worn and dirty but clearly serviceable. He gives the impression of vast cleanliness. He wears a green turban, which keeps slipping showing wisps of clean hair, so he reties it. Grace feels a sense of enormous well being, humbled to be in the presence of a yogi Hilda wrote 'is helping the whole world' with every casual seeming movement and sound.'

Grace thinks I would like GOD to be just like him, if we are to have an anthropomorphic One at all. She notes three tanned ladies in orange saris sit like a Greek chorus on one side of the tiny room filled with the yogi, a young attendant and herself. Soon three men in white come in, prostrate, (which she realizes she should have done but knows still somehow forgiven the protocol lapse. At least she knew to take off her sandals). YRSK blesses the men, gesturing they go through a curtained door with him, where they speak in another language, drink tea and laugh. Grace stays with the ladies, very happy in the ambiance of sacred India.

One of the ladies whispers, "Do you have your question ready? Keep it in your mind and he will work on it." Grace opens *Saints Alive* for guidance to the JJ Krishnamurti section, 'Heal the past hurts from your mind.' Grace thinks of the German voices, Mike's reaction, and seizes the opportunity with gratitude.

Then an image of the guard slapping her face, as a child when she screamed at the rats in the barracks. Then an image of her not yet ex-husband shaking her until her front tooth chips. As these thoughts rise, Grace holds very still, stilling her reactions, watching as if at a distance instead of being drawn into the pain. Suddenly she feels 'it's all just part of the plan to be free.' Lightness fills her being, the thoughts dissolve as she hears the ladies chanting the mantra on the name of Ram: Yogi Rama Surat Kumara, jai guru, jai guru jai guru raya until Grace feels she is in a paradise of flowers and the urine smell from the street becomes jasmine, although it's still urine.

Her perception changes. With that shift of consciousness, Grace lets go of past grievances, terrible, hurtful, seemingly justified rage and grief of the past, and simply goes on. In the high, pure vibration of love, she becomes anchored in the present, an invisible gift from the Father.

Grace and the ladies sit for three hours after the yogi came back to the front room, blessing one by one prostrating people, who had been outside the front grille clamouring to get in, including one American boy who left at the door, not wanting to wait in line for an hour he said. One by one they came in, prostrated, offering a flower, fruit or wrapped candy, tapped by YRSK with a seeming nonchalant 'Ram, Ram' and they leave. Children come, and receive candy. One lady receives a beautiful hair ornament of fresh flowers, recycled from a previous donor. Grace has a grand time sitting and loving being there. She notes her bottom and legs do not hurt all the time she sits with them folded, although they do go to sleep but without stinging prickles.

Then, when everybody leaves but the three singers, he signals for Grace to stay. Yet courteously as she is the only English speaker there, he speaks in English to a wealthy devotee who says she comes from the huge city of Chennai to see him. Together the yogi and the rich householder talk keenly about interest rates, income tax, investments, despite the obvious fact he has none himself. At no time was money collected or received.

Now, he says, "O, O, O!" as she recounts money and tax woes. Then he asks about her mother, her mother's servant, her political patronage. Grace is amazed for it's not high spiritual talk but the wealthy woman's concerns, her world. Grace could see the devotee is deeply grateful. "I thought gurus only talked about spiritual things," she muses silently. Instead they speak of what the woman thinks she needs. Later Grace was to read Sai Baba's words: "I give people what they want until they want what I have to give."

After the expensively dressed woman leaves, YRSK bestows a fancy armful of flowers she brought to the chief singer, who chanted the one mantra during the long queue, fruit to the other ladies and calls Grace close.

Grace bows.

"Where from?"

"New York."

"Name?"

"Grace."

"Please spell." She does then he replies:

"Yes. Kripa, My father blesses you."

Tears fly from her eyes, this time in gratitude. She asks:

"May I come tomorrow?" It is the only question she can think of, in the presence of Love.

"Yes, yes."

Grace goes out into the dazzling white-hot heat. "Four hours. So simple, just hanging out with Love Eternal.

The next day, when she comes back to her ashram room at siesta time, she goes directly to the journal, concerned she will leave out one precious moment of the astonishing second meeting with the yogi, her gratitude for meeting a realized Hindu holy man and sitting only inches away:

Journal

"Left room at 9:22 a.m., returned at 1:22 p.m. Four blissful hours at Yogi Ramsuratkumar darshan again. He blessed me. He said, 'My Father blesses you. Come back tomorrow.' I had no problem getting there today. Just walked out of the ashram, actually found my sandals with no problem, right onto the main road from Bangaluru to a waiting riksha with the leper driver. We are friends now; as it seems he was waiting for me.

"Carefully I negotiated the fare as Christi recommended, seven rupees. But what do I know, that seems cheap to me, just to get a seven mile ride for $1.40, but the hauler seemed pleased so it must have been too much. I say, 'Temple,' he nods and we take off with him running. I'm still uncomfortable with a human being pulling me – Who am I? The town is thoroughly packed with people and animals, shops and stalls, the closer we come to the Temple the more raucous and jammed it is.

The driver stops, points to an alley, says *Yogi Ram,* and gestures to a flower stall. I get the message. Purchase ten pink roses for five rupees; the vendor puts in three extra and then gives me one more. He gives me also a very big smile, so dazzling in fact, I return it happily. Since yesterday's darshan, I am in a buzz of anticipation and happiness as I wander down the dirt alley along the west side of the ancient temple's wall. I see men going in and out of the main entrance of the Temple, but no women.

"While the venerable temple is famous for its massive *gopurams* (towers) some of which reach as high as 66 meters, I'm focused on seeing the yogi in its protective shade. The venerable temple is made up of three nested rectangular walls, each of which was built during different periods; the innermost could have been built as early as the 11th century, the guidebook says, and is renowned for some of the remarkable carvings on the walls.

"But in the small dusky, sunpacked alley, I find the house again easily, the one with a line of five or six sari-clad women outside in the February searing glare. They see me hesitate, beckon me over with 'We wait here until Swami opens the door.' We wait long enough, about a half hour, that I start worrying about sunstroke but oddly a sweet breeze comes, so OK without hat.

"The women fill me in kindly on the protocol I did not know yesterday, fortunately speaking English. 'He will be sitting on the left near a cloth-covered arch. As each of us enters, we pause on the threshold, prostrate with folded hands outstretched. If you cannot bow like that, just do your best, and if you have trouble getting up, we will brace you. Do not touch him, although he may touch the top of your head. Then get up, back up, and leave the room. If he allows you to stay again, it will be unusual and a great privilege, most of the throng will have to exit immediately. If he permits, then sit as small as you can near the door. We each have our own places so you must not sit by us. Only by the outer door.'

"The young Tamil man in white opens the door finally, and when all the waiting women enter inside, the yogi gestures and the attendant closes the door behind us. The cool darkness of the concrete room is welcome after the sun drenched wait. Thanks to my Princeton Hatha yoga with Barbara Waaben, I was able to perform the stern directions fairly well, although balancing the bouquet of roses with one hand was a bit complicated while squatting, then prostrating."

"He was smoking another cigarette, but Hilda said he blesses you with the smoke, not to think it's anything like the mundane blowing of tobacco smoke in your face. 'Do not react. Do not think. Pay attention and sit quietly,' the book said. When he takes out a cigarette, first he looks at each person on the porch, one by one, deliberately. Then he cups his hands around the cigarette and inhales using his two thumbs like a filter. Then he slowly blows white smoke out, wafting it towards each person. When the smoke comes to me, with blessings in it, I feel like a kite suddenly released from its string, woo, woo, woo and away. There seem to be no limits to his kindness, charm, delight and mystery. What he was doing I do not know except thank God for Hilda's chapter on him in Saints Alive otherwise I might have missed it. I am so glad I decided to seek out this being after reading Hilda; otherwise I would not have understood or even had the opportunity. I would have gone straight to the office never to know him.

"I still was so full of worry I would do the wrong guru thing, that when I bowed awkwardly, thrusting the flowers out so enthusiastically they actually touched his feet. He laughed and laughed. I feel that what I had done was wrong somehow according to guru protocol of putting my karma on him. However he handled it masterfully, his laughter erasing both my error and my fear of not being guru-socially graceful. He also took my letter telling about job, Mike and German curse and taps it, since he already knows the contents obviously."

"He cleans me up, like so many others, taking the 'dirt and grime' accumulation. For YRSK has a reputation of collecting dirt, bits of paper, seeming just trash and keeping it for some cosmic purpose known only to him. Sure enough it was there, a big neat pile of debris shaped cone-like in an alcove. My letter hopefully will go there too. It is said he bathes once a year but how could that be possible? His long pure white beard is immaculate as is his light brown skin. He may be in his 60-70- even 80's. I could not tell because there were no wrinkles and his hands were firm and strong. He wore an artistically tied turban. His feet, because none of us present were wearing shoes, neat and clean without blemish. I felt like I wanted to stay at his feet forever such was the tenderness poured upon me.

"I continued trying to give him the roses while he laughed. There was kindness and love in the laughter, he was not laughing at me at all. It seemed like he was tickled by my ineptness or something else. He took the paper-wrapped bouquet with all the roses for I had put in the extra the vendor gave me. He pointed to the rug across from him, but I remembered what the Indian women had said, so I backed into the corner. He laughed, said something to the women in Tamil perhaps, it could have been moon-talk for all I knew. They bowed to him again. Perhaps he was reprimanding them but who knew? There as was so much love in the air. He called me back, across from him.

"After the brief drama, he starts to read my letter, so I bring out a picture of the Princeton Woodrow Wilson house. He seems to search the air, the ethers, like a computer scan, then he exclaims with a power not so much to me as to the air: IT IS POSSIBLE. He blesses the photo with a flick of his index finger and gives it back to me. I bow again. From the paper packet, he takes the gift rose out tenderly, with a cultured gesture, inhales the rose perfume, traced its long stem, finally holding it like a wand, taps me with it, and gives it back to me. A very gentlemanly gesture full of gracious good manners. I rose in love with him again instantly. We both laugh this time. How did he know which rose had been the gift, as all were seemingly the same pink, I wondered.

"But when I get up, my feet are atickle with pin-like prickles, and this time losing my balance, I fall awkwardly back by the door, landing amidst the orange sari ladies away at the side. O O O, everyone said as I nearly die of embarrassment. I am feeling like a western cow but they quickly hush themselves and me, and keep me there among them. I had literally fallen for him, humiliated at my lack of grace.

"But that feeling so quickly passes. I have a view of his tanned foot – and after an hour or so, he leans forward so I could see his profile frequently.

"Once my drama/his leela is over, I cannot call it an interview although I did expose my inner-view, YRSK gestured to the young man in white at the door, to open it, and for three hours a long stream of Indian men, women and children came in, the first few receiving the roses I had given, then wrapped pieces of hard candy. I saw the disappointed looks on the children's faces and knew they would have preferred candy to a girly pink rose.

"At one point, a man in white, just like the others it seems, is prone before him bowing and YRSK, just like the professor he once was, yells 'Scoundrel!' and gestures the assistant hustle the man out. Then YRSK said in a calm voice, 'these smugglers of sandalwood are making a high profit.' So he's an environmentalist with a Cap E. It's getting better and better as my gaucherie and awe subside – somewhat.

"Another wealthy woman from Chennai comes in dressed in a fabulous sari; she's very plump which also indicates her husband's wealth I've been told. She flips open a gold trimmed fan, which she waves back and forth before him. He jokes with her about income tax and asks about how her sister is – She replies with a litany of troubles, then asks him to arrange an interview for her with Sai Baba. There that name is again. But I wonder if it was good protocol to ask one guru for help manipulating another? YRSK turns and talks instead to us ladies by his side saying, 'so many people there at Baba's now, hard to get private interview.' Chennai Ma would not let up, repeating, 'Swami, you can arrange it with Swami.' YRSK said, O! O! O! Then: 'My Father Blesses you.' I wonder what her frenzy is about? Why is a Baba interview so vital? If I go there, I will remain centered as this yogi models.

"She stays firmly in place, ignoring his remarks. Shortly he comments 'again 'so many people are coming here now, he doesn't know how.' Chennai Ma says, 'word of mouth, Swami.' YRSK repeats, "Don't know how they come." I felt guilty and crass although it rolled right off her back so determined was she.

"Finally around 11:30, he gestures for the door to be closed after she leaves, although there was still a long line of supplicants, some children repeating I guessed, hoping for their candy this time around. We are once again alone in the tiny darkened room with him, only slanted sunlight pouring in the closed door.

One by one he calls the ladies who chanted forward. When he calls me again, he blesses me, telling me to look up as I hide my forehead on the floor. As I looked into his eyes, I see no end. Then, he laughs, and asks me if I am learning Tamil? I couldn't comprehend the question as I was reeling from the energy of the darshan look, called *diksha*. Then I got it, and burst out laughing also, "Not possible, Swami, my brain does not work that way." He laughs more, raises his hand, palm out in the *abishaya* (do not fear) mudra gesture, sometimes seen in Romanized churches and in Buddhism, known as the priestly blessing for fearlessness and protection.

"Everything is funny now, all shame and uncertainty vanish from my ken.

"He then signals for the door to open again for another session in quick processions of prostrating people and candy prasad, finally he dismisses us also. I came out into the brilliant sun of the marketplace around the Temple. I feel strong and confident. The Frenchwoman in orange sari said something about rubber *parottas* (bread) and rice that confused me, so I decided to give the idea up of a restaurant for lunch and signaled for a riksha to return to the serenity of Ramanasrama. One guru in *mahasamadi*; another guru in the thick of market. Funny-odd. Hilda had said just that, one comes up, another comes down. She also said the great saints live in the markets rather than seclusion.

"Seems Hilda shares wisdom for everyday life – whether reading it at home, and even in India!

"And as I bask in bliss, thinking about being in the midst of turmoil of the market, the riksha driver suddenly wheels us around to the front of the thousand-year-old temple, having spotted a skirmish beginning between several young men of his ilk. Shouting over his shoulder as he scrambles out of the riksha and starts at random punching other young men, he calls out to me: 'Wait! One minute.'"

Grace puts down her mobile, thinking of the abrupt change from the sanctity of the saint's dimly lit sanctuary and the strong sunlight with frenzied young men hitting hard at each other. Police began arriving on motor scooters blowing whistles at the screams, shouting and confusion. But something of the Yogi's peace has penetrated her.

"Oh no. Trivandrum incident all over again. Mumbai with Uzies. Now I'm in a melee in Tiru. But this time I know what to do, and it's not to grab for the paring knife.

"I jump out of the other side of the open riksha; walking calmly back towards the flower stall. The rose vendor sees me, hears the roars, pulls me into the stall and then escorts me through back alleys to a placid side street, flags a vehicle driven by an older, blue turbaned man. "He's Sikh, no one will mess with you, lady," he whispers as he puts, literally puts me, in the cab.

"To Ramana!" he shouts to the elder peddling the riksha. I should have been pulling him but I'm grateful, and so was he with the fare. And suddenly I'm back in the garden of beauty and quiet exactly four hours to the minute that I left. Completely transformed, I dine on the big green fruit prasad from YRSK at my desk. That along with cashews and a turmeric hard pretzel with a whole bottle of purified mineral water."

Grace chuckles: "More grace for Grace from YRSK!"

After recording the astonishing morning, Grace sleeps for two hours, again missing the midday dinner of the tropics.

When she wakes, it is late afternoon, but a still few hours before meditation, supper and dark. She decides to explore Arunachala on her own.

It is the most important holy place for people practicing relentlessly *Atma vichara* (self enquiry – Who am I) until realization comes of its truth as taught by Sri Ramana Maharshi, Christi pointed out that a very early reference to Arunachala could be found in *Rigveda*, the foremost of the four *Vedas*, Hindu scriptures.

As she takes up an ashram booklet, Grace reads a verse in the *Arunachala Mahatmyam*:

"Arunachala is truly the holy place. Of all holy places it is the most sacred! Know that it is the heart of the world. It is truly Shiva himself! It is his heart-abode, a secret *kshetra* (refuge). In that place the Lord ever abides on the hill of light named Arunachala."

"Asked about the special sanctity of Arunachala, Ramana Maharshi explained that other holy places such as Kailas, Kasi and Chidambaram are sacred because they are the abodes of Lord Shiva whereas Arunachala is Lord Siva himself. However, as the above verse of *Arunachala Mahatmyam* says, Arunachala is a secret *kshetra* (refuge). It is this place that bestows *jnana* (Self-knowledge) taking away impermanence in order to find that which is permanent, indivisible. Yet because most people have so many desires and do not truly want to know their True Self, Arunachala has always remained comparatively little known. But to those few who seek, Arunachala always makes itself known through some means or other." Grace picks up her mobile, performs a key word search and finds a twenty-four hour camera viewing the mountain now as she sits below it. She looks up in delight to see the moon rising and down in joy to see it on the smart phone. So I can 'see' Arunachala anywhere I am by the www. I have to tell Mike . . . opps where did that thought come from?

"The circumambulation of Arunachala is known as *Giri Pradakshina* in Sanskrit and *Giri Valam* in Tamil. Performing pradakshina (walking entirely the 2.5 miles around the mountain) of Arunachala is considered to be beneficial in all ways. Typically, pradakshina is done in bare feet, with the Hill on the right. Sri Ramana Maharshi once explained the meaning of the word pradakshina and how it should be done by a devotee: "The letter "Pra" stands for removal of all kinds of sins; "da" stands for fulfilling the desires; "kshi" stands for freedom from future births; "na" stands for giving deliverance through jnana.

"If by way of Pradakshina you walk one step it gives happiness in this world, two steps, it gives happiness in heaven, three steps, it gives bliss of Sathyaloka (realm of Truth). One should go round either in *mouna* (silence) or *dhyana* (meditation) or *japa* (repetition of Lord's name) or *sankeertana* (bhajan chanting) and thereby thinking of God all the time. One should walk slowly like a woman who is in the ninth month of pregnancy."

No problem, Grace says to herself, I have to do barefoot slowly, feeling my way because of the stones in my path.

Sri Ramana Maharshi described the meaning in this way:

"Getting rid of the `I am the body' idea and merging the mind into the Heart to realize the Self as non-dual being and the light of all is the real significance of darshan of the beacon of light on Arunachala, as the center of the universe." So much for her being worried about barefeet.

Grace laughs, for she stands very small at the bottom of the rocky iconic moonscape rising over her. The path is lonely, winding and steep. 'Here I am climbing the rocky path of God.' And gathers three pebbles for her Bangaluru team leaders, forgetting they are not hers but Mike's now.

Just then three German women come up to her on the path, chatting in their language but switching politely so she can understand. They are talking about a guru in North India who is saying he is a realized being. When she does not seem duly impressed they explain realized beings have ten liberations to give away as a result of their enlightenment. "We know he has given one to an American woman from Hawaii, but there are still some more. You should go there."

Grace, not up to date on guru protocol, looks doubtful. "I really don't know how that's for me . . . " They laugh at her. Or Grace thinks are they laughing at her ignorance about the Great Getting Enlightenment Rush among travelers to India.

"I'm just here on a business trip. Doing some consulting in Bangaluru. I need to go to Puducherry first, then I will do my job and go home." Even to her ears it sounds lame but then Grace is beginning to realize something is going on here in India she doesn't get, but Mike knew. These women know. Even the businessmen on the train had it. 'Sacred India. Technological India. Is there a gap in me?'

Ortrude, named for one of the Valkyries, she says off handedly, suddenly says, 'O, see the garuda.' Pointing to the brown eagle in the sky circling the mountain. They sit on a boulder watching the bird with the huge wingspan. He circles the ashram buildings, spiraling ever upward, until he flies over their heads, seemingly close enough to touch. Grace sees his feet tucked like landing gear to the dark feathered body. It takes her breath away to be so close to his power.

The women tell her "this Garuda flying over us now is very auspicious. Shiva blesses us." Then they launch into an admonition, repeating it over and over, that Grace is not to continue walking around the mountain alone. Grace listens, thinks 'that's too bad, I thought Hilda said one goes to God alone.' Just then a young man, who looks completely French, strolls down the path. The Germans latch onto him, laughing and flirting. He bows with disinterest and moves on.

The trio's leader says 'we should be going also. We're trying to get the cute Swami to play his flute. We heard him in the garden this morning, he is so cute. Maybe he will play after Aarthi,' and they scamper off after the Frenchman. Grace is left alone on the mountain path, the sun at the horizon casting long shadows.

Knowing as breathless and hot as she is now, there is no time to reach the goal before dark falls swiftly, Grace says, "At least I had a great walk up to this point, and saw an eagle." She holds on to the yogi's blessing with equanimity and goes back to her room.

All stones in that place (Arunachala) are *lingams* (ovoid shape representing Shiva). It is indeed the abode of Lord Shiva. All trees are the wish-granting trees of Indra's heaven. Its rippling waters are the Ganges, flowing through our Lord's matted locks. The food eaten there is the ambrosia of the Gods. When people move about that place it is the Earth performing *pradakshina* (intentional circling) around it. Words spoken there are holy scripture, and to fall asleep there is to be absorbed in *samadhi* (higher level of motionless meditation), beyond the mind's delusion. Could there be any other place which is its equal?" – *Arunachala Puranam*, Sri Ramana Maharshi.

After bathing: O the privilege to be able to pour bucket after bucket of fresh cool water over her head, Grace dresses in fresh clothes for meditation. With the blessings of YRSK from the morning seemingly waiting for her, just over her head, she closes her eyes sitting in the meditation hall. Her mind fills not with the usual dark red one used to see behind the eyelids, but now brilliant white light. Then she recognizes from his shrine photograph, Ramana Maharshi standing before her, towering before her closed eyes as if lit with a blazing radiance of golden light. With her Christian training Grace recognizes his stance as like the paintings of Jesus risen in glory from the cross, blessing, sending waves of light out to the world, like the old fashioned painting in her grandmother's living room of 'The Light of the World.' What she sees now is Ramana's pure energy sending light to the enormous Temple room, as this light rains gently on all sitting there. She marvels at the gift of this vision without wondering how it occurs, accepting the gift.

Once full dark rises, Grace finds dinner, having had only the green-skinned fruit since Ashram breakfast, using her right hand's fingers to eat every grain of curd rice from the banana leaf, while sitting silently next to her German guides. Declining to join in enticing the young Swami into a flute concert, she returns to her monk's cell, dictates into the journal and prays for a good, uninterrupted night's sleep. Which is exactly what she gets after murmuring "perhaps tomorrow I can find the library and a companion to circumnavigate the mountain."

Her wish for a companion – like Mike, but not of course Mike – is based on her theory that sharing makes the experience fuller. Forgetting that talking away an experience is less fruitful than journaling it.

Her last thought before deep sleep: *I wish you well. My Father blesses you* – YRSK

Grace goes happily each of more three mornings to YRSK, her heart going bing, bing, bing in the ride through the crowded market to his modest concrete dwelling. Each morning waiting in line with the Indian women, she shields herself the best she can from the blistering sun. Each morning he motions to her after her bow of respect that she may stay. Grace grows happier and lighter, at one point suddenly feeling as if something that had been on her left shoulder, something a bit bitter, fly away. Every day she finds herself more and more sensitive to the sweetness in the air of his spare and immaculate quarters – immaculate even in that precise pile of dirt in the alcove. What's that about?

With each puff of cigarette smoke a wonderful sense of peace and purity, sweetness and light fills Grace. The yogi is working so simply 'yet I have a moment of feeling we are changing the world through sitting here in this small room with a pile of debris in the alcove, changing the world with kindness, persistent, unremitting kindness' she writes in her journal. 'And changing me right along with everyone else.' That pile must be a symbol of the world's debris symbolically cleansed.

Continuing in her cyber journal, "When I was getting dressed this morning, I realize I am thrilled to be going to his 'class' on nonverbally practicing the presence. And then when I get there I just sit, keeping my mind as still and quiet as I can, bringing it back to attention when it wanders away into thoughts, and I am as happy as I've ever been for those three hours. When I come back to the ashram, I lie on my single bed in a bliss daze, singing *Yogi Ramsuratkumar jai guru riya* over and over. I visualize my whole body as cells full of light, body, mind, emotions and everything else that could be called Grace anchors in light. I seem to want all my being to get it, to remember vividly – even when I go back to seeming problems of money, job, where to live, what to do in the world again – that I have sat with the Light in India."

"Today he says, 'I wish you well.' He laughs and laughs and laughs. I am so shy with him I don't have a question. I tried to ask him something life changing like that Chennai woman who wanted an interview with Sai Baba even as she was having an interview with YRSK. That didn't seem according to protocol but what do I know? I don't even know what to ask. All questions seem perishable. For my job back? For another husband? For what? One chance to ask the wish-fulfilling tree for something. What would it be, my mother's diamond ring and my pearls stolen for a short-term girl friend? One chance. It's not that I don't want. I could ask for Self-realization, but without doing the work? That seems vain. Yet it is your one chance only, says the mind.

"I could say, I'm tempted to say 'to stay with you?' But I've a suspicion that India and this body are not well matched. Good work? What would that be? I've always been in business. No matter, I am so joyfully happy at being in his presence, I start crying, tears rolling silently down my cheeks, dripping on my tunic.

"Never mind, it seems he's given me a technique for being in his presence. For it's too hard to keep up with my mind, thoughts persist in coming in even when all I want is to be still and know. His gift is that I suddenly develop this belief that every single thing that comes into my mind is his cleaning it all out, useless thoughts and patterns. This theory seems to be serving momentarily well, I don't get attached to the thoughts so don't ride them into full-fledged absorption away from the present moment. I just say to the thought, I give this to you, Swami – and really believe he's doing it, pulling those thoughts up out of me. Old thoughts, about my mother, that guy I used to call husband, career, my so-called life, all fear thoughts imbedded in the past. I do believe he is doing this. And since I know now that all my thoughts are projections impinged on the screen of my mind by the energy, colored by my history – that I am doing the best thing I possibly could to get free. I know I am safe and acting correctly. It is so clear here.

"Because all thoughts are God's thoughts – just colored by our small personal histories." Hilda Charlton, *Saints Alive*.

"When I am leaving today, YRSK sorts through a pile of offerings and carefully selects a small paper packet and a green orange and bestows them on me. Later, I eat the orange as a substitute for the missed Ashram mid-day dinner. As delicious as poet William Carlos Williams' ripe wild plums. I feel completely comfortable eating the orange, peeling away thick bumpy skin for the luscious ripeness within. What a metaphor for this whole trip, to find the beauty within. I am still obeying the encomium to avoid street amoeba-filled food and fruit without thick peels – definitely.

"However, when I open the packet of that India coarse paper barely recycled but so evocative, I gaze on green grapes. Ninety percent water, Indian water. With who knows what swimming happily and productively within?

"Yet blessed, these grapes.

"The agony. To discard a blessing. Not conceivable. To eat the fresh grapes and face weeks, or possibly, the rest of my life battling with sick tummy as British India called it. So like the quandary in the dining room. We are sitting on concrete floors, which they sweep but that's hardly sanitized. Food on a fresh delightfully green banana leaf. Maybe an eighth of an inch, if that, from the floor we just walked in on with our bare feet that have been everywhere. Everyone eats with his or her fingers. Handy not to have to wash or care for silverware. But I know where my fingers have been since I last washed them, riksha, market stall, door handles, money, oh my, oh my. I ate with bare fingers once and didn't care for it at all. So I purchased a shiny metal soupspoon, washed it from my handy bottle of diluted hydrogen peroxide after each use once I'm back in my Spartan cell. No use pretending I am anything but what I am, a New Yawkah. So I use my runcible spoon quite happily.

"But here are lovely juicy grapes – a gift blessed and given by the yogi. Like his cigarette smoke which normally, by normally I mean back in the States, I would abhor, avoid, here I can feel the blessing in each billowing puff heading my way. Blessed grapes – but I just cannot get my lips to introduce them to my mouth – which is watering for them.

"O quandary of quandaries. But why worry; it is solved for me by the mystical laughing energy that is guiding me here.

"So simple really for as I come back from the library, which I finally had the guts to find, the great grape dilemma is solved nicely. Returning through the placid garden, walking barefoot on the flagstones set in the sandy soil, it is solved hilariously. It's late afternoon just before cow dust time. The peacocks for once are not surly but content, other birds settling in for the quick night with lots of chatter about the weather and tomorrow. Two local women, carrying cleaning tools, come out of one of the cottages, presumably day's work done. The younger, seeing me, puts out her hand, asking for money with her eyes. The older woman puts a cautionary hand on her arm, and shakes her head 'no' to me.

"But I am opening my chest purse ready to comply. It's a puzzle in a puzzle for there sits the packet of grapes. The blessed grapes, probably with a vibe on them that would release me from all my karma. But caution wins out, and so I give her the packet.

"She's delighted. Opens it, thrilled to see the rare treats. Then before I can move, she snatches a perfect grape off its stem and pops it in my mouth.

"My mouth is a perfect oval. I cannot spit it out – too late anyway. And it's holy blessed food, a gift.

"So I eat it.

"They laugh and go on with many bows. I am in agony picturing an army of hungry microscopic monsters racing for my New York intestines. O, o, o, a drama beyond belief. And a great yogi laughing somewhere near-by knowing that I would receive the blessing either way.

"But what to do? I take a drop of the eatable peroxide in a liter of bottled water, laugh and laugh, again at myself. If I was set up for a blessing, by golly, India is going to see that I get it by golly.

"Later I have some trouble about walking around Arunachala at sunset after the great grape incident. I am praying I not get sick and that furthermore, I can share the bus ride back to Bangaluru with someone safe. I wave to two of the German women who want me to chase the guru in North India for enlightenment in case I found him but they didn't see me I guess. Two Tamil Nadu young men walk up the path. They seem to be enjoying the peace of the sunset too. I remember the Germans warning about strangers hassled on the hill. But they just smile. I think they were just hanging out with Shiva also.

"At dinner, I see a stranger nearby, smiling and waving at me. Later, he thanks me again for the ride in Mumbai from the airport. Niles Dashwood, the old India hand. He takes me on a tour of the ashram, explaining what the different rooms and places are, even shows the senior swamis in the kitchen cleaning up so humbly after having served the dinner.

"Ramana had them do the work of serving the guests. No one was too high not to work, serving the people. That's why you see even the senior men scrubbing pots and taking out the garbage," he said. "Fastest way to enlightenment is to work in a noisy, busy kitchen cooking for others and keeping your cool no matter what."

I tell Niles about my guidebook to India after he asks how I got myself to Tiru as he calls it. "Hilda Charlton, I used to attend her classes at the Cathedral Church of St. John the Divine in New York, in the late seventies. Now there was an enlightened sadhu, she is amazing. You are blessed if you have her books.

"I kind of got that."

"So who've you been seeing?"

"For the last four days, YRSK."

"What?"

"Well, Hilda wrote about him, so I found out where he is, and went there. He's so gracious, he lets me sit there all morning."

"Jesus," he pauses, "You think I could go with you tomorrow?"

"I don't see why not? Streams of folk seem to just walk in. Why? Is there a protocol?"

Niles looks at her, stunned out of his scruffy cool but does not answer. For once he has no snappy comeback.

It is night, the moon not yet half, wall to wall stars, tiny blue wallflowers in the courtyard outside Ramana's meditation room. Beyond on the mountain, Niles points out a garuda circling. Grace's eagle. A blessing comes. "In Tamil, when you ask someone how they are, they say 'fine' which means 'happy,' so are you happy?'"

"Yes," Grace affirms, "I am happy at last. Good-night, Niles."

Kabir says:

There is a strange tree, which stands without roots

And bears fruits without blossoming:

It has no branches and no leaves, it is lotus all over.

Two birds sing there; one is the Guru, and the other,

the disciple:

The disciple chooses the manifold fruits of life

and tastes them,

And the Guru beholds him in joy.

What Kabir said is hard to understand:

'The bird is beyond seeking, yet is most clearly visible.

The Formless is in the midst of all forms.

I sing the glory of forms.'

CHAPTER 6, Sharada Devi

My Father Blesses You – Yogi Ramsuratkumar

Mike wakes unable to place where he is: views some age-long filthy green, peeling walls, noxious odors coming from the thin mattress, smeared windows showing a vast polluted sky, the sound of honking from a major traffic jam . . . wait this is not New York or Sydney, where the hell am I? Then he catches sight of his floral shirt thrown over his Vuitton backpack on the floor. "India. No hotel, wandering into this haven. Well, at least I slept somewhere."

He swings his feet towards the floor, pauses, grabs his sandals, and shod gets out of the cot. Fumbling with his Android, he calls the office. "Good morning, Mike McCall here. Put me through to Amrita Mukerji at once." (pause) "Mike McCall. Get her now."

He snarls into the device: "I'm in Bangaluru but need a hotel suite right away. Arrange it, and then let me know where. I have about five minutes of patience left, honey. You get me?"

He slips on his shirt without bothering with the greenish brown stained sink, swings his bag over his shoulder and rumbles down the steep stairs. Anything's better than Grace the Wacko, he thinks as the familiar tone signals an incoming call. "Good work, darlin," he says, only to hear Phil's laugh. "I knew you cared, buckaroo, all along."

"Where were you last night, buddy, when I needed this blarney?" Mike barks, still aggravated.

"What's up? If it were anyone but you, I'd say you were flustered."

"Spent the night in the Krishna Hotel, one star, Bangaluru's best where fortunately the bugs were vegetarian."

"Mike, I am so sorry. If I had been in the city, you would have come to us, of course. What are you going to do now?"

"As soon as you stop bothering me, I will be on my way to a first class hotel for a shower and shave before going into the Mystix office. I upset an entire tech team about five minutes ago. You better believe they are arranging something as we speak."

"Mike, I am calling for my mother, she wants you to come to Puttaparthi with her this afternoon. Can you arrange to escort her up there? It's about four hours. We both invite you to join us in our quarters for a day or two. Can you make that happen at work?"

Mike pauses. Thinking quickly, he confirms acceptance of the invitation. "Your mother made a powerful impression on me," he confesses. "I would love to spend four hours on a journey with her. What is this place, by the way?"

"Call her. She's expecting your call. She'll tell you all about it in the car. Must go. See you later today then," and he rushes off the call.

Mike stands looking at the call ended light. The device blips again, "Yeah?"

Amrita gives him the name and direction of the Woodlands as Mike responds, "Thanks, good work. I will talk to you again in a few hours. Meanwhile, don't get into an uproar; I won't be in for a couple of days. Reschedule the appointments with the team, and don't tell me they will not mind. And yeah, there's that Grace Avery due. Put her off; tell her to see the sights, shop. Reschedule that too. Ok? Bye, see you possibly on Friday. What?"

"Yeah, I had a good time at Kovalam, nice beach, great food. Thanks for the hotel. If you need to talk to me, I keep the thing on."

Mike punches in Phil's parents' Bangaluru number. Embraced by the hospitality Sharada Devi extends, soon on his way to refresh himself before they meet at her quarters, having refused to let her pick him up at his hotel. "Why do that? I can easily get there through this traffic and save you a trip into what seems to be a perpetual traffic jam. Ok, be there at 11. Yes, I promise not to eat first."

Margaret Wilson

In the morning before time to sit silently with YRSK, Grace decides to do some research on the next stage of her journey. She loves going to the spacious and placid library at the Ashram. But she by-passes overseas editions of European and US newspapers and magazines, determined to track down just why Margaret Woodrow Wilson, who also had grown up in Princeton, on Library Place, would leave a written legacy stating that she was Living in Bliss in India. How had a President's daughter, a southerner, a Presbyterian, a concert performer, come to India and according to her obituary in the *New York Times* say she had found perfect peace. And what is perfect peace anyway? Grace puts her considerable strength of mind to solving the puzzle. First she finds, also reported in the *Times*, that Miss Wilson once had refused to prosecute a burglar, caught in the act of robbing her New York City upper east side apartment.

Grace thought there must be something spiritual going on here. She thought about Margaret Wilson's possible circle of friends. She was a trained classical singer, giving numerous concerts during World War I, even going overseas to entertain the troops. She was well enough to travel the country giving concerts for a while after the war. Therefore she must have known other performers. Then the connection dawns on Grace. The famed Ole Bull, Norwegian violinist and composer, married Sara Bull. The Sara Bull who recognized Swami Vivekananda, the monk who brought to the US the deep spirituality of India. Delighted at her intuitive leap, Grace ponders further. Who in New York would know Sara Bull and Swami Vivekananda but Josephine McLeod, socialite, dedicated to the Swami. Jo traveled in circles that would know President Wilson's daughter. It was a leap but reasonable. At last, Grace pictured what she knew about the musical and the prestigious in New York City in the first third of the Twentieth Century, as the shift inched from religious to spiritual, from European to Asian traditions. Travel to new horizons calling to both the leisure monied and to seekers, often combined.

Grace could relate to seeking now. Although new to higher dimensions, her recent taste of bliss calls her to live continually in the on-going ineffable calm that fills the air. And there in the Ashram Library on-line she found on-line various letters and commentaries.

Journal

"Jo McLeod returned to New York to live after her trips to Belur Math near Kolkatta, touchstone of Sri Ramakrishna and Swami Vivekananda. So her conversation must have led Margaret in 1936, to Sri Aurobindo's *Essays on the Bhagavad Gita* in the New York City Public Library. There Margaret struck gold she yearned for as she sat in the main reading room so engrossed she lost sense of time as her legend goes. She returned the next day to finish the book, as she wrote, for she found her path, her missing aim, which she had been searching throughout her life and above all, her Guru. The ground had been laid, her spiritual upbringing, the years devoted to studying and editing Vedanta at the Ramakrishna center in New York. She was ready to comprehend the depth of the essays. Immediately she sent a letter to Sri Aurobindo asking to practice his Integral Yoga. Most poignantly to me, she sought to find a way turning 'mental seeking into a living spiritual experience'. If I can only calm my mind so I can have a peaceful life those circling thoughts I can find true happiness for once.

"Then I discover even more treasure for not only does Yogi Ram honor Sri Aurobindo but he is honored globally as the theoretical architect of India's Independence from British rule. Moreover in the utter deprivation of solitary confinement, meant by the Raj as severe punishment to break him if not kill him outright, irrevocably changes him in 1910 from revolutionary patriot to supreme mystic visionary. Called the Lion of India a generation before, Swami Vivekananda (1863-1902) who forged a national identity for India, appears victoriously in the lightless cell. Vivekananda! His triumphant return to India after the Chicago World Parliament of Religions ignited India's independence from British bondage changing the course of India's history. Mystically, Vivekananda appears to Aurobindo where instead of the Raj breaking the prisoner in the solitary black hole, he experiences the ultimate. When Aurobindo is taken into court thereafter, he sees everyone as Krishna, judge, jury, advocates, prisoners, audience – his cosmic consciousness endures. After release, he slips away to French-controlled Pondicherry, finally free of the British dominion. He found the self, the Divine. His work for Independence would continue as freedom of the self. Sri Aurobindo answered Margaret Wilson a long letter in reply in 1936:

"'To find the Divine is indeed the first reason for seeking the spiritual Truth and the spiritual life, it is the one thing indispensable and all the rest is nothing without it. The Divine once found, to manifest Him that is, first of all to transform one's own limited consciousness into the Divine Consciousness, to live in the infinite Peace, Light, Love, Strength, Bliss to become that in one's essential nature and, as a consequence, to be its vessel, channel, instrument in one's active nature.

"'To bring into activity the Principle of Oneness on the material plane or to work for humanity is a mental mistranslation of the Truth—these things cannot be the first or true object of spiritual seeking. **We must find the self, the Divine**, then only can we know what is the work the self or the Divine demands from us. Until then our life and action can only be a help or means towards finding the Divine and it ought not to have any other purpose. As we grow in the inner consciousness, or as the spiritual Truth of the Divine grows in us, our life and action must indeed more and more flow from that, be one with that. But to decide beforehand by our limited mental conceptions what they must be is to hamper the growth of the spiritual Truth within. As that grows we shall feel the Divine Light and Truth, the Divine Power and Force, the Divine Purity and Peace working within us, dealing with our actions as well as our consciousness, making use of them to reshape us into the Divine Image, removing the dross, substituting the pure gold of the spirit. Only when the Divine Presence is there in us always and the consciousness transformed, can we have the right to say that we are ready to manifest the Divine on the material plane. To hold up a mental ideal or principle and impose that on the inner working brings the danger of limiting ourselves to a mental realisation or of impeding or even falsifying by half way formation the true growth into the full communion and union with the Divine and the free and intimate outflowing of His will in our life. This is a mistake of orientation to which the mind of today is especially prone and we are glad to see that you are free from it. It is far better to approach the Divine for the Peace or Light or Bliss that the realisation of Him gives than to bring in these minor things, which can divert us from the one thing needful. The divinisation of the material life also as well as the inner life is part of what we see as the Divine Plan, but it can only be fulfilled by an outflowing of the inner realisation, something that grows from within outward, not by the working out of a mental principle...

"'You have asked what is the discipline to be followed in order to convert the mental seeking into a living spiritual experience. The first necessity is the practice of concentration of your consciousness within yourself. The ordinary human mind has an activity on the surface, which veils the real self. But there is another, a hidden consciousness within behind the surface one in which we can become aware of the real self and of a larger deeper truth of nature, can realize the self and liberate and transform the nature. To quiet the surface mind and begin to live within is the object of this concentration. Of this true consciousness other than the superficial there are two main centres, one in the heart (not the physical heart, but the cardiac centre in the middle of the chest), one in the head. The concentration in the heart opens within and by following this inward opening and going deep one becomes aware of the soul or psychic being, the divine element in the individual. This being unveiled begins to come forward, to govern the nature, to turn it and all its movements towards the Truth, towards the Divine, and to call down into it all that is above. It brings the consciousness of the Presence, the dedication of the being to the Highest and invites the descent into our nature of a greater Force and Consciousness, which is waiting above us. To concentrate in the heart centre with the offering of oneself to the Divine and the aspiration for this inward opening and for the Presence in the heart is the first way and, if it can be done, the natural beginning; for its result once obtained makes the spiritual path far more easy and safe than if one begins from the other way.

"'That other way is the concentration in the head, in the mental centre. This, if it brings about the silence of the surface mind, opens up an inner, larger, deeper mind within which is more capable of receiving spiritual experience and spiritual knowledge. But once concentrated here one must open the silent mental consciousness upward to all that is above mind. After a time one feels the consciousness rising upward and in the end it rises beyond the lid (Hilda's term is cork) that has so long kept it tied in the body and finds a centre above the head where it is liberated into the Infinite. There it begins to come in contact with the universal Self, the Divine Peace, Light, Power, Knowledge, Bliss, to enter into that and become that, to feel the descent of these things into the nature. To concentrate in the head with the aspiration for quietude in the mind and the realisation of the Self and Divine above is the second way of concentration. It is important, however, to remember that the concentration of the consciousness in the head is only a preparation for its rising to the centre above; otherwise one may get shut up in one's own mind and its experiences or at best attain only to a reflection of the Truth above instead of rising into the spiritual transcendence to live there. For some the mental concentration is easier, for some the concentration in the heart centre; some are capable of doing both alternatively—but to begin with the heart centre, if one can do it, is the more desirable.

"'The other side of discipline is with regard to the activities of the nature, of the mind, of the life-self or vital, of the physical being. Here the principle is to accord the nature with the inner realisation so that one may not be divided into two discordant parts. There are here several disciplines or processes possible. One is to offer all the activities to the Divine and call for the inner guidance and the taking up of one's nature by a Higher Power. If there is the inward soul-opening, if the psychic being comes forward, then there is no great difficulty—there comes with it a psychic discrimination, a constant intimation, finally a governance which discloses and quietly and patiently removes all imperfections, brings the right mental and vital movements and reshapes the physical consciousness also. Another method is to stand back detached from the movements of the mind, life, physical being, to regard their activities as only a habitual formation of general Nature in the individual imposed on us by past workings, not as any part of our real being; in proportion as one succeeds in this, becomes detached, sees mind and its activities as not oneself, life and its activities as not oneself, the body and its activities as not oneself, one becomes aware of a Being within—mental, vital, physical—silent, calm, unbound and unattached which reflects the true Self above and be its representative; from this inner silent Being proceeds a rejection of all that is to be rejected, an acceptance only of what can be kept and transformed, an inmost Will to perfection or a call to the Divine Power to do at each step what is necessary for the change of the Nature. In most cases these two methods emerge and work together and finally fuse into one. But one can begin with either, the one that one feels most natural and easy to follow.

"'Finally, it will help you in your meditation and practice to keep yourself turned towards us and call for our help in all difficulties; for where personal effort is hampered, the help of the Teacher can intervene and bring about what is needed for the realisation or for the immediate step that is necessary.

"'We are doubtful about the advisability of your coming here the next winter. Your illness and the fact that you suffer from the heat stand in the way, for in Southern India the heat is extreme. The sudden change of climate and ways of life may be hard to bear. Moreover there will not be truly competent medical aid and advice available here as it would be in America. Finally, you do not know perhaps that I am living for the present in an entire retirement, not seeing or speaking with anyone, even the disciples in the Ashram, only coming out to give a silent blessing three times in a year. The Mother also has not time to give free or frequent access to those who are here. You would therefore probably be disappointed if you came here with the idea of a personal contact with us to help you in your spiritual endeavour. The personal touch is there but it is more of an inward closeness with only a few points of physical contact to support it. But this inner contact, inner help can very well be received at a distance. We have not any disciples in America, though several Americans have come recently here and became interested in the Yoga. But we have disciples in France and some of these have been able already to establish an inner closeness with us and to become aware of our nearness and help in their spiritual endeavour and experience. We would advise you therefore to try this way where you are rather than face the difficulty and inconveniences of a journey and stay here which, if necessary, could be undertaken with more advantage after you have gone some way in the path rather than at present.

"'You can write to us always about your experiences or difficulties and we shall give the necessary replies—between the written letter and reply there will necessarily at this distance be a rather long interval; but the silent answer and help can always go to you immediately—for here distance does not count.'"

*

With this letter, Margaret's life – and Grace's on reading it decades later: **We must find the self, the Divine**, changes focus. Miss Wilson and a young Joseph Campbell had edited Swami Nikhilananda's translation of *The Gospel of Sri Ramakrishna* during the early thirties. Grace thought one couldn't do that without both information and an interest in the Hindu teachings. Joseph Campbell was even then known for his work in comparative world mythologies, and would later fascinate viewers of the public television series, *The Power of Myth* with Bill Moyers. And Margaret must have known Jo McLeod. Grace takes Sri Aurobindo's letter to heart, as if it were written to her as well as

Margaret. Perhaps it was. **We must find the self, the Divine - Sri Aurobindo**

Aha, Grace shouts silently, Miss Wilson already was interested in the spiritual, deeper inner meanings of religion. I knew it. I could feel it in that Library Place house. Her mother, first wife of President Wilson was her first teacher – not only in education as the girls were taught at home, but in the inner life. Now I find the whole family spiritual and involved in the Way of God. And here's Margaret turning to Asia for its wisdom. I always wondered about that house on Library Place. Something mystical in the timbers, it got even me interested. Perhaps those migraines when I first went there were from spiritual causes. "And I thought it was haunted with memories and scholarship, maybe there was more present in the air than I could fathom."

Grace continues tapping: "After Sri Aurobindo's deeply helpful response, Margaret continues her practice on the principles of Integral Yoga: finding the self, the Divine. She also arranged the publication of an article on Sri Aurobindo and his Yoga written by Swami Nikhilananda in the American paper *Asia*. Ill health had required her to retire from her singing engagements, so she was living quietly on the Upper East Side in Manhattan. The Depression was in full force. She had only her father's small legacy after a failed attempt at bond trading. War again, despite President Wilson foresight in trying to end war, was at hand in Europe. Japan was arming. Margaret, in ill health, made a bold decision in an attempt to find peace on Earth.

"On October 1938, at age 52, she came to Puducherry ignoring the warning of her physicians regarding the difficult effects of the hot climate of South India on her severe arthritic condition. As First Daughter of a President of the United States, she was considered newsworthy and a concern of FDR in Washington. Yet she left quietly, determined on India. By November, Sri Aurobindo gives her the name of *Nishtha* meaning "one-pointed, fixed and steady concentration, devotion and faith in the single aim on the Divine and Divine Realisation."

On receiving her new name, she wrote to her younger sister Eleanor: "Do you remember those beautiful words in the Bible? *And I shall keep him in perfect peace whose mind is stayed (or fixed) on me?* That is what we must do, learn to stay our minds on Him."

Grace finds a commentary by Nirodbaran: On November 23, 1938 before the scheduled 'Darshan Day' when the devotees and followers of Sri Aurobindo and the Mother were to have their Darshan: Visitors had swollen the even flow of our life; among them, Miss Wilson, daughter of President Wilson, had come from far-off America for the Master's

Darshan. That there could be someone who could write such a wonderful book in this materialistic age was beyond her imagination. She could hear the Voice of the Lord saying to "Abandon all dharma. Take refuge in me alone. I shall deliver thee from all Sin.' The book was her bible. She decided she must have the Darshan of such a unique person. But on that night Sri Aurobindo caught his foot on a gift tiger-skin rug in his room and fell with his right knee striking the head. Darshan was cancelled due to a severe fracture."

Nirodbaran continues: "All hopes and aspirations of hundreds of people were set at naught by this single blow. They gathered in the courtyard of the Ashram to know the truth and went back sullen-hearted with a fervent prayer addressed to the Mother and the Lord for his speedy recovery…The Mother, out of compassion for the disappointed devotees, gave darshan to all in the evening. Thus she wiped away their gloom with the sunshine of her smile and the power of her touch."

And about Nishtha, Nirodbaran writes: "Miss Wilson accepted Fate's decree with a calm submission." When on 18 December, Dr. Manilal who was treating Sri Aurobindo said to him that Nishtha must have been disappointed because of the lack of Darshan, Sri Aurobindo replied:

"No. She has taken it with the right attitude—unlike many."

Nishtha was told by The Mother that the members of the Ashram were free to follow their own 'promptings' and that there were no pledges of any kind as they were all untrue. "Here it is only the Divine," the Mother had told Nishtha. Soon after, Nishtha wrote to her friend Lois Kellogg Roth: (with)"That pregnant saying I am only gradually learning to recognise, the significance of this place. I am beginning to see that all the bondage here as elsewhere and everywhere are our own making—that the Divine imposes no bondage of any kind whatsoever."

Grace ponders what it would mean for her to sweep away all her belief systems like Margaret Wilson had. Discard the sense of betrayal at losing her profession, disbelieve the hateful voice, and give up her hatred of Germans, tidy up her long-held opinions on, oh, everything. But how? Wouldn't she then be a bore? She develops an aspiration, from that moment on, to go beyond her prejudices and limitations in that Ramana Ashram library.

Grace reads on. 'In 1938, Christmas was celebrated in the Ashram for the first time at 'The Red House', which was owned by Udar Pinto. The guests included Nishtha, Ambu (the Hatha yoga teacher who also looked after Nishtha) and François Sammer (one of the architects of Golconda and his assistant architect George Nakashima). "Nishtha made a big star to place on the top of the tree that year," remembers Gauri Pinto.

Nakashima, Grace exclaims out loud in the library reading room, "My grandmother purchased several pieces of furniture from his New Hope studio. I remember his taking us out to lunch in New Hope at a restaurant called 'Mother's.' What a pun, so even he was into The Mother. My gran told me that the public heard little of Miss Wilson after she retired from concertizing until 1940, when Nakashima, an American born architect, returned from Pondicherry. He had spent two years overseeing the building of Golconda Guest House. On his return to Seattle yet before his internment in a Japanese-American prison camp, Nakashima made the announcement to the press that Miss Wilson had found peace and seclusion from the world." Grace pauses, and yet he is a national treasure now. "Something is going on here, I never thought about all these subtle connections. Maybe my grandmother was onto something. Perhaps it's similar to what's in that book, *Saints Alive*."

Grace continues taking notes: 'Miss Wilson wrote to her friend Lois: "Since seeing Sri Aurobindo and the Mother together, I have been surer than ever that their way is my way—that my soul brought me here where it belongs." She spent her days in the Ashram in prayer and meditation. She worked in the flower garden of the Ashram and she also helped in typing Sri Aurobindo's writings on her manual Corona typewriter. Another privilege that she enjoyed with others was washing Sri Aurobindo's dishes. She contributed one hundred dollars a month to the Ashram from the stipend that her father had arranged for her; from whatever money that remained, she brought fresh fruits and her favourite facial lotions.'

"The Mother too, took extreme care of Nishtha. She provided Nishtha with a spacious building across the Playground building for accommodation (this building was converted into 'Sri Smriti' in 1989). The Mother made Nishtha feel comfortable in the best possible ways; she was given a special cook and a servant. Once the Mother told Nishtha in Lalita's presence that since she was unaccustomed to vegetarian diet, she must not hesitate to have non-vegetarian food if her health required it. Nishtha replied: "No, Mother, I will not have it—even if I have to die as a result." Later, in 1941 she had to resort to non-vegetarian diet when she began to suffer from gout.

"When the United States joined the Second World War, President Franklin D. Roosevelt called for the evacuation of all Americans residing in India but despite extreme pressure and requests from her family, friends and the U.S. government, Nishtha would not leave. "Few can show the strength of character which came so easily to her," writes Amal Kiran about Nishtha.

Grace taps in excerpts from Nishtha's letters to her friend Lois Kellogg Roth regarding her thoughts, spiritual experiences in the Ashram and above all, Sri Aurobindo and the Mother:

"Sometimes I feel as if the Divine were whispering to my soul and I, in order to catch the faintest word, am listening as I have never listened before. Sometimes it is as if the Beloved and I were telling each other secrets that none can share except in a wordless communion with us.

"But I will note, simply as one notes a "happening", that the closer I feel to Mother and Sri Aurobindo, the closer I feel too as an immediate result sometimes, to those other dear ones . . . I was transported into an inner plane of being which I recognise as the same one I was in inwardly at certain moments when my singing was more than ordinarily subjective.

"But when I look at the Mother in the morning sunlight on her terrace from which she sends each of us a shaft of love more brilliant than any light that was ever seen on snowy crests, or when in the evening I see her standing in the meditation hall, still in the immutable calm, the Unchanging One, I know that the vast stillness of Mont Blanc is but a faint imitation of that other Peace that She is.

"Oh, Lois, one cannot talk about Sri Aurobindo and the Mother—one can only suggest in some such words as these that they are what we are seeking, that which we will be in the outer man as now we are in the inner Reality. They are consciously that.'

". . . One day in a California garden, when the intensity of my enjoyment provoked the rather humorous thought—"I wonder if God enjoys this in exactly this way—if he doesn't, I'm sorry for him"—then came the idea as a kind of realisation, "it is He that is enjoying this way—perhaps that is the reason for me."

About Sri Aurobindo, Nishtha said: "Here is one on earth whom one can love all one's life and in whom one can lose oneself."

"Excited with the success of her search, Grace finds that on January 21, 1943 Margaret

Wilson told *The New York Times* correspondent Herbert L. Matthews - "I don't want to return to the United States. I am not homesick. In fact I never felt more at home anywhere any time in my life.

"To her friend Lois again, she wrote in 1939: 'Since seeing Sri Aurobindo and the Mother together, I have been surer than ever that their way is my way - that my soul brought me here where it belongs.'

The Ashramites remember her as an 'imperious, fastidious lady of remarkable mind and character.' True to her new name, Nishtha, she seems to have had only one intense aspiration, that of realizing the Divine according to journalist Matthews. Grace ponders why a woman who knows her way is called 'imperious.' What Grace admires is just that very strength and one-pointedness. She feels she knows Margaret Wilson, having lived in her home. Somehow she knows her."

In another letter to her dear friend Lois, Grace quotes: "I think I can say that some kind of 'experience' has begun for me, for I strike a quiet nearly every day." Peace of mind, o, how I long for that, Grace whispers to herself, if only my mind would leave me in peace.

Grace looks up the obituary printed in the *New York Times*, which calls her a "recluse," as though she were some sad hermit, but Grace decides that's a jaundiced view. For Margaret chose to live in a spiritual community dedicated to beauty, culture and world peace, inner and outer peace. Not a 'recluse' at all, but like her father, a contributor to ending wars. I could commit to that, maybe I could start with Mike? Once the war stops in my own mind, peace must be possible, look at Yogi Ram. He has it.

"In the forties Margaret's body, which had suffered ill health for much of her life, began to give way." Grace surmises at the ironic twist of fate, she suffered periodic occurrences of kidney problems that had eventually killed her mother of Bright's Disease while the Wilsons were in the White House. But, such was her comfort level in India, "She begged the Indian doctor not to send her back to New York. For several days she hovered between life and death. On April 24, 1944 Margaret Woodrow Wilson, or *Nishtha*, died of uremia. She was buried in the Protestant section of the cemetery at the Ashram in Puducherry."

Then to complete the picture, Grace finds this excerpt: "Risha Blackand, an Indian student at the Ashram who had been assigned the task of escorting Margaret back to her apartment every evening after meditation, wrote of her death. 'So lived Nishtha in her spacious apartment fanned by the fresh breeze from the sea (Bay of Bengal) and caressed by the balmy breath of her garden blossoms. So she thought and felt and dreamed: so she loved God and her fellow men...Suddenly, like a flower, she drooped and languished and faded away. But the unfading bloom and aroma of her soul still hovered over the atmosphere in which she aspired and prayed and adored her beloved Lord.'"

No wonder, Margaret Wilson felt at home in Pondicherry, President Wilson and Sri Aurobindo both envision world peace.

(Text excerpts on-line from Aurobindo Ashram Publications Department and private correspondence.)

Kabir says:

I have stilled my restless mind, and my heart is radiant:

For in Thatness I have seen beyond Thatness,

In company I have seen the Friend Himself.

Living in bondage, I have set myself free:

I have broken away from the clutch of all narrowness.

Kabir says: 'I have attained the unattainable,

And my heart is coloured with the colour of love.

Mike at Baba's

Sharada Devi and her husband, Dr. S.R. Patel, are waiting in the lobby when Mike's taxi arrives at the front gate. Dr. Patel releases the gate's electronic lock, standing at the open carved mahogany door welcoming his son's friend into the foyer. "So now you are the visitor to my country, welcome to India," he says, his bright eyes twinkling with the same charm as his youngest son. "We knew when we met you in Sydney that someday you would be called to India. And now we have the chance to show you the real spiritual India you have heard of for years. Welcome, son."

Mike's eyes suddenly moist at the kind greeting, sticks out his hand to press the other's but Dr. Patel, gracefully folds his hands in the traditional Hindu greeting, at his heart, and bows. "Here we do this instead of exchanging germs the English way. As a heart surgeon, I find it triply interesting. We humble ourselves by bowing; we touch our hearts in order to touch yours since we are one, and we press our hands to our own hearts, awakening compassion and sharing it with you. A practical custom, do you not agree?"

Mike bows, hands to his heart, gladly. "And most sanitary," the medical man proposes with a laugh. Mike suddenly laughs back. "Yes, sir, an excellent idea, especially if you had seen the so-called hotel-hovel I stayed in last night."

"Mike," Sharada Devi, by the elevator in the marble tiled hall, "Come, son, we are sorry you had that experience."

"But it just makes me appreciate your hospitality more, ma'am."

"Oh, now that's more like the cheeky, young Michael who introduced me to his beautiful grandmother. Mike, come upstairs, before we leave, come with me up to the terrace. I want to show you my garden, which is on the roof."

Mike and Dr. Patel perform *Namaskar* again, the same small bow while holding the palms together raised before the heart, Mike going up the elevator as the surgeon leaves for the hospital. "We will see each other soon," he promises Mike.

Leaving the elevator which opens directly into the apartment, she says "Yes, leave your sandals here; choose house slippers so you will be comfortable. Come in."

As Sharada Devi leads their son's friend out onto the same terrace where she and Sushil had spoken of the sad changes in Mike since their college days in Sydney, she gestures to the wall hanging. "Your grandmother gave this to me, fresh from her loom. That time you escorted us out into the bush to her studio. You remember?"

Mike replies tersely: "Yes." Then changes his tone, "You and she became like sisters in that moment, did you not?"

"Yes, we recognized each other by our love for God. And now she is gone on into the

Light. Sit here Mike, I am going to speak to you, as I know she would. You have changed since those days? You have lost yourself, is it not so?" Nodding, Mike sits obediently at her gesture in a wicker chair next to the jasmine vines.

"You know we are devotees of Sathya Sai Baba. Sushil had a photograph of him in your apartment."

Mile replies, "And an altar with incense and fresh flowers daily. He meditated. Oh, yes, I remember those eyes of Baba. I loved that place we shared; it was like a refuge from classes and sports. We were happy there in those college days."

Silence as Sharada listens, giving him time to recall his life in Australia. "Then we graduated, Sushil went to flight school and I went into graduate school for what we called computer science then."

He stopped right up against the memory.

"And then Oma died."

"Yes, you greatly missed her."

"She was my guiding light. Everything in our family centered on her. She wasn't religious, you know? In fact I think she secretly was bored by my grandfather's dedication to the church. But how kind she was. She never saw a stranger, spoke kindly to everyone, and instinctively knew if someone was in need. She made soup, bread, gave away baskets of food, no one could ever trace how much money she just handed over at the back door. God, I can still feel how good it was to be in her embrace. That loving touch is my first memory – not my mother, seems she was busy, but my grandmother. And then, and then," he fights to control his voice, "to watch her die after a brutal attack by vandals. She just turned bone white, lost consciousness for days, still beautiful, all her wrinkles were from laughter, but she never opened her eyes again. And then she was gone, just like that. No goodbyes, nothing medicine could do."

Sharada Devi listens without comment. Mike takes a deep breath, controlling himself visibly.

"Just gone. So I went to New York and joined the toughest, meanest corporations I could find. Otherwise it hurt too much, you know?"

Sharada looks at Mike, her full attention on his whole being. She sees the tight lines around his mouth and eyes, hard blue eyes now, not the bright laughing ones she remembers. Although he just spent two days in a resort beach hotel over MahaShivaratri, his skin is a greenish white hue, she knows by this he has lived indoors by artificial light too long.

"So you went to the Big Time and turned into a stone. You lost your heart, gave away your soul and buried your pain."

"Now, don't coddle me . . ."

"Mike, your grandmother did not die, she did not leave you, and there is no death. She died paying off karma on a global scale as she is a pure soul, no karma of her own. Can you accept that?" No response comes from Mike, still as iron.

"Have you heard of St. Thérèse of Liseaux?" Mike nods remembering Grace at Kovalam. "The Little Flower died at age 24, she died believing her suffering was that others might have less suffering. It takes a great soul to be willing do take on others' suffering. . .Wait, don't reject my words, at least keep an open mind until your own experience can tell you this. I am so sorry for the situation you find yourself in. I want to give you a gift that never dies. Will you allow me to do that?"

Struggling at her incomprehensible words, yet from their history together, knowing she is reaching out to him, Mike nods. A sharp, reluctant *yes* as if wrenched from his depths.

"So. Good. Sushil is there now, waiting for us. We have long thought Baba sent Sushil to college in Sydney for your sake. Here you are, you have found a way to India, so now I am taking you to Sathya Sai Baba. I know that is where your oma is. I am taking you to heaven on Earth, where else would she be?"

And then from memory, in English, Sharada Devi quotes her Baba:

> "Riches and wealth are short-lived; office and authority are temporary; life-breath is a flickering flame in the wind. Youth is a three-day fair and pleasures and fortunes are bundles of sorrow. Knowing this, if you devote this limited term of life to the service of the Lord, then you are indeed blessed. Seek refuge at the Lord's feet early on. Everything is untrue, impermanent and akin to castles in the air. Contemplate on this truth, approach God and glorify Him; that alone

confers permanent joy. Inside the room called the body, in the safe called the heart, the precious gem of wisdom (*jnana*) exists. Four wily thieves - lust, anger, greed and envy (*kama, krodha, lobha* and *asuya*) are lying in wait to rob it. Awaken to this danger before it is too late. Reinforce yourself with the support of the Universal Guardian, the Lord, and keep the gem intact. That will make you rich in love (*prema*), and peace (*shanthi*)." She quotes from *Sathya Sai Speaks, Vol. 6, Chapter 38.*

"None of this is my belief system," Mike says, "Nor my experience. I like my job, I like the money, sorrow can be dealt with by forgetting it, and love doesn't interest me any longer: it hurts too much. But if you and Sushil want to take an unbeliever there, I will be a good boy and behave well. I respect both of you too much to reject your proposal."

"Oh, Mike, terrific honesty. What a ride we are going to have. Let's get started with, what, eggs, bacon, toast for you?"

"Thank you for your consideration but I can have that anytime, how about a real Indian breakfast? And you can tell me more about what I'm getting into."

After idles and huli are put before Mike, he shoots a questioning glance at Sharada Devi. "The vegetable stew I recognize, what's it called? But what are these little white packets that look somewhat like Proust's *petite madeleine*?"

She laughs, "And when you bite into one does it take you back to your grandmother's breakfasts?"

"No, not at all, she would have given me oatmeal with brown sugar and real milk from her own cows. But that would be horrible in Bangaluru, temperature too intense for a German breakfast. Do I taste rice?"

"Of course, our Indian staple. These rice cakes are the shape of a woman's palm. Before electricity, an amma would have stored any left-over cooked white rice in water overnight, scooped it out of the clay pot, squeezed and shaped a handful then steamed it to make an idli. Get used to them, you will find them everywhere. Have some curd, what we call yoghurt, and eat along with the huli. My cook made the huli - vegetable stew, mild just for you. Extremely nourishing for our car trip."

Mike looks at her over the delicious perfectly made Chai, "Yes, ma'am. And I will learn to love it all."

Later they walk into the front courtyard to find the driver standing by a dark green Mercedes C320. The trunk is open, filled with hampers and soft suitcases. Mike sees his fancy backpack, which he had left on the terrace, now among the baskets of fruits and vegetables.

"I will cook for you and Sushil in our quarters," promises the mother of the family. "We will stay together at the Ashram. Since you probably do not have the white shirt and pants you will need for Darshan, I have instructed extras of Sushil's be packed for you. No worries."

"But Mataji, I will buy some there."

"You will do as I say if you choose to call me mataji – which of course I would welcome. Let's go, I hope to reach 'Parthi' in time for 4 p.m. Darshan. Get in, we will have time for conversation on the road."

As the driver weaves the comfortable and strong car through the boiling, roiling streets of the Garden City of India, to the howling of horns, Sharada explains what Mike can expect at the end of the journey.

"Everything is organized around Darshan that is sight of the holy. If we arrive without mishap, we will go directly to the courtyard of the Temple as directed by the Seva Dals, volunteer service workers, one of whom today will probably be Sushil. We will sit on the ground, men on the right facing the altar, we women on the other and wait until our number is chosen, and then file in by lines to the assigned seating. Then we will relax, if you meditate . . . " she pauses.

"I don't."

"Then you will calm your thoughts, allow them to focus not on business, or your past, or your hopes and fears, for you will be in a vibration of sublime peace and may rest in it. The waiting is a time to tame the outer world that is so busy in you, not to cut it out but to focus on the touch of the air on your face, the silence around you, the beauty of the opportunity to be present."

"Present for what? Or rather do you mean a gift?"

Laughing, "Good, I am glad you are relaxing and your good humor is coming back. To be present. Just know that the atmosphere of this place is intense, filled with the echoes of eighty years of sacred chanting, holy discourses, healings beyond description, meditation, seva and miracles no one on Earth except our Sai can know."

"Miracles? Is this a Hindu Lourdes? Oma went there before she left for Australia. She wanted permission to escape from Europe. She didn't want to run away and leave her family. Actually I don't know why she went there, she just said to pay her respects and ask for a miracle," he choked. Sharada waited. "She said I was the answer."

"Ah, now all this is coming into focus. Your oma asked the Blessed Mother Mary for a blessing for her grandchildren when she went into the waters at Lourdes. No matter why you think you came to India, Swamiji has invited you here. And so your soul journey continues."

"What if I cannot meditate while we are waiting?"

"Then I will give you a book to read, a holy book, by a woman who came from California to give dance benefits to raise money for convents and schools. But ended up digging in with the masters of spirituality. She spent two years at Baba's, invited to live in his household in those early days, before going back to guide what she called her kids. They published this book of her teachings after she passed over in 1988."

"Don't tell me. I know it. I don't want it. It's *Saints Alive* isn't it? A wacko woman I used to know made it her guidebook to India. And she's nuts."

"So anyone who reads a certain book who you've had a hard time with, then that book is not to be touched? Mike, what's the sense in that? Guilt by association. Come on. I love this book, and so does Sushil. She has an amazing wit as well as a truly deep understanding of the universality of the great masters of which she is one, a great soul come back to Earth to help - but she would never tell you that. So you must read her chapter on Baba while waiting in Darshan. That's settled."

"Ok, boss, if you say so."

"Now, Mike, that was sweet. It felt good to me, not harsh like your comments on the woman. No, no, you do not have to tell me about how she hurt you now. Later if you want, now I want you to know about the miracles I mentioned. Aren't you curious about these healings?

"Not especially. I'm just surprised to hear he's a magician. I'm not into magic and wizards and am astonished for I saw that photo everyday for four years in college. He looks like pure love to me."

"Well, that's it, Mike. Divine Love is the miracle. Look around, do you see love in action out the car window?"

"I see one hell of a traffic jam, gasoline pollution, hordes of people packed in an over-populated city, all shades of poverty, filth, commercial greed, I see the horrors of our western civilization layered on the ancient culture of a poisoned Asia with violence, disease, greed, lust and anger taking us all into hell in a hand basket. And I am sorry to despoil your comfortable life with these words, Ma." He glances at his travel companion expecting to see rejection.

"Yes, Michael, your assessment, while only the surface, is correct. And what would you say about a man who can, with the flick of an eyelash, bring a dead child, certified dead, to life, heal impossible blindness, lead the broken-hearted to help others, to provide 1.2 million people with drinkable water, a whole district of India, which includes Chennai and instigate SuperSpeciality hospitals that are totally free to patients. One where my husband and I, now retired, are volunteers along with all the other staff. The list of miracles you will come to find out is endless, what Love can do in this place we call our planet Earth. Millions of people have benefited from his love in action. I am taking you there so you can see what you, in turn, can learn to do about furthering that list of miracles yourself."

Mike sits silently, absorbing her words.

"Mataji, I can do nothing about the world. I cannot even do anything about my life."

"Just so."

"And how does he do all this, one little man, now in his eighties? Make miracles from his hair?"

Kabir says:

Who are you, and whence do you come?

Where dwells that Supreme Spirit, and how

Does He have His sport with all created things?

The fire is in the wood; but who awakens it suddenly?

Then it turns to ashes, and where goes the force of the fire?

The true guru teaches that He has neither limit

nor infinitude.

Kabir says: Brahma suits His language

to the understanding of His Hearer.

CHAPTER 7, Pondi Bus

Sri Aurobindo solves the problem of the linkage between the ineffable Brahman, or The Supreme Absolute, with creation – Puducherry Tourism booklet

Cyber Journal in Tiru

"Last night after talking with Niles about Ramana Maharshi's Self Inquiry, I pledge to keep asking ever deeper and deeper *Who am I*? As a result I observe my mind at work for the first time from a place outside the mind. From a clear observation point I didn't know I had, above the mind. The mind's grotesqueness horrifies me. Re-occurring thoughts, this constant refrain of wanting, wanting, wanting. Wanting Mike, although I don't really. Wanting to leave YRSK for Puducherry. But not ever part from him either.

"Historical likes and dislikes seem the same energy. Strengths the same as hates: hate Germans, love the British Isles: But in India some Englishmen behaved brutally, some Germans spiritual seekers. Rile. Jack the Ripper. Bennie Hill, Beethoven. Grace, Mike. I could scream with the inner confusion once I really notice the mind has a pattern of duality. Clearly I am not my mind only but something more vast.

"Now the mind is obsessing, it is greedy for experiences and more thoughts come as if there are not enough of them. 'Shall I break this magical circle in Tiru with the yogi just because something inside is urging me to continue on east?' And then, is it a miracle that Niles Dashwood shows up, a seasoned Indian traveler, sensitive to the spiritual, offering to accompany me there on the bus? No question of romance. 'Hardly,' the mind says, 'he's too disorganized and scruffy to think of romance. Wonder when he last combed his hair, what little there is of it?' I feel guided to go there. Yogi Ramsuratkumar frequented the Aurobindo ashram, talked with the yogi and the Mother. Calls him Teacher.' I wonders if I'm being sent there?"

"STOP. I take charge of the wandering thoughts with discipline, pledging contentment. What is true at this moment is that somehow I know I must go on to Puducherry. The Universe has kindly provided a guide.

"Simple enough. But I so love sitting with YRSK, to move on, depart without taking leave is without courtesy. The conflict about leaving, even for two days, unbearable."

Grace ends her journal entry by writing, "I am wishing for peace to get away from my mind's repetitions. Where is the mind anyway? In the brain? The Tibetans say the Big Mind, the true mind, is in the heart. To Ramana and the Advaitists (non-dual) not the mind but the True Self. I am Episcopalian, I believe my soul, aka my higher consciousness is my true self."

Yet something of the Tiru yogi's peace penetrates her, transforms her into a new way of being. She does get in bed, but instead of falling into unconsciousness, sits cross-legged in meditation. And lo, by itself with no spiritual techniques like breathing, visualizing, certainly no special spiritual music, just Grace, her mind and body and emotions concentrate on one point in her heart as if she has a nose there breathing in love, as Hilda guided. By itself seemingly, an energy called the Kundalini, sparkles straight up her spine. Briefly she notices the sensation is like the one occurring on the airplane as she flew into Mumbai less than a week ago. And again, it is so sweet Grace simply enjoys.

From inside a strong quiet voice, very distinctly, says: *You are very beloved, my daughter. I surround you in love.* Grace feels as if she is in a rosy mist and hears: *You can trust this because your mind has never thought of this image before. I give it to you that you may be in peace.*

After a period of time wrapped in gentleness, happily still in that rose mist.

Grace hears in the silent air: *This would be your work. Take the fear of the world and transform it through your consciousness into peace. Not your fear, the world's fear but it would run through your consciousness. Because you have learned how, now do it yourself, turn it over to the Father. This is the only way to overcome fear. Do not hold onto to it, give it to God, who will take it; transform it and newly purified, send the energy out to those who need it.*

Grace knows Jesus said, "Those who follow me must take on the suffering of the world.' This is what YRSK is doing. Who can I ask who knows the straight answer?"

At some point, Grace knows not when, she must have lain down for when she was last aware of her body, she was sitting cross legged on the thin mattress of her cot in the India night. Silence settles outside in the heavy vegetation behind her back window. Silence before with the balcony overlooking the ashram gardens. Even silence to her right over the high clay wall running along the main road to Bangaluru. Silence with Grace enrapt. She enters a dream through the rosy mist.
I am with a man with a big halo of hair appears raises a golden goblet, saluting me yet drinking what in the dream seems to be blood. I fear he is a vampire, and worry if I have wandered into a wrong place? Then I remember the mass – where we symbolically drink the blood of Christ every week. Many non-Christians have for two centuries misunderstood the symbolic act of communion with God through the Eucharist wine as

drinking blood. Not so, Grace believes the act commemorates union with the Divine, the embrace of God.

Next dream: YRSK comes to Grace as she sits in a Hindu Temple with sandy floors; all is dark except for flicking ghee lights in clay bowls. He signals her, "Ah, Grace, My Father blesses you." Then Grace realizes she is lost walking through the dark in a labyrinth of Indian streets. Yogi Ram holds out his hand, leading her to the way out. "My Father blesses you." To the Greeks, the mind is a labyrinth. To neural scholars the brain is a labyrinth shape. It all clicks for Grace in an instant flash. Labyrinths are same way in as the way out, one step at a time, breathing calmly, preserving and focusing.

Then late in the night before leaving for Puducherry, by the light of the 40-watt bulb, Grace wakes, so reads from *MahaYoga*, the writings of Ramana. "There is no mind. If you believe in the mind, it is impossible to meditate."

Grace, new to flexing the meditation muscle, accordingly in her innocence, prays to her True Self to be present, which Ramana's teachings said is the only thing worth meditating on. But true to her Christian upbringing also asks Ramana Maharshi for his blessing.

Slowly, majestically, irrevocably, an essence of Presence pours in stalwartly. Searching for a metaphor Grace thinks: like the beginning of Gustav Holst' *Jupiter* from *The Planets*. Then silence, sleep and the end of dreaming.

Dawn chattering of the monkeys, skittering along the front balcony, wakes her. Her hand moves instinctively towards the clock on her device to find it is just minutes before she's to meet Niles for ashram breakfast then the bus to Puducherry. Pondi he calls it, like an old friend.

She puts mobile, change of clothes, tooth and hair brush in her carryall, leaving all else, grabs a fresh bottle of water, and dressed, runs out among the monkeys. She's been careful, avoiding their sharp fruit-eating teeth, their little white hands imploring, plucking, demanding from her. Now she startles them, as they startle her, and all scurry in opposite directions.

Niles finished with his idlis, plucks a bumpy-skinned yellow fruit and two bananas on his way out the door, pulling a hungry Grace in his footsteps. "We do not want to be on the local bus," he warns and strides on, leaving her to follow him. In the taxi on the way to the Shiva Temple, Grace calls silently to YRSK, 'please smooth the way and don't let me be lost in India please, please, with this strange guy.'

Journal

Suddenly, inexplicably, now Niles wants to be introduced to the yogi. I cannot say no. Who am I to do that? But it's a lesson 'don't talk so much,' seems like bragging, one-upping on the latest guru, like those women on the mountain. Then Niles spots another woman, a Hindu wearing an orange sari and brings her along.

At the session, YRSK is the same. As I enter with Niles, an orange sari woman whispers sternly KRIPA! they buzz softly to each other. Have I done something wrong letting Niles come and bring the woman?

YRSK is so patient, first there's the Chennai woman wanting him to arrange an interview with Sathya Sai Baba. Today, a woman comes with a very sulky teen-age daughter. The mother explains this girl is doing her exams. "Why bring her, woman? She needs to study."

Then he looks at the girl. "You will do well," he says it many, many times, repeating it, stroking her right wrist, giving her rock candy, puffing smoke at her, peering into her eyes with kindness. "Take her home, she needs to study," he indicates they should leave, and after prostrating they do. The girl is beaming, the mother content with the blessing, ignoring the reprimand for she has gotten what she wants.

At that the orange sari guest departs in a huff because it seems to her, he did not 'help' the student. She didn't understand, reacting to YRSK's smoking and the appearance of his tiny dwelling, that pile of debris. Although I had suggested on the ride over she read *Saints Alive* with Hilda's teachings about hidden saints who disguise themselves as 'beggars' which YRSK calls himself not guru or yogi but 'this beggar.' She has her mind set on appearances and misses the kripa.

Unperturbed, out of nowhere the yogi says to me, "You can come Friday." And gives an apple to me – no more grape tests.

Niles winks. We bow and walk through the market crowd to the bus station. It's Wednesday, I have my two days for Puducherry – confirmed and blessed."

Invisible in India

After the Yogi's darshan, they immediately run to the packed bus station. Grace can read neither the signs, travel destinations and arrivals nor the bus placards. Without Niles she would have been, what? Lost. No, helped by kripa. What a change in her. But then hadn't she been helped all along the way in India? Even by Mike on MahaShivaratri to get to take part in the celebration? And it had been an enchanted evening . . .

The packed bus from Tiru to Chennai bumps and winds along at the same tremendous headlong pace as in her journey from Bangaluru – except this time, Grace sits next to a big-boned, wiry Brit, an old India hand, scruffy, scattered, self-absorbed, but his company keeps the eyes off her unlike the bus in. Suddenly she's become invisible, like in New York. Here it is because she is with a man, any man it appears would do, and therefore not such an object of curiosity. A woman alone is public curiosity, a woman pigeonholed with a man the usual mere nothing, she assumes. When she asks Niles, he says of course and goes to sleep with his straw hat over his eyes.

Grace gazes out the streaky window, as villages flash by the ratcheting bus, most no more than a few small dwellings along the road with outlying fields full of bright green. Alternating with these villages of Gandhi's India, are the larger towns, packed with people. Then bang, back out into the country. Grace wishes she had a guide who would tell her what the miles and miles of women in their bright colored saris are doing sitting on the side of the road. All have legs folded. All sit very straight. Bareheaded in the searing sun. All have the same hair style, shiny, perhaps oiled, black hair pulled back tightly in a wavy shock that falls below their shoulders. None have flowers. There are no children. Few men. Piles of rock at the side of each woman. Miles and miles of womankind, sitting in the searing sun pounding rocks.

It's mesmerizing, and in the hot sun herself (the only seats available to them are on the south side of the bus) she too falls asleep slathered with sun block. Although the water bottle soon empties, the Yogi's prasad apple sustains her nicely. A blessing since Niles does not offer to share his Ramana Ashram fruit.

When the bus approaches world famous Chennai, Grace wakes in a pool of sweat, her travel pants sticking tight, to feel Niles less than gently shaking her shoulder. She straightens her hiking hat, trying to rearrange herself. Outside the window, more people than she had ever seen were going about their lives in an enormous sprawling city – Chennai, called Madras for a blink of the city's history.

Signs were definitely not in English, but in the ornate scripts for shops in shocking colors and designs. Occasionally she would recognize Ganesh Travel, Devi Photocopying, Krishna, Krishna, Krishna everything from one star hotel to food to video stores. Grace, overwhelmed, turns her gaze into the bus. The white-clad men. who are the majority of passengers, are in single file in the aisle. The tourists would be the last to leave the bus obviously. But no, the bus driver turns, gets up, shouting something harsh, the sea parts, and Niles pulls her first off the bus unceremoniously.

As rude as he is, does this diminish he's highly spiritual? Grace thinks perhaps not with her clearer thinking. He does manage to get them safely through the bus terminal without being run over by buses, hand trolleys, porters, passengers and outnumbering them all, seemingly thousands of beggars and travelers. "Keep your hands in your pockets. And, for God's sake, don't let anyone catch your eyes. Follow me."

Grace briefly considers rebelling but one quick glance at her alternative: being alone, and certainly lost, she scrambles on after him. He pushes and snarls his way to the other side of the terminal, finds the Puducherry bus. Then leaps on it as it is moves out. It squeals stop, the driver shouting. Niles waves to Grace to come up the steps. They find seats amid the angry shouts of the passengers and driver, Grace keeping her eyelids down as commanded.

"Couldn't we have taken another?"

"Sure."

Grace gives it up; he's the one who says he's been to India twenty-six times. "I will do it his way, but as soon as I can, he's history," she decides and pulls out her journal to record the passing mélange.

Later, the vista changes from sprawl. They are no longer in the mobbed crazy quilt of mass civilization but in a bus riding on paved, broad avenues shaded by tall and elegant Royal palm and flowering mimosas trees. There is a sense of decorum and delicacy. Finally for the last leg to Sri Aurobindo, they change to a taxi.

Journal notes from travel brochure

"Of late, Puducherry is also considered an educational hub of southern India, having one central university, eight medical colleges, ten engineering colleges, three dental colleges, two law colleges, one veterinary college, one agricultural college, ten arts and science colleges, and five polytechnic colleges functioning within its territory. Many medical and engineering colleges including one national institute of technology and a state-owned university are also reported in planning.

"A Roman trading center, in 1742 Joseph François Dupleix became the Governor of the French Territory. Then the British and French squabbled over the land but it remained French until 1954. There's a decided Gallic flavor to the place, buildings, streets in grid patterns, plantings, quite French feeling still.

"Puducherry helped in the freedom movement in British India since 1910 when came Sri Aurobindo of Bengal followed by other patriots. In 1954, finalized in 1962, joining the India Union became a reality.

"Puducherry is one of the most popular tourist destinations in South India. The city has many colonial buildings, churches, temples, and statues, which, combined with the systematic town planning and the well-planned French style avenues, still preserve much of the colonial ambience. Puducherry is also known as La Côte d'Azur de l'Est meaning 'The French Riviera of the East.'

"The Auroville Beach and Serenity Beach. Sri Aurobindo Ashram, located on rue de la Marine, is one of the best-known and wealthiest ashrams in India. Auroville (City of Dawn) is a township located 8 km North-West of Puducherry. Auroville is a universal town where men and women of all countries are able to live in peace and progressive harmony, above all creeds, all politics and all nationalities in ecological and sustainable balance.

"In Puducherry, Sri Aurobindo completely dedicated himself to his spiritual and philosophical pursuits. In 1914, after four years of concentrated yoga, Sri Aurobindo was proposed to express his vision in intellectual terms. This resulted in the launch of *Arya*, a 64 page monthly review. For the next six and a half years this became the vehicle for most of his most important writings, which appeared in serialized form. These included *The Life Divine, The Synthesis of Yoga, Essays on The Gita, The Secret of The Veda, Hymns to the Mystic Fire, The Upanishads, The Renaissance in India, War and Self-determination, The Human Cycle, The Ideal of Human Unity,* and *The Future Poetry.*

"Many years later, Sri Aurobindo revised some of these works before they were published in book form. It was about his prose writing of this period that *Times Literary Supplement,* London wrote on 8th July 1944, "Sri Aurobindo is the most significant and perhaps the most interesting . . . He is a new type of thinker, one who combines in his vision the alacrity of the West with the illumination of the East. He is a yogi who writes as though he were standing among the stars, with the constellations for his companions."

The bus wends through the lively commercial districts of the city. Grace wonders about the teachings of the ashram that so suited Margaret Wilson and she is about to visit.

Swaying with the bus motion, as Grace reads the booklet she automatically puts it into the God of her understanding, her own words. Thinking it's not God evolving as our understanding of God evolves. She continues pondering the brochure: "For Aurobindo, the connection between the Absolute and the world of multiplicity manifested was The Supermind."

Grace tells herself it's complex theology for only when she puts the esoteric teaching into her own words, and culture, can she even begin to understand a bit. Something like Jesus upgrading the fierce father image of is times to language translated as daddy, *abba*.

Grace remembers reading Yogi Ram frequently walked to Pondi in his early seeking days to listen to Sri Aurobindo and bows to him as a most profound influence. She knows she is being guided on her Indian journey every step of the way and is thankful to grow.

The one aim of my yoga is an inner self-development

by which each one who follows

it can in time discover the One Self in all

and evolve a higher consciousness than the mental,

to a spiritual and supramental consciousness

which will transform and divinize human nature.

— Sri Aurobindo On Himself

Arriving at the Ashram, Niles barges out of the taxi. This leaves Grace to pay, tip the driver and handle the entire luggage. Then, she stands awed by beauty in front the high white walls of Mansion Street, an exclusive section along the shining and fabled Bay of Bengal.

Flower stalls on wheels across the street attract Grace by their exotic scents. As she carefully selects a bouquet of lilies, she joins a queue of Indian women in saris so elegant they remind her of Parisian couture. Grace is in love with the graceful sari enveloping Indian women with beauty. Most are slim and graceful, and some not so, but it doesn't seem to matter in saris. These saris are silk, not like the polyester of the city women or nubby cotton of the villagers. They are hand-dyed by professional colorists, many decorated with soignée designs of gold. The earrings and necklaces (which she later learns are called chains although Grace abhors the image of women in chains that such jewelry-term invokes. This grates on her in an extraordinary way, she shivers at the thought of feeling chained sometime, somewhere in the past). However these pieces are elegant. Diamonds, rubies, emeralds, especially sapphires seem the gems of choice, yet each designer-wrought and sophisticated, many with priceless pearls.

"What is this place?" Grace wonders as she crosses the tree-shaded street. As she comes to the open gate of the Aurobindo Ashram, she can see the elegant women with their bouquets pacing sedately along the curving path. Prize specimen blooms border the path. Grace steps on the welcoming path, and hears, way high up above her, a cultured voice whispering in ecstatic tones:

"I'm home. I'm Home. I AM HOME."

She gazes around bemused, there's a two-story white building with broad balcony but it's as if someone beautiful had just been standing there, smiling. The doorkeeper is an elderly man, dressed in tailor-made whites. Others before her are steadily advancing meditatively, gracefully, on the path.

Grace looks up as if the voice comes from above, a rather breathless and high-pitched, like a 19th century American lady's voice. Trees in full flower, the strong sunlight shining through the canopy. Nothing up in the trees except beauty.

Yet, with that voice, Grace is released from the indefinable something that had propelled her towards India since she lived in Princeton.

She had long thought that with that along with the house blessing, in all its charm, that there was also a curse on her. Hadn't she lost essentially everything she cared for there? Then by hard work, she'd joined the technological world, ok, became a geek, and secured a satisfying position in management, hadn't that gone also – as if cursed. Everything she touches, eventually turning sour, ending up depleting her dragging her into fearfulness.

Yes, the curse is there, the Hatha yogi told her in Kovalam Beach. Make the most of it. For seventeen years you have been under a Saturn Return, meaning you could easily have become addicted. He said: "I had it, for me it was marijuana. But because of the other aspects in your chart, you have an awareness of the choice. I'm telling you, you can, and must, choose the addiction. No way you can avoid it, you choose your chart before birth. You have the rare opportunity to select your path. From this chart, I see that your past lives, and the suffering of them, have earned you the kripa to make decisions."

"Choose your addiction."

So Grace, with her analytical mind, develops and runs an internal program with various choices of her favorite addictions. Her list included: marriage, homeownership, raising children, higher education, working on Wall Street, traveling first class, become an expert on food, wine, poetry, the Blue Ridge Mountains, gardening, travel writing. All interested her, none encompassing, as each had endings: divorce or death, children growing up and away, houses needing constant maintenance, markets collapsing, travel disaccommodating, food fattening, wine and alcohol becoming traps, plants dying or weed-bound, writing tedious. She had tried all on her list. Now none interest her.

Spirituality finally comes down to be her working choice. She decides to throw herself in patience, loving kindness, ethical behavior, working for other's well-being, cultivating compassion.

An ineffable persona shapes her decisions, like this sudden impulse to travel to India on a contract project. The Mike episode as she now thinks of it. And what is there to return to in New York? Not even a dog who cares if she comes home. But with the joy in the voice saying, "I'm home" Grace knows to her depths, release is happening. She believes that by setting foot on the Aurobindo Ashram she had been mystically, mysteriously, marvelously freed from 'her curse.' And it's her natal day as well. How did Yogi Ram know, this is where she needs to be?

Renewed vigor, as if energy had been tied and strangled let loose now, Grace shakes her shoulders to pace forward. "If Sri Aurobindo is truly the Master of the Occult my research says he is, I welcome meeting his gift in its stunning, life changing potentially."

The path leads to a marble tomb in the midst of the garden bower. The women, brilliant like their jewels and saris, are sitting or kneeling around a handsome white memorial. Their flowers placed at the foot of the memorial are being arranged, each bloom counted, into a mandala design on the top. It is the sacred tomb of Sri Aurobindo and The Mother. Service tree. Flower game. Still being honored here.

A volunteer hostess comes to greet Grace, welcoming her to the Ashram. Grace finds that guests do not stay on the premises but at a resort motel on the beach. A call is made to reserve a room for her. But in the meantime the hostess escorts Grace through the Ashram, past the bookstall and an easy walk into the Dining Hall where breakfast is being served. There is no sign of Niles; she's on her own.

Her guide, Giselle, a Parisian, is a long time devotee of the Mother, having been to the Ashram many times over the years. "I always make my plans to come here on my birthday," she says as she shows Grace how to secure the generous sized cup of hot chocolate, whole wheat freshly baked rolls, a small cup of plain yoghurt with jewel-like bites of banana with lime. For dining it's Open Air on a tall colonnaded terrace surrounded by plants so full of vital life force they are bursting with blooms, attracting butterflies and small yellow birds.

"Sri Aurobindo's private rooms are upstairs near the main courtyard. You know once he retired to seclusion only the Mother and close attendants were allowed in his sanctuary. The Mother formed and ran the Ashram around him. She is the Shakti to his Shiva, the active role to his meditative energy"

Grace nods, she had done her research well at the Ramana library.

"However since his Mahasamadhi, people come from all over the world to spend time in his room. Only on your birthday are you allowed the kripa of being in the room. That is why I am here on this date."

Grace gasps, it is her birthday also. When she mentions this to Giselle, the graceful woman turns to her with pleasure.

"Ah, the day of your birth. You must certainly tell the gatekeeper, he will provide you with the voucher."

"Oh, no, I am not a devotee. I just felt compelled to be here at this time. It was as if an invisible voice were calling me here."

Giselle laughs lightly, "Never underestimate the power of the Divine Mother. She brought you here. Since it's your birthday, you are invited to the party. So enjoy the blessing." Giselle presents a beautifully hand-woven platter heaped with wrapped candies. "Here, we give presents to everyone on our birthdays, to reverse greed. Please, accept my best wishes on the birthday we share." She bows, making her offering. Grace is delighted with the blessing.

Grace blushes now, she did nothing to be eligible for the opportunity, should she really partake? "Thank you, how delightful, this gives another layer to the meaning of birth. Giselle, I wonder if you could clarify something that just happened? For many years, I have wondered if I had a curse on me. So many things happened before I had a peaceful life that flowed harmoniously. But then awful things, I couldn't find a job when I graduated, my good husband turned abusive and unfaithful, we divorced, I lost everything that mattered family, home, friends. Then when I do finally achieve a worthwhile position, it's gone too, in a corporate dirty deal. And yet, just now . . ."

Giselle listens thoughtfully, crumbling the remaining roll into bits. She nods to Grace encouraging her to go on.

"I felt something fly up off my aura when I entered this gate."

"You would," she said. "I see you are developing your sensitivity. I cannot know about a curse but you are describing the duality of life on Earth. Yet I do know that house, so you lived on Library Place in Princeton?"

"Yes, not long enough for me, only after I was at university."

"Margaret Wilson grew up in that house. Her mother designed and oversaw the building of it."

Grace, eagerly, "Yes, yes, I read Volume Nine of the Wilson Papers. It has the letters the Wilsons wrote each other as he was lecturing at Johns Hopkins to pay for construction of the clay model she made and sent to the architect."

"There's somebody I want you to meet. Udar, he knew Margaret Wilson when she was here. Sri Aurobindo gave her the name *Nishtha*, meaning "one-pointed, fixed and steady concentration, devotion and faith in the single aim, the Divine and the Divine Realisation." On receiving her new name, she wrote to her sister Eleanor: "Do you remember those beautiful words in the Bible? *And I shall keep him in perfect peace whose mind is stayed (or fixed) on me?* That is what we must do, learn to stay our minds on Him.""

So here it is again, this important quote, linking Grace's love of the Christian Way with the Asian way. 'Stayed on Him.' One of the four basic principles of Aikido, so many strands coming together for Grace in India. The other three are: be completely relaxed, extend Ki (chi, qi) and keep weight underside, as in grounded.

They look at each other in dawning understanding: "So Nishtha's beneficence has brought you here, on your birthday. O, know the Mother is truly still here in her subtle world."

At the appointed time, a long line of members with birthdays of the global family of Sri Aurobindo waits in the courtyard for entrance to the upstairs sanctuary. Grace stands with them, feeling like an imposter a bit since she is not a member only drawn here. An elder very dark skinned in contrast to his sparkling fresh whites sits Indian male style on a near-by stairway. He catches her eyes, staring profoundly, holding her gaze long after good manners seemingly would allow. Grace feels a benediction stirring deeply inward. He only breaks the connection when the line starts moving up the stairs at the guide's signal.

"I must ask Giselle about this staring. It means something, something good. I feel it." Later Giselle confirms this strong directed gaze is actually the Hindu initiation called 'drik diksha' – the transmittal by sight of spiritual power.

Grace enters Sri Aurobindo suite of rooms believing she is entering a sacred realm. Before her the line moves slowly, awed by the extreme beauty. The rooms preserved are as they were. A glass screen etched with Monet-like visions, which Grace perceives with a golden garuda; water, ivory and verdigris. Swami-orange Chinese rug. Polished dark wood bed with white satin cover. Handsome wood, polished into sheen for a working writer's long desk.

The group is allowed to sit in meditation. To Grace it nurtures a new birth after the diksha from the ancient sadhu sitting on the stairs, she is now open to tune into the energy in Sri Aurobindo's pristine quarters.

As the group is escorted from the private quarters, Grace stands on an inlaid symbol. She hears confirmation inside just for her. "It *is* my birth." And she leaves feeling that wherever she may be she is therefore at home.

Downstairs at the Samadhi, Grace sits on a stone bench amid cinnamon ferns as directed by the guide: To Absorb The Energy, he says with such peculiar emphasis Grace hears the initial caps.

After a timeless flash, perhaps in clock time an hour, Grace stirs from meditation. She decides to go to the Perfumeries, one of the many specialty handcraft/artisan workshops started by the Mother in the traditional Indian cultural arts. There she purchases Jasmine Absolute for 56 rupees – since the aroma had been seemingly following her around India wherever, Kovalam Beach, Abdul's shop, the hotel restaurant, her room, the train and bus north to Bangaluru and then in Tiru, on the mountain, in the courtyard and in meditation room in Sri Aurobindo retreat. The overwhelming aroma of jasmine, as strong and uplifting as bliss. "I want to take this aroma home with me," she says naively without understanding yet the wafts of jasmine that surround her like a protective cloak, are blessings on her.

Grace sees Niles at lunch. He is at a table of similarly scruffy men. She pauses with a question of joining them, and he waves her on. She's quite content to do so. "I was only being polite, must not be something that sticks with him."

Giselle comes up with her platter of sweets while Grace is waiting in the buffet line. "Will you join us for luncheon, we are sitting over there."

Grace selects clear soup with julienne vegetables, a curried dal of orange lentils and rice, small cup of fresh yoghurt and pineapple. At the table Giselle sits with a fit older couple in pressed whites, Udar and his wife. He stands, bows, gesturing her to sit next to him. "You want to know about Margaret Wilson, we called her Nishtha. The Mother assigned me to her as I speak English. I was Nishtha's secretary in the 1940's until her death here in 1944."

"Thank you, I was wondering, how the eldest daughter of a President of the United States came to live – and die – in India, in an ashram. I've been curious about her since I lived in the Wilson House in Princeton."

"Yes, we know. She came from a religious family who were also deeply spiritual, both grandfather's were ministers. Woodrow Wilson had a vision of peace, of nations working together for the good of all. Her mother guided her daughters into a spiritual appreciation of life through music, art, reading and doing good works. Extraordinary family, ahead of their times. Margaret left a organized religion service one day and never returned. She also, despite frailty, during World War I, raised funds for the Red Cross performing, singing at concerts, even traveling to battle-torn Europe to sing until the strain forced her to retire from public life. After her mother's death, she lived in New York City, studied Vedanta (the Vedas) at the Sri Ramakrishna Society, was close to Swami Nikhilananda a direct disciple with Swami Vivekananda, heard Swami

Yogananda when he first came to America, whose later book was *Autobiography of a Yogi*. Have you read it?"

"No, second time this has been mentioned to me, I would be interested. I am learning so much in India. But I would also like to read more about Sri Aurobindo and the Mother – If you have suggestions where to start? There are so many pearls to choose among the books."

"Start with The Mother! But you must come to my office. We read each morning. We are reading what Nishtha read in the New York Public Library: *Essays on the Gita*. Mind you, I have to be home in time for the World Cup. Did you hear the scores yesterday, despite the riot in Bangaluru?"

"Riots, no! I was just there briefly three days ago."

"Ah, it seems that too many tickets were sold, huge numbers more than seats. Some counterfeit possibly. Thousands, or more, disappointed fans in the streets around the stadium could not get in. Some traveled so far. There was a great to do."

Grace thought of her four kind escorts on the Bangaluru train. She hoped they were safely inside the stadium. Such considerate, well-mannered and gentle men, hope they got into the stadium. She thought of Niles, who claims to be more spiritually evolved but rude always. The scales tip to the Good Samaritan. But Udar is saying:

"Your birthday today, amazing! A good portent for you to be here, on this day. The Mother said that if there is human birth then there is death. So we must call her back, call her down so she will manifest without birth. She is the mother of the new golden race preparing the thousand years of peace, pioneers of the soul coming in now. Write this, Grace, tell mothers-to-be that the soul of their child comes in at three months into the pregnancy. Write your journey, help the golden children to come in."

Grace wonders with awe at his comments, Niles told her that Sri Aurobindo and the Mother were beyond the cycle of birth and death. Still present at the ashram. To expect contact. They live within her heart she decides. *I know he lives within my heart*, as the truth of the old gospel hymn comes back from Sunday school.

Then Udar looks at Grace significantly. "You want to know more about Nishtha? Come to Golconda for tea this afternoon. I will have some people for you to meet. I hope you like chocolate cake!"

So even birthday cake is to be Grace's lot today. Golconda, George Nakashima's project at the ashram. She is truly in joy here.
Grace signals a riksha in order to register at the recommended motel on the Bay. It is a

144

complex of charming low wooden buildings with winding paths through ornamental grasses and pungent gardens. Grace's room is on the first floor facing a border of flowering ginger at a shell and rock wall separating the perfect grass lawn from the sand and waves of the Bay of Bengal. "You will see the sunrise if you are up," the porter says.

As Grace tips him gratefully, "I must be, what a treasure to see the sun rise over the Bay of Bengal."

"The dawn roars up across the bay," Grace muses on this, for romance comes from her old-movie loving mind quoting Rex Harrison to Gene Tierney, in *The Ghost and Mrs. Muir*. But now, I'm living the *adventure in spirituality* not watching it on the screen."

Inside the elegant room, Grace rests on the bed, taking her journal in hand to key in a thank you note to The Mother of the Ashram:

Cyber Journal

"Beautiful Mother, thank you for showering me today with beauty. May this kripa carry me on to the Shore of God.

"I feel so filled and thrilled by the holy ones of India, Lord Shiva, Yogi Ram, Ramana, the tiny man on the stairs to your balcony, countless, nameless others have nourished, caressed, purified, blessed, succored me with all the love I longed for with Mike, and in my past. It was to be not forthcoming, even as I knew somehow it could be. Yet here, here in India, love is lavished on me. How to explain it? I cannot even try. Why do I want to go back to the States? – Ever?"

For afternoon tea, Grace parks her bike; turns to enter the smooth-lined polished wood Guest House called Golconda. As she enters the lobby, she stops in astonishment to stare at the full wall sized mural of the blue and gold ocean. Before its vastness, the back of a slim, elegant woman, her arms upraised in ecstatic appreciation and/or blessing. In a dream an hour ago, she saw this scene alive. It is the same view of the ocean she merged with on MahaShivaratri. Grace stands, awed, mesmerized, unmovable, blessed. The mural confirms that she has been sent here – perhaps by Yogi Ramsuratkumar, master of Divine Love. She feels his laughter echoing in her, "My Father Blesses You."

Udar, in fresh whites after either his siesta or *fotbol*, sporting a fully blooming red rose in his shirt pocket, welcomes and escorts her into the tea party. The people around the table, who all seem to work in the Publications Department, laugh with him about the importance of Cricket versus Soccer. They laugh, eating rich dark double chocolate cake; drinking hot Ceylon tea with milk and sugar, fully at ease with life although the late sun is as strong as the tea.
Grace faces these ashramites as a neophyte, hesitant to speak up to their kind questions.

Then Udar quotes the Mother: "Challenge. May I remind you, the Mother said, "You must come to like a challenge – I Do!"

They talk about Margaret Wilson as archivists; only Udar knew her personally but highly recommend Grace be in touch with a playwright in Colorado. She's writing a play, she has the research; "She'll be glad to talk with you."

After tea, Grace goes to the Archives, where the precious, and now fragile, original works of Sri Aurobindo are being carefully transcribed and catalogued. Grace longs to touch the ink to feel the vibration directly but that's off limits for preservation reasons. So after a pleasant half-hour she leaves to attend the evening meditation in the Samadhi courtyard.

While she is sitting, Niles comes up, interrupts her meditation and asks if she would like to take a bike ride along the ocean highway at sunset as if he had been courteous all day. Seems he had heard about Udar, tea at Golconda and her room at the motel. Grace accepts his offer for the bike ride. They set off to a soft breeze with the sound of the waves caressing the shore on her right side. Graceful mansions with their gardens behind high walls flash by. Grace, so relieved to be steering her own craft, revels in the coolness of the wind sweeping her hair back. The day hot beyond belief but the balmy winds filled with sweetness of rose and jasmine. The tall street lamps come on in the gathering quick dusk of cow dust time as they return to the motel.

"Thanks, Niles, enjoyed it," she says, turning to go.

"Umm, just a moment, you have a room here, right?"

"Yes, a very nice room."

"Two beds?"

"As a matter of fact."

"Mind if I bunk in with you there."

"Yes, I mind very much."

"Ouch. It would save a bundle."

"No, I want to be alone."

"Oh well, can't hurt to try," he smiles, goes into the reception area for his own room.

Alone by choice, Grace goes into her serenely beautiful teak room, for a rest and journaling, then a shower. A real overhead shower head just another magnificent gift for her birthday from her hosts, Sri Aurobindo and the Mother. Later she accepts Niles joining her table at dinner. They walk along the boulevard under the stars after the French chef version of the Indian meal of curry and rice. A beggar with white stubs for fingers, approaches, leprous hands out. Grace unhesitatingly gives him his due. It's a peaceful exchange. Grace now changed after the glorious beauty of the day. Nishtha safely 'home.' Her own self, Grace, clean and at home in herself. Somehow fear flees also, perhaps a parting gift from Nishtha. She understands now, she has been led home to her Self, guided ever since those days in Princeton to this very moment. *Taken by hand and led home.* A-lone before, now All-One. Beauty overwhelms her.

They find an outdoor cafe, with a projected terrace out into the Bay. It's high tide; waves crash uproariously on the concrete sea wall of the café, turning away the gulls. Overhead the mystical Southern constellations dance as Indian Ocean spray leaps at them only to be spun away by the wind. "This is hilarious," Grace shouts, the uproar and the gulls gyrations and squawking making it impossible for conversation.

Neither mentions the question hovering in the air over the tea table, why would Grace want to spend the spiritual energy of the Birth-day in casual sex? Grace now knows the answer. Not she. She wants to dream her own dreams, meditate before sleeping, and wake up in her own energy. It's the end of the road for recreational sex so she raises her ginger-lime juice like a cocktail and toasts her second chakra freedom.

Later in her dreamtime, Grace sees Mike wrapped in a white cocoon, sleeping unconsciously on the side of the road. Grace is in a fast Indian bus traveling, traveling, traveling and wonders where she is going. She sees the Mother of Sri Aurobindo Ashram bending over Mike, so she leaps off the moving bus, to kneel before her. At that, the Mother knights Grace with a sword-like flower stem. A red tulip. Grace knows without a doubt she is blessed as the Mother speaks: 'Go forth, my child. All your steps are guided.'

With the sun coming up across the Bay of Bengal, Grace puts reaches for her mobile journal, knowing she must capture this important dream – or was it a visitation? It's clarity still palpable in the air. That accomplished, she slips on her sandals to walk on the lawn above the beach and soft surf. Pondering the dream, she realizes she is all three: sleeping Mike her male energy, also questing feminine and the wise guide. The Mother stops this helter-skelter lifestyle as Grace surrenders to the Divine energy by kneeling in the prayer of surrender. And cleanses Grace of any possession, or idea of possession. There is no curse just because we believe there is one. However, the Mother, an adept who released myriads of genuine possessions and spent many years releasing clinging spirits who had not managed to find home, releases Grace's concern. It had all been a mind game to make sense of natural order of life on Earth: *To every life some rain must fall.* A honeymoon life of rest is not for Grace. She wants to grow and with that comes experiencing duality of life, the yin and yang, the ups and downs, the hard the soft, the journey of life.

"I release you with love to your true Mother's arms. Go in peace. You are a free soul."

Following The Mother's words, Grace hears Nishtha's characteristic fine soprano voice: "Thank you for all you have done for me," Grace replies 'ditto.' Without the Wilsons, Grace would have ground her wheels in a comfortable enough situation; perhaps only near the end of life wondering what was the point of it all. But with the journey towards the Divine, Grace sees new horizons ahead.

For Grace listened deeply to Giselle's anecdote about the Mother at one point in time:

"To change the ashram, which she saw had gone stagnant, she went within, saw she was the center and so changed herself. And the ashram began thriving again with spiritual activity."

Grace knows she has changed inwardly with the help of Sri Aurobindo and the Mother, Yogi Ram and Ramana – even Mike although that's still obscure, cocooned, as she looks forward to the next challenge. No more curses, only challenges to be met, and enjoyed.

The whole tremendous theorem is Thou completely

Sri Aurobindo

CHAPTER 8, Return to Tiru

Who Am I – Sri Ramana Maharshi

After her sunrise walk by the Bay of Bengal, Niles meets Grace as planned for the four-hour bus back to Tiru. Both seem satisfied in their own way with the outing, as he calls it. She's glad to be invisible due to traveling with a guy. Grace watches village life flashing past: schoolgirls in blazers, herders with plucky goats, three boys playing on an irrigation gate, a determined woman circumnavigating a modest Devi shrine reciting her mantra vigorously, an itinerant shoemaker with his lasts, the blacksmith at his forge. The fast pace with the hot wind and fumes from the diesel engine rush by, her hair blowing from the open windows, they cover only sixty miles in four hours. It would have taken one hour on the New York Thruway but without such different ambiance.

Niles says, "That's fifteen miles in an hour, so we are actually traveling at an average of 40 mph's. But it is painted with Lord Vishnu and has colored lights strung across the front. Photos of Sri Sai Baba mounted on the dash. Look ahead, the villagers have spread their wheat stalks across the road, so the bus can winnow the chaff."

"But the pollution of the diesel goes into their food."

"Sadly, their good idea does not include knowledge of the dangers," he replies.

"There it is again, the heights of truth, beauty and bliss contrasts with the horrible."

"Yes, that's not only India. It's life, is it not?"

Journal entry, Ramana Ashram

So glad to be home to my comfortable lavender walls in Tiru. Traveling with Niles defines odd; he's spiritually inclined but culturally rude. We parted cordially, no karma between us and a final good-bye. Now to unpack, shower with bucketsful of water, buy the precious nectar, i.e. bottled mineral water, then a white rose to leave for YRSK doorstep if the mysterious door closed. She wouldn't dream of knocking on it.

Grace returns to find YRSK the same: eternal, mysterious, kind, funny, austere, smoking that somehow clean tobacco, the ladies in saris who wait for the open door in the hot sunlight, the blessing of the dusky-shaded small room, the neat cone of dirt, streams of men, women and children prostrating receiving fruit and candy, and the inquirers.

To Padma, who had come with tears to report her jewelry had been stolen, he says, "Day, Night. Pleasure, Pain. Happiness, Unhappiness comes to every life."

Then he laughs and laughs and laughs, his long snow white beard pristine, rising at a comical angle in the air when he throws back his head with joy. He says:

"God stole your jewels so he could give them back." And laughs and laughs and laughs.

"Wouldn't you like inner flowers instead?"

Padma now smiling and nodding, transforms. And Grace also, for her ex-husband had lifted her pearls and diamond earrings during their marriage for his lover. She now knows that harboring angry memories is useless, to just go on. Yes, inner flowers indeed, there must have been some good times. Yes, unhappiness happens in every life. It just is. Something else drops out of Grace's bundle of grievances to be replaced by the inner flowers of gratitude. No matter that she loved those pearls, they are gone.

Journal – Cast out all malice.

Grace looks up the phrase on her smart phone: *Cast out all malice*. It's been ringing in her ears since Yogi Ram's" My Father blesses you" rings through her being/consciousness.

"As I thought. King James version, Mathew 15. So free of that anchor, I have no hesitation having lunch at Udijri Bhavananda restaurant on my own. Come back to room for siesta, and begin thinking of my soul, my sanctuary always with me.

"'*Now that I've found you, I'll never let you go.*' What's that from? My soul rejoices. I am my soul, not 'I have a soul.' Ah, it's *Some Enchanted Evening* again, from *Saints Alive*. Now not about Mike and romance at Kovalam Beach but my love song of my True Self.

"Pray to your True Self, only thing worth doing" Ramana

An incredible vibration comes in so Grace turns off her mobile to sit within the peace. After a while she prays for everybody she has met in India. It's a long list. Then she thanks all the teachers, another long list. Then free and quiet, she opens to read from *Sri Aurobindo's Sonnets*.

And suddenly realizes what the gift of the trip to Puducherry is: to be free of pressure and wanting. The pressure of wanting. "Have I ever been free of such pressure? And the pressure is fear-based, feeling lack and scarcity. Has my mind ever been free of it before? To live without pressure, without inner pressure, without outer pressure, all the same inner and outer. Margaret had surely led her to sanctuary, the sanctuary within her own Self."

After Ashram siesta in the heat of the day, Grace goes across the road near the Library to an Ayurvedic appointment.

"Too Vatta, too much air. Avoid potatoes, peas, bread, yeast, bananas, sugar. Have yogurt, oranges, lime, rice, greens. But you have a very healthy body. Take care of it and you will live to age 92."

Grace is horrified: "Live to 92! I don't want to do that!"

"Well, you are going to. So take care of the body."

Evening walk around Arunachala. Followed by meditation in Ramana's room at sunset. Grace is happy to be back in the serene routine of the ashram. She looks forward to seeing YRSK many more times. She vows, "I will never leave here. To be quiet so wonderful" noting the complete transformation of her thinking into freedom from fear.

> One cannot belong to any cult or group whatever
>
> if one is to come upon truth" – JJ Krishnamurti

Back in her lavender room, Grace notices it is in disorder and by lamplight starts tidying. Before she realizes it, she completely packs her basket and her carryall. Only the sheet and shawl remain for sleeping.

"What does this mean? I want to stay with YRSK, see him in the morning if I must go, ask for his Father's blessing to leave, ask him to bless my business in Bangaluru.

But here I am all packed."

And Grace knows suddenly, she packs at her soul's direction. It is time to leave Heaven. What on Earth next?

Australians Everywhere

In the morning at the Ashram office before breakfast, the flute player who had successfully resisted the German women's lionizing, frowns at Grace. "You cannot take the bus to Bangaluru."

"I came on the bus from Bangaluru."

"No, you cannot return on the bus. It is not seemly for you to travel thus. I will arrange you share a taxi with two other people. One is a lawyer, one a doctor. You will go with them."

"I don't know them; I don't want to impose on them. And I don't like lawyers."

"I don't care about your likes and dislikes."

Realizing she is talking to an implacable will, Grace says, "Well, then, perhaps you would introduce me to them at breakfast. Then I will see."

"Yes, I will do that."

Grace is astonished that the two Hindu cousins, one an attorney from Sydney, the other a pediatrician in her seventies from Canberra, would consent to the Ashramite's travel arrangement. But they are quite cordial, telling her to be in front of the ashram after breakfast as they are leaving immediately.

Chastened, recognizing her reactions the same as feckless Padma bemoaning her fate in the jewelry leela at Yogi Ram's, thanks both the Ashramite and the cultured women for the arrangements. As she walks back to her room to pick up her already packed luggage, she suddenly realizes she would not be able to say good-by to the yogi.

There is no coming, no going, she hears in the air. So no good-bye, yet surely she knows she goes with His Father's Blessings, as he so often impressed on her. My Father's blessings! That means GOD.

It is Sunday morning as the diesel taxi leaves for Bangaluru, grinding and stripping its gears. All three women sit in the back seat, the Australians in saris, Grace in her now clean western travel clothes. What astonishes the women is that Grace is traveling alone.

Grace soon sees this is why they agreed to a stranger sharing the taxi. They are avidly interested by their questions to her stories of YRSK, who they inform her left his body on February 20, 2001.

"Do you have no clue what grace you met?" asks Dr. Ganapati, "Arunachala has given you visions of mystical India."

"But I don't understand, he was smoking, people came in, there was a scuffle outside the temple, I bought roses."

"And what evidence do you have these acts were on the physical plane?"

"Well, well . . . actually none, except what I saw and felt. But what evidence do you have he's dead?"

"Of course he's not dead. You sat with him on the divine plane."

"This is too much for me. No wonder Niles was astonished. It's not possible."

"Wait until you go to Sai Baba, then talk to us about *impossible.*"

Even though the women have said they are making their annual pilgrimages of the South Indian temples, they are astounded by Grace's reception in spiritual India. Look at each other in silence as they question her about her adventures. Clearly India is working its sublime magic on this tourist. Instead of the fruitless act of explaining the ancient mysteries, they accept and ask her what hotel? She replies with a name given her in New York by the office. Once Mystix would have paid all her expenses; this trip's not on an expense account, it's out of pocket.

"Not possible for you to stay there," Dr. Ganapati, the senior asserts.

"You would not like this place," Saraswati adds reasonably like a good attorney advising a client ready to invest foolishly.

"You will stay at our hotel, The Ashreya." The medical doctor asserts, brooking no opposition.

Grace recognizes the name as the hotel the pilot wrote on his calling card. Feeling a bit managed, she thinks hadn't she done well for herself in Kovalam, Tiru, Puducherry. Also she wonders if she can afford the three star hotel they mention. The Ashreya. Yet her pride does not want to reveal her rupees are dwindling. Now she notes she is slipping back into worry and pride so soon. At least she notices her thought processes so she can choose a peaceful way instead.

Thus it turns out they all enjoy each other, sharing books, music, films they had seen over the years. Dr. Ganapati directs the driver to stop periodically for fresh Chai and Indian snacks at the roadside stands. Grace happily joins in, when they show her how to discreetly go behind the taxi, shielded from other eyes, lift their saris just enough to form curtains, and relieve themselves. They give Grace a pashmina, with which she drapes herself and thus avoids the great pee-drama of the incoming bus trip.

"Are you glad you came with us now?"

Laughing, "I admit it with pleasure."

"Then you will stay at the same hotel we do. That's settled." Senior Doctor commands, whose name is a form of Lord Ganesha, the famed elephant headed deity, whose auspiciously breaks through obstructions for those who love him. His image is omnipresent in India. Even Grace recognizes the artists' images of Ganesh, Ganapati everywhere on heavy machinery to roadside shops. She surmises nothing favorable happens without Ganesha.

"Yes, ma'am."

"That's better."

"O look at that field of marigolds, like Krishna's golden carpet." It's the very field the villager companion on the bus pointed out on the way into Tiru. Now, it reminds Grace of the silk rug in Sri Aurobindo's private quarters. Rooms so filled with beauty but astoundingly small to an American to have been lived in exclusively for many years.

It was a most pleasant ride back to Bangaluru, leaving Grace feeling pampered and enveloped in such sweetness that she forgets the difficulties ahead in upcoming job assignment.

"You must see Baba," they say as the taxi weaves through Mahatma Gandhi Avenue and other broad city streets lined with the overarching trees of Bangaluru. To Grace with her consciousness still filled with the beauty of Puducherry, this sprawling major city appears to be kin to Paris. But her companions settle that with, *not possible. Bangaluru is ruined now, too much pollution, all those high tech companies. Ruined.*

"So you only stay here briefly, then go to Baba's," they direct.

The hotel much to Grace's trepidation turns out to be quite classy, located on a row of former great mansion properties nestled in tall, dignified, pink-flowering rain trees (fragrant Mimosas). However she is beyond relief when the credit card cost for a deluxe room is approximately seven dollars a night. The room with highly polished furnishings, ivory drapes with light saffron roses, soft mattress, western bath and a view overlooks a garden with a little Shiva Nandi shrine under a stately Magnolia with creamy white blossoms. Jacarandas scatter their purple petals on the packed red dirt. Quiet, cool, safe. And there is Asian television, Grace's first experience with it in India. "Tonight the news of Asia" with a drum roll and excited woman journalist's voice ASIA!!!! – Grace gets a strange thrill hearing those words. It's still hard for her to grasp she is halfway around the globe, but not as alone as it seemed it would be.

The Australian émigrés-guardian angels insist they all meet in the Indian dining room for the English restaurant, Dr. Ganapati says, is "ridiculously expensive." After lunch of *chithranna*, or lemon rice, and thick soup with lots of vegetables, Grace takes her now habitual afternoon nap in the tropics, without the air conditioning, and then meditates. Refreshed and eager to see the city, she dresses in the peach salwar chemise and leaves the hotel for a walk. She stops at a flower stall for a jasmine strand to pin in her red hair. The city is quiet, comparably little traffic in the late Sunday afternoon. She soon finds a park on her map given by the bellman. Thrust into her hands more accurately by the bellman, who urges her to go to the Roman Catholic Church when she asks for directions to the Anglican Church. "Many miracles, there, prayers answered, crippled walk, jobs come," he says.

The Jacaranda trees that make violet carpets of blossoms in the ocher dust are everywhere thorough out Chubbon Park so she walks through them bemused by beauty. In a distance she glimpses a herd of brown horses running loose, thankfully away. On the other side of the winding park is St. Mark's Church of South India, mass just starting. Grace enters, on home ground with the Book of Common Prayer, responding in English. It is the kind of formal church she has known since baptism and confirmation. A church she has left and returned to many times but home ultimately. She knows all the words without the prayer book. When communion comes, the parishioners take off their shoes and approach the altar. Grace, delighted at the respect, does the same. As the priest serves the bread and wine, he whispers, "You should keep your shoes on." But it's too late and she does not regret the devotion. Healing Service follows, with an enormous outpouring of the Holy Spirit. She sings: *O How I Love Jesus* softly to herself as she emerges on the street after the nostalgically familiar service. She does not notice it rather odd she found the church so easily as unfamiliar with the vast city as she is. Further it's completely reasonable to her that she walks for miles as if in a cocoon of protection. No importune beggars or tricksters in view the entire stroll. Grace would have used more caution in Central Park where she understood the easy target she offers. However trouble did not trouble her at all.

Wandering back following the paper map instead of her built-in GSP, Grace spots the Hotel Rama, notes the Dalai Lama's sister started a restaurant here - The Rice Bowl with Tibetan and international offerings. Once well fed and satisfied, Grace wanders back to the hotel, congratulating herself on having flexed her confidence muscle in anticipation of tomorrow's meeting with Mike at Mystix located in a High Tech park only one kilometer from Whitefields and Baba's Brindaven.

Journal

"I bought a papaya in the park without negotiating because I did not mind paying the price. I feasted on it in my room for dessert after dinner at a Tibetan restaurant. Both Saraswati and Ganapati are presiding over my travels. I discovered Sathya Sai Baba photographs all over the lobby here. Miracles? What does it matter that I have this meeting tomorrow? I know where to find Baba now I reckon he's never lost track of me."

Then Grace searches the web for the meaning of her new friends' names: Saraswati. Dozens of responses pop up. She chooses one at random:

"In the Rigveda, Saraswati is a river as well as its personification as a goddess, sister of Shiva, married to Brahma, increasingly associated with literature, arts, music. In Hinduism, Saraswati represents intelligence, consciousness, cosmic knowledge, creativity, education, enlightenment, music, the arts, power. Hindus worship her not only for secular knowledge but also for divine knowledge, essential to achieve *moksha*, liberation. Her Mantra: **Om Eim Saraswatyei Swaha**."

Grace sighs, she is familiar with the First Americans whose ancient teachings also symbolically, give personification to river, tree, sky, animals. The old religions with roots in the mythological realms often depict personal characteristics in form. But what had Hilda Charlton written: "Behind all lore is truth. Find the jewel hidden within. Then all you wish to know will unfold." Grace continues her search on-line:

"Lord Ganesha, first-born son of Shiva, is depicted around the world as the Hindu Elephant god, the breaker of devotee's obstacles." Grace sees the image everywhere, wonders without ridicule who would worship an elephant – until she saw a live one from the bus to Chennai: - tremendously huge and so strong he could uproot a tree something human people could not do alone. Yes, we humans cannot describe the Divine except by attributes: Love, Compassion, Almighty Strength. And to early people naturally who better than the enormous elephant as the Remover of Obstacles? "His mantra is **Aum Sri Ganeshaya Namah**, Praise to Lord Ganesha. This is the mantra of prayer, love and adoration. It is chanted to obtain Ganesha's blessings for the positive starting of a project, work or simply to offer praise and pleas for the removal of obstructions. Ganapati is an affectionate nickname for Ganesh."

Glad to be under her traveling companions' protection, Grace thinks, exiting the search engine. Wisdom must make a great attorney! Maybe I should talk to her about Mike and Mystix? And a physician who removes obstacles, perfectly named.

Monday morning, Grace rises determining to go directly to Sathya Sai Baba, feeling an irresistible urge to just brush off Mystix. She dresses, goes down to the lobby where a larger than life-sized blow-up photograph of Sai Baba hangs over a desk. Several men in white clothing, lounge completely relaxed, just hanging out in the South Indian way, behind this desk.

"Is this the place where I can reserve a taxi to take me to Puttaparthi, to Sathya Sai Baba?"

"Yes, it is, most certainly it is the desk."

"O good. When can I get one and at what time does it leave?" She says politely matching the speakers' tone.

"You cannot go."

"Awk, ump, why can I not go?"

"You cannot, that's all. Go away."

Grace stunned after the beautiful and gracious receptions at ashrams in both in Tiru and Pondi can only stare at the man. He turns back to his cronies and henceforth ignores her.

Grace, tears in her eyes, knocks on the door of the elder Doctor Ganapati and Saras. No answer. She goes to her room, lies down on the freshly made bed, cries a bit, and then reviews her options like a good manager.

"I suppose I could go to Mystix this one day and then find another way to get to Baba later." Finally having made a plan, she dresses carefully in her re-laundered western clothes, goes back through the lobby careful not to attract the attention of the rude men at the desk. When the doorman whistles in a waiting taxi, she gives him the Mystix address. He nods, wobbling his neck, points out the circling garuda overhead. "Good omen, you are very lucky today to be in Bangaluru."

She smiles, wryly, than laughs with him. "Yes, I am blessed. Wish me more!"

"Go to St. Mary's Basilica, in Shivajinager," the doorman instructs the taxi driver.

Grace, from the back seat of the taxi gasps: "But I said to my office."

"Not to worry, you will like the church. I told you yesterday you must go. Many miracles happen there." And he salutes, closing the back door with a snap and a smile.

"OK, madam, it shall be done," the driver confirms.

Shortly they leave the broad commercial streets of Bangaluru, to wind through narrow lanes, crowded on either side by milling people and animals with displayed goods outside minimalist shops, albeit colorfully packed. Grace is fascinated to view up close 'behind the scenes' of the city. There are no tourists or techies in sight.

The taxi slows amid the crush of people, animals and vehicles. Grace is reminded of her repeated adventures in India with taxis and rickshaws, whose drivers have wills of their own. She reminds herself of Thomas Jefferson's advice to *Americans Traveling Abroad*: recollecting she "may never again be so near and she may have to repent not having seen it", so settling down into acceptance of the unexpected.

"Cathedral. Time for Mass. You go there. See St. Thérèse, the Little Flower. She's looking for you. Meditate. I wait."

When Grace leaves the brilliant sunlight to enter the high church filled with worshippers, her eyes slow to adjust to the sudden dimness with hundreds of ghee/butter lights on shrine alcoves. Crutches by the score, canes, curling photographs of smiling children fill the walls.

"This must be the healing church Hilda knew. She had a tiny house near here when she was a wandering sadhu. That time she was ill, when she prayed in the church. When she came home, Sri Ramakrishna and the Mother appear over her meager bed. This was no mistake, I've been called here. I will stay for the mass, welcome the blessing of walking where Hilda walked."

After merging with the solace of the Blessed Holy Mother in her mind and a feeling of being embraced by the Holy Spirit, Grace finds the taxi driver lounging outside. She is dazzled by the experience and the bright sunlight outside after the peaceful dark interior of the shrine.

"This is healing church," the driver says, closing the door.

"I'll say it is. Thank you."

"Now to office?" As the taxi wends it way through the swarming city, Grace reads the prayer card pressed into her hands by a beggar when she dropped coins into the care-worn hands:

The Memorare
Remember, O most gracious Virgin Mary that never was it known that anyone who fled to thy protection, implored the help or sought thy intercession, was left unaided. Inspired with this

confidence, I fly unto thee, O Virgin of virgins and Mother, to Thee do I come, before thee I stand, lost and sorrowful. O Mother of the Word Incarnate despise not my petitions, but in thy mercy hear and answer me. Amen.

Peacefully now, in the aqua glass skyscraper, Grace approaches the receptionist, showing her badge and letter of assignment.

"Go right up, Mr. McCall left word you should go right up. Twenty-first floor. Elevators to your right."

As Grace steps off the elevator, a slim Indian man greets her, "Ms Avery, I am Arjuna, this way please."

Her escort chats kindly with her about her flight as they walk down the freshly waxed floors into a department of cubicles, past the buzz of men and women with headsets and quiet taps of keyboards. Grace notes name plate after nameplate bearing names she recognizes when she was their editor. She smiles, enjoying the freedom.

"Mr. McCall asked me to see you," said a svelte, efficient worker. "You will be doing a training for us?"

"I was expecting Mr. McCall . . .?'

"Umm, no, he's out of the office. Nothing important, not ill, you understand. Personal time. He asked me to assist you with anything you might require?"

"Ok, then. The room I imagine is set? What is the schedule for the training?"

"At your wish, Ms Avery. Anytime after the next ten days."

Startled Grace pulls out her mobile, points and clicks, "Then Friday, that is in a week from this Friday would work for me."

"Done," said the assistant entering the information. "All will be ready for you. Now, is there anything I can arrange for you in Bangaluru? I can take some time to escort you on a tech tour. Or Gap, maybe you would like to shop. I know all the shops," she taps her slim Prada boots, smiling widely.

"No, thank you."

"But Mike said I am to take care of you . . ."

"No, not necessary at all, I have friends I'm traveling with, we have plans. See you next

Friday."

And silently as she goes back down in the blue-green glass elevator, "He's such a chicken."

*

Grace spends the rest of Monday alone happily, meditating, thinking about Yogi Ram and coming Darshan with Sai Baba, then a long walk in Chubbon Park, but with no sign of the wild horses, the park full of bustle as vendors and walkers mill purposefully around. The garudas soar overhead, aloft, playing the wind in the brilliant blue sky. She is at peace, cocooned after her visit to the healing cathedral from the raucous traffic. 450,000 auto-rickshaws in Bangaluru plus every other imaginable scooting vehicle.

Late afternoon around three, she returns to the Ashreya to find a note inviting her to a noted swami's lecture on the Bhagavad-Gita. "My cousin Leela and her son Ananda will collect you, myself and Dr. Ganapati. Can you be ready at 4? Please join us, where have you been all day? – Saras

Sri Ganapati looks critically over Grace's pale turquoise salwar chemise noting the accompanying shawl. "You must dress respectfully for Swami Chimayananda tonight. This you have on is fine, although a sari would be more appropriate. Just sit behind me quietly. This is a talk for Hindus on our sacred literature revealing deep truths. Keep your mind open. And do be quiet. Do not argue inside yourself with him. It would not be respectful. Listen only. And take no notes. You will remember." Then the pediatrician drops her stern aspect and smiles primly, kindly, "You do not know what good karma this is that you may attend this talk. He is elderly, has been ill, we did not know if we would see him again. We have patron's tickets for the third row. You are blessed to be able to hear the Swami. It is God's kripa that we do. The Devi Saraswati has made this possible for you."

"And Lord Ganesh perhaps?"

"Of course."

The car is again a mid-size black Taurus as in Mumbai. As there, a Muslim chauffeur drives. Leela, the owner, is a strong and gregarious woman, whose husband retired after an important position in Malaysia. She says she is a thirty-five year devotee of Sai Baba to Grace's astonishment, as another Kripa unfolds.

"I am a Hindu raised in Indonesia, I moved to Bangaluru to be near Sai Baba," she says to Grace over her shoulder. Grace, the two aunties as Anand calls them and Anand himself are in the back seat, matchsticks in a box. "My cousin is flammable," Saras had coached her, "We never know what will set off her short fuse. Be a little more tactful than usual," she coaches Grace beforehand in the wide lobby.

As the car weaves through crowds of men in white, Grace notes they are wending their way to a large soccer field. However the driver skillfully avoids the distant parking lots, steering the car directly to the garland-decked platform. Their seats are in roped-off stalls at the front. Grace is awed that her 'chance' escorts are VIP's. They sit so close to the stage that Grace can see the remarkable expressions on the guru's face. He is a strong, dynamic speaker who announces his text for the week will be the first ten verses of Chapter Seven of the Bhagavad Gita.

While they are waiting for the sizeable crowd to settle and the Guru to begin: Grace searches for an overview of Chapter Seven. She finds it on http://www.bhagavad-gita.org.

"When warrior prince Arjuna accepts the position as a disciple of his cousin Lord Krishna, he takes complete obedience to Him requesting the Lord instructions on how to dispel grief. This chapter is often deemed as a summary to the entire Bhagavad-Gita. Here are explained such Hindu concepts as: karma yoga, jnana yoga, sankhya yoga, buddhi yoga and the Atma which is the soul. Predominance has been given to the immortal nature of the soul existing within all living entities in great detail. Thus this chapter is entitled: The Eternal Reality of the Souls' Immortality."

Again India is amazing Grace. Someone arranged for her companions, her taxi to Bangaluru, her hotel, now this extraordinary opportunity to be in an intimate Hindu setting, only 10,000 attendees, to hear an illuminated scholar discourse on the basic text, some would say of all Hindu theology. In her inner ear, runs the tune to Somebody Loves Me, I wonder who it can be? The song is too precise to the moment to be a coincidence. Somebody is broadcasting American jazz tunes to her. What's up with that? These recurring songs uplift her spirit, make her feel light-hearted, like nothing can faze her. What manna. She settles in, easy now despite not having a sari. She's alert and receptive, maintaining her attitude of receptivity as Dr. Ganapati directed.

Swami Chinmayananda speaks simply, directly, clearly, with jokes that arouse a polite wave of humor flowing back through the audience. Nothing rowdy. "Not to know the Self is indeed the greatest of tragedies. It is to lay waste our powers and miss a chance that has been given to us, so rare, so sacred, so divine." His teachings are Advaita, or formless rather than devotional yet again reminds Grace of *Saints Alive*, the guidebook thrust upon her as she left New York just ten days ago, this message to accept the kripa being offered.

It is quick dark when the driver finds them and full dark when they arrive back in the hotel. After tea and refreshments with Dr. Ganapati and Saras, Grace excuses herself, longing to be alone in her room.

Journal entry – first day – who was that man?

"What a day this has been! Full of astonishing incidents, so glad Mystix was easy without Mike there complicating things, so puzzled by being turned away from going to Baba, so amazed to meet Leela who knows Him, so beautifully informed by the Advaita Swami. Someone is pulling my strings. Someone powerful, omniscient, loving, protecting, as if He knew my every move. *Somebody loves me, I wonder who it could be?*

Journal Entry – second day at Advaita program

"Alone but minded it today, I dearly want to go to Sai Baba's. Instead, went to British Library and read last weeks' newspapers which included a notice that there's 'Satsang by Sai Baba. Brindaven. Kadugodi, Whitefield, 4 p.m. Ate at Rice Bowl again. But again in the evening, Leela picks us up to go to the lecture. Still on Chapter Seven, every word has deep implications. And this time, she offers to drive me to see Baba!"

Grace slings down her electronic, jumps up and dances in a state of spiritual enthusiasm, delight and joy, dancing around saying Baba, Baba, Baba. When she calms herself with a cool shower, she meditates. "What had the Advaita Swami said? If bored, there is always something spiritual to do."

Dream: I am in an ancient temple of stone with a dirt floor just like the images of Ganesh during a holy puja (ceremony). Baba, from a high seat, throws gray powdery dust on me

Grace awakes in the morning feeling the sweetest ever, like subtle nectar has been poured slowly over her all night. As agreed, she is ready when Leela's car arrives in early morning for the group at the hotel. As she walks by the Sai Baba desk, the man calls her, stubbornly Grace turns her head away, so he runs over:

"See, I told you not to go to Puttaparthi two days ago. Baba has come here, to Whitefield. It would have been a waste for you to go five hours to Him in all the confusion and try to find a ride back again, when He is now one half hour from here."

Grace blushes for her rudeness despite his earlier chauvinism, in withholding information. She nods, "Thank you. Thank you."

He says, "Not me, Baba did it all. Baba does it all. You understand!"

"I'm starting to," she replies and waves joyously.

"Do you want to arrange a ride now?"

"No thanks, Baba has arranged a chauffeur and car to escort me."

"Oooh, you must be a queen, my lady," he says. Grace assumes he is mocking her but just smiles back. Perhaps not mocking, truly saving her from inconvenience. Her perceptions seem to be singularly off about people's motives in India. But are they off just in India? She sweeps that thought aside, strides on to the car. Leela, which means divine play, announces she is escorting them to Sai Baba's darshan so they must do what she tells them.

Bangaluru is not asleep at 6:30 a.m. but in full-blown rush hour. "Always rush hour, auntie," Anand says expansively. Dr. Ganapati chooses not to travel to Brindaven, as the ashram of Sai Baba in the section of Whitefields is named. On the ride out through the uproar of roads and building construction, including shopping centers, supermarkets and tech highrises. "Do you know what happens at Darshan, Grace? After some time, perhaps hours, He will come out, walk around blessing people, giving vibhuti. Taking letters. You know what vibhuti is?"

"No, this is not a word I have heard. Please tell me."

"Vibhuti is sacred, holy ash. Vibhuti may refer to glorious attributes of the divine, however from Baba it is 'all pervading' and 'superhuman power', and so on," Leela says briefly.

"Do you mind if I look it up online?" Grace can still not yet picture what Leela is talking about.

"Not at all, Anand always has his head in one." Grace taps in vibhuti and reads aloud to the Hindus in the car: ·

"Vibhuti: The ash of any burnt object is not regarded as holy ash. Bhasma (the holy ash) is the ash from the Homa (sacrificial fire) where special wood along with ghee and other herbs are offered as worship of the Lord. Or the deity is worshipped by pouring ash as abhisheka (blessing) and is then distributed as holy. It is generally applied on the forehead. Some apply it on other parts of the body, like the upper arms, chest, etc.

"The word means, 'that by which our sins are destroyed and the Lord is remembered'. The application of vibhuti therefore signifies destruction of the evil and remembrance of the divine. Vibhuti means glory as it gives glory to one who applies it and raksha (protection) as it protects the wearer from ill health and evil, by purifying him or her. The ash we apply indicates that we should burn false identification with body and become free of the limitations of birth and death. It also reminds us that the body is perishable and shall one day be reduced to ashes. As death can come at any moment, this awareness must increase our making the best use of the short time of our lives. This is not to be misconstrued as a morose reminder of death, but as a powerful pointer towards the fact that time and tide wait for none.

"Vibhuti is specially associated with Lord Shiva, who applies it all over His body. When applied with a red spot in the centre, the mark symbolizes Shiva-Shakti (the unity of energy and matter that creates the entire seen and unseen universe)."

Grace looks up, "May I put this into my words? Shiva is passive, non-interfering. Shakti is active, creating. Together these constructs transcend polarity."

Anand says, "Well, auntie, so long as you remember that 'constructs' are also constructions of the human mind. And Shiva and Shakti are real." Grace nods, "So like all words, limited by the users' point of view?"

Leela harrumphs. "Read on, Grace, do not get involved in speculation."

Grace continues: "Holy Ash is believed to have medicinal value and is used in many ayurvedic medicines. It absorbs excess moisture from the body and prevents colds and headaches. The Upanishads say that the famous Mrutyunjaya mantra should be chanted whilst applying ash on the forehead:

Grace pauses, her tongue tripping over the Sanskrit verses of the Life-Giving Prayer, so hands the display to Ananda saying, 'would you read this aloud please."

Om Tryambakam yaja mahe

Sugandhim pushti vardhanam

Urva rukamiva bandhanaan

Mrityor Mukshiya amritat !!

We worship the three-eyed Lord Shiva who nourishes and spreads fragrance in our lives. May He free us from the shackles of sorrow, change and death effortlessly, like the fall of a ripe cucumber from its stem.

With this, Grace recalls the beautiful server at Kovalam on MahaShivaratri, chanting this same mantra as she dines with Mike. Here it is again, in the car on the way to Sai Baba's.

When he hands the mobile back, Grace reads aloud that Chapter Ten of the Bhagavad Gita, she's been reading it all, since they heard Swami Chinmayananda's discourse, is titled *Vibhuti Yoga.* Saras laughs. Then Grace reads again: "Krishna uses the term vibhuti to describe divine attributes such as magnificence, splendour, glory and prosperity.

Grace stops, tears in her eyes, hand to her heart which seems to be expanding like a balloon, to remark how truly astounded she is by this synchronicity due to her dream of being showered by vibhuti from Baba's hand.

"But that's how Baba is," Leela says laughing joyously. "He makes vibhuti from the air, one of his ways of blessing and astonishing people into bliss. And healing, even from seeming death."

Grace listens. So many things unfamiliar to her but she knows that the dead can be raised. She thought, however, that was a long time ago, by one man who walked this Earth as the Christ. "What is going on here?"

When the car arrives in the small village outside Whitefields, traffic stalls in a mass of all kinds of vehicles and people. Leela says to the driver, "We will get out here, wait for us until after Darshan." Saras says to Grace, "Darshan is the sight of holiness. A guru gives darshan to followers. It is a gift to be in presence of God in the form of guru, one who is God on Earth Sai Baba's followers believe. You already had your Darshan in your dream last night, so do not worry. That dream was Baba letting you he knows you are finally here."

Meanwhile Leela in her inimitable way has managed the group to the front of the waiting horde of people. She is negotiating with the organizers, called Seva Dals (service volunteers in charge of policing and order), notable for their identical neckwear and authoritative ways.

"Come, Grace, come. You must go into the VIP line. I have told them you are important person." Grace, a puppet in Leela's masterful hands meekly obeys, thinking, "Such a big heart, big presence, big courage. I love her! She is so vivid."

Saras and Grace settle down to wait in the first line, as Leela insists for she must be obeyed. They are sitting cross-legged in a great courtyard on a poured concrete floor, no shade, easily ten thousand people Grace estimates, having no idea really how many, as everyone sits meshed together with no personal space American style. Knee to knee, shoulder-to-shoulder, front to back, the only space with air is upward. Grace wonders how long she can sit this Asian way, her bones and sinews already in shock. Yet she has her little book of Kabir in her pocket, so she pulls it out and quickly becomes immersed in Tagore's translation:

> Kabir says:
>
> O servant, where dost thou seek Me?
>
> Lo! I am beside thee.
>
> I am neither in temple or in mosque:
>
> I am neither in Kaaba nor in Kailash:
>
> Neither am I in rites or ceremonies, nor in Yoga and renunciation.
>
> If thou are a true seeker, thou shalt at once see Me;
>
> Thou shalt meet Me in a moment of time.
>
>
> Kabir says: O Sadhu! God is the breath of all breath.

All at once after waiting for more than two hours, an unknown signal causes the crowd to rise, Grace and Saras helping each other up. Their line, the first, paces slowly into the great hall, which is covered with green and yellow plastic sunshades crisscrossed over metal poles acting as protection from the hot sun. Grace has long been awash with perspiration, her cotton clothing limp and damp with the moisture, humidity and heat of thousands of bodies in the Indian sun. She clutches her Kabir booklet to her chest as she paces slowly inside. Following the directions they are passed on to one Seva Dal then another, until finally although they are first, they sit last at the end of the VIP enclosure. Grace whispers 'funny arranging' but is severely hushed by a fierce Seva Dal.

Exhausted with sitting on concrete flooring, cross-legged, but thankful for the green panel to sit under instead of the yellow one which offers little barrier to the intense sun, she closes her eyes in meditation repeating her mantra Christi in Tiru suggested to keep the mind engaged inwardly: *Lord Jesus Christ, have mercy on us.* Some time passes as the long lines file in line-by-line until all sit and settle. It is very quiet – and hot. Grace feels a Chinese heritage woman breathing next to her. Suddenly, the air changes, lightens.

166

Journal Entry

"Then a power comes out, like through a tunnel directly towards my heart and Baba walks behind it, so softly, so little, so tender, so sorrowful for all, the whole world and all in it. With a gentle mischievousness, he seems to have white sparks and golden blue flashes of light emanating from him. Baba in a silk geranium-colored floor length sheath of a robe is gliding around the maze of people, sitting in ordered blocks with polished pathways of open space. I am amazed at his crowd control, at the rainbow lights, looking around for the spotlights doing it but there is nothing shining on him from outside, he is actually emanating the sparks and flashes of light. I am wowed. Then my eyes change and all I see is pure Love, the special effects vanish.

"I feel an instant of eye contact that carries a blessing as he scans briefly pass the huge roomful of our staring eyes. The mantra changes inside me: OUR Jesus Christ HAS mercy on us. Tears come bursting out of my eyes. Then his hand rises in blessing and as it comes in like a wave something lifts off my right temple, a headache from the sun and perhaps even more than that. Then it's as if a long knitting needle, a laser beam of light piercing the slight indention in the middle of my forehead, like it was a clock face, the energy pierces at 5 o'clock position. Then my heart begins hurting, oh hurting, hurting, horrible hurting with memories of it closing when my parents died long ago, husband abuse, a quick kaleidoscope of images to the recent loss of my position and then, even Mike's note. Tears hurting, burning and suddenly, instantly all the pain is washed away and I find myself saying 'Thank You, Baba,' thank you with deep sincere gratitude for what I know I have received in the slightest glance from his eyes.

"I am expecting to feel the light and heat in my stomach area next but instead it goes to my colon, which seems to be full of air and is painful suddenly. That settles too, into a smoothness. The Bhagavad-Gita says, "There is nothing that is not God doing." Imagine that God would be personally interested in how my body does and does not work harmoniously. The Darshan Hall is tremendously charged yet completely silent, all eyes on the gliding figure.

"Baba glides on, pausing before the men's section, creating vibhuti by a graceful swish of his wrist, seemingly making it release from the open empty space between his thumb and forefinger, the white sacred ash dusting down into the waiting hands of an elderly man who has tears of joy also like mine streaming down his face. Then coming into the women's section, Baba takes a handful of wrapped candy from the upheld tray offered by a German woman with old fashioned braids. He scatters the candy through the air to the delight of all of us. The handful of candy arcs towards us, in slow motion it seems, scattering, our hands cupped hoping to garner a piece of the blessing. Ahead women scramble to catch their piece as if it is a precious gem. Then a perfectly aimed candy arcs directly towards me, prinks the exact center of my crown, bounces off into my lap into the folds of my long sheath. The soft part of the top of my head stings with the impact, as I, dazed, watch a deeply tanned woman's hand snatch the sweet away before I can comprehend what is happening. So stunned by the bonk, I cannot move. I'm blissful with the reverberations of the candy, which felt like an arrow centering on bull's eye. Baba is already passing by, only his retreating saffron robe shaking with his laughter at the leela (Krishna's play).

"'I've missed my chance,'" a small feeling wells up, hot tears come, but from some place new inside me. So I give the feeling to Baba and the angst evaporates. The tears of joy flow like satin. Then another thought arises, 'I've been cheated. She stole my blessing.' And as quickly as the thought arises, it is stilled, stopped. Instead, I am savoring the correction of my thoughts. I just go on beyond the grievance to great peace.

"As Baba walks on, he collects letters held out with eagerness, yearning, inexplicable why he takes some, ignores others. After the Aarthi, Baba near the entrance door, suddenly slips away to his private quarters.

"Saras and I are overwhelmed, sharing hugs and loving tears, realizing we must join the crowd that now rises and moves out. We cannot mediate in the press of bodies rising, so join the dispersing crowd. Leela is chatting with those she had been sitting with on a side bench, comes up and says, "Nice darshan."

"Nice darshan? I am amazed. Baba has walked two feet away from me and looked into my eyes. Nice darshan? Everything inside clicks into place. Nice darshan, perhaps her understatement is the best way to say it. I look at my mobile, it had only been one half hour of his walking silkily around the hall but I have new eyes and perhaps a new heart. Tomorrow I come alone.

"Leela herds us to her car, where the driver sleeps on the back seat. She yells at him as he scrambles to escape. Anand joins us, unperturbed and unmoved by his mother's chastising the driver. 'Baba welcomed you nicely, auntie. I couldn't see did you get the sweet he tossed you?'

"Definitely." For I knew I received something better than sugar candy, something life changing.

"What a welcome our Baba has given us," Leela adds. "We will celebrate it now."

Back in Bangaluru at Leela's spacious villa, a caterer serves an elaborate Indian breakfast. Next Leela introduces a shy girl, a *jimso* (cowrie shell reading fortune teller). Who tells Grace that she and Leela were sisters in a past life, devotees of Shirdi Sai Baba, she will marry soon and so have grandchildren to love. Grace is by now accustomed to the Indian determination to see her married as if that would bring happiness. She doubts it; she wants to be free; she wants her job back, she wants people to stop calling her queen.

Later, Leela decides they must go shopping in Commercial Street, where she enjoys supervising and deciding on which saris Grace must buy. Grace loves submitting to Leela's powerful will – especially since she's right. Then on to the Taj Hotel and its Jockey Club for lunch including fresh salad and tall frosted glasses of scarlet watermelon juice, which Leela guarantees are germ and amoeba free. Astonished, Grace says, "Delicious." And prays.

On the way, passing a large, glitzy shopping mall, Leela calls for the car to stop on the side of the road. "Come, this man has fresh green coconut." Grace sees an artifact country cart, oddly juxtaposed to the blue reflecting glass of the mall. A tattered hemp mat is flung back to reveal stacks of coconuts. "Cut," commands Leela, so the man pulls out a rusty scimitar (knife sharp as a razor) and chops off the top including the stem. He offers her a straw, Grace deliriously happy it's wrapped in paper, sips happily. She's adjusting nicely under Leela's guidance.

"The new crop is ripe," Leela says, bargaining with the vendor. "Good, I pay. Now fill the trunk."

They return to Leela's house, named she said by Baba, for afternoon rest. And in the evening they are driven in the car, to the last night of the lecture series. The topic is On Karma Raga, spiritual power without desire or attachment as in strength like steel. Grace thinks she understands what he is saying is the power to be gentle.

Journal

"Life is looking up! Will Baba go back to Puttaparthi? If so, I will also."

Grace, a new strength in her now and sleeps the best sleep of her life.

Kabir says:

The Vedas say that the Unconditional stands

Beyond the world of Conditions.

O woman, what does it avail thee to dispute

Whether He is beyond all or in all?

See thou everything as thine own dwelling place;

The mist of pleasure and pain can never spread there.

There Brahma is revealed day and night:

There light is His garment, light is His seat,

Light rests on thy head.

Kabir says: 'The Master, who is true,

He is all light.

CHAPTER 9, Help ever, hurt never

From today onwards, always help others, hurt never – Baba

Unwrapping his sleeping cocoon of sheer linen, Mike wakes in perfect bliss. Granted he slumbers on a flower-lined veranda in a peaceful ashram in Andwar Pradesh, South India. To pale peach dawn air edged with a cool breeze, bird song, monkeys chattering overhead. Yet something unnamable in Mike's vocabulary, something ineffable, a strong current of – could he say it, a current of unconditional lightness.

Bending over him with a light touch, Sharada Devi gently lays a hand on his cheek. She is the mother of his college friend and now his as well. Mike tries to concentrate, his mind completely relaxed, he would rather float on this sea of tranquility.

"Mike, if you open your eyes you will find that the prevailing bliss will stay with you. Come, Mike, you are in the direct domain of Sathya Sai Baba, you are feeling his radiation. You will experience this awake also."

She laughs, shaking him shoulder gently, "And Sushil arrived late last night. Do come, son."

"Yes, Mataji, but what a dream I had. It was so clear, so real. I was by an elevator and that woman Hilda Charlton, the spiritual dancer in Grace's guide book *Saints Alive*, Hilda standing over me, saying, 'Don't worry, you are going straight up' so I got in her elevator and whoosh – straight up. It was out of sight."

Sharada does not laugh. She beams at Mike, "Son, you have hit the jackpot, as Hilda said when she came to Baba's in the 1960's. He gave her a room in his household. You should read her story of making him chapattis then you will begin to understand she is a perfected being. I knew her well. What fun she was, her laugh" – here Sharada Devi pauses, a deeply loving look on her face. "She was here when Baba married the 'two Petals, One Flower' as he calls us. He gave her a sari; he gave all the women in the ashram a sari that day. Baba makes grand gestures like that. He was exuberant and full of fun then and so were we all. Those early days, just small groups. Now, so many thousands. You must be collected and ready for Darshan. So rise now and soon I will have my boys' breakfast ready."

After chapattis and spicy vegetable stew, the trio leave the family quarters in the Prasanthi Nilayam Ashram at Puttaparthi and walk a few minutes to the gathering place to prepare for morning Darshan.

Mike tucks under his arm Sharada's copy of *Blessings, Hilda*. While strolling to the lines, Sharada says, "Hilda was born to parents who were fruitarians at the time. She was a natural life-long vegetarian, completely pure in all ways. She came into this Earth enlightened for she is a Master Soul. In her early dreams, even at four, she called to her mother about 'those whirling energies' which we know are the Chakras. She could see the lights in the air.

"I personally believe she practiced austerities, intense yoga, extended meditation, sadhanas to teach others how to 'go the whole way.' She forged a path to the heaven world for her students and now for all the readers of her books. She left as she came, teaching how to be completely one pointed to the Ocean of Light as she called God. She left with no ties, no rules, no organization, no deputies, yet she blazed a trail even a regular guy like you, Mike, can find. And how she divinely loved Sathya Sai Baba. When she told Baba she must go back to 'her America' he said 'Don't go, only troubles.' She said, 'I must Baba, the young people are in trouble.' So he replied, 'Then go, Hilda, and write to me.' Which she did and he answered beautifully. There is no separation, Mike, from Pure Love, from Prema."

In due time Mike, with *Blessings, Hilda*, to read follows Sushil to the men's side on the right and Mrs. Patel to the ladies' area. Neither needing to occupy their minds during the wait, as they carry meditation with them.

Having been coached by Sushil's mother that the main *sadhana*, spiritual practice, is waiting at Parthi, in Mike settles. So unlike his frantic workday, all wait two or three hours in the morning heat, seated in equal sections, row upon row of sections with wide pathways in between.

Sitting on the floor, devotees and visitors alike facing front, silently waiting. Eventually the mind runs out of thoughts as the vibration of decades of concentration, consecration and devotion silence the atmosphere. As Mike dives into the deepest peace he ever experienced, he stops observing, naming and judging procedures. He sits next to Sushil, both dressed as the other men in whites, eventually with quiet eyes and mind. Training in waiting, she had said, distills and purifies the ego. Intense training, Mike finds, as he had never been someone to wait for anything patiently. At first, it's not easy for Mike to even sit still on the hard ground, packed with others' waiting, yearning, sweating profusely. Sushil says in a low voice, "The weather is not causing this spiritual heat, Mike, Swami is burning off your karma."

"It's like a global sauna inside me," Mike whispers back his face fire-red, "I could faint like a girl." The possibility of pain as a blessing is totally out of Mike's context. Across the sea of bodies, Dr. Patel zips lips to them. Suddenly with her gesture Mike sees the horribleness of his ego, his actions, the way he's been living, the way he's treated others, cheating Grace, spurning her instead of comforting her – thoughts race full speed through his mind, so he squirms to get away from them. Sushil puts a hand briefly, softly on his knee. So no talking, no moving, how about no thinking then? "Might be a relief," Mike mutters under his breath.

As soon as Mike posits this ancient, sacred initiative, another layer of peace emerges. He'd heard that the body is a reflection of the mind, in fact that the one body-mind-emotions-spirit is a wave. If peace in mind and heart, then peace in body even for a second. As Mike holds firm to this inner wave, his eyes soft, his heart willing to feel, an ocean of *prema*, divine love, swamps him. But here's the thing, he realizes, this Prema does not come from somewhere up or over or outside himself, it wells up from the deepest place within. Ever practical, Mike decides to have no opinions about this Love. He does not want to disturb the still water flowing through him, his ego engulfed. From his Australian boyhood, he's been surfing long enough to ride on the wave, not by force or fighting or trying to hold on to it, but by surrender, by floating free.

Then a long suppressed memory comes by, in their dorm, Sushil at his small altar, lighting incense, waving it before the photograph of Sai Baba, softly chanting into the silence of meditation. Mike waking up every morning those years to this same vibration, not joining in, but the recipient of the mood. *Bhava*, Sushil called it, divine mood that fills the air. The current always broadcasting, Sushil says, just tune yourself inside to Radio Sai and you too will experience it. And now, here he is, in the gigantic hall, waiting peacefully to find out more about the Real.

As Mike notes his willingness to sit still, his mind becomes like deep still water. There, but not processing. There, yet quiet. Here.

When the massive crowd rustles, Mike opens his eyes in time to see Sushil's hands lifted as if in Christian prayer, Hindu prayer, palms together touching the chest at the heart. He had seen this salutation in Kovalam yet here the prayers of so many thousands focused on the slight orange clad figure of Sai Baba gliding into the enormous auditorium. The space to Mike becomes electric, suddenly charged by the presence that at least one hundred million people around the globe love, like millions of butter lights lit with love. Following Sushil's gesture, Mike also gazes unwaveringly, his eyes resting on the small figure walking through the silent and calm crowd.

Do not look for God in the world around you.

Have firm faith that you are the eternal soul,

that the divine spark is in you.

Move out into the world like heroes

whom success does not spoil

and defeat does not discourage.

There is no need to call on God to come

from somewhere outside of you.

Become aware of God as your inner Self.

– Sathya Sai Baba

Baba flows towards the well-ordered men's section, gazing or not at individuals; perhaps taking letters or not; stopping for brief exchanges or not. Mike sees that the Holy Man is present, alert, aware of far more than Mike is – but concurrently detached, approachable yet unapproachable. As he comes up the aisle towards them, he smiles directly at Sushil, who takes padanamascar while Baba looks at Mike. After the devotion, Baba says to Sushil, "Bring to interview" indicating Mike. Sushil beams. Mike blanches stone white. Baba moves on up the row, as Sushil rises to a half crouch, lugging Mike up to follow him and they walk out in a gait known as the Groucho Marx. Mrs. Patel slips out to meet them at the Mandir. Still no talking. He gets a smile and pat from her. He beams like a boy but it's mixed with trepidation. "Uh oh, I'm in for it now, this guy sees me, his laser look reads me like a chalk board."

If there is a boil on the body, we apply some ointment and cover it with a bandage until it heals. If you do not do this, it is likely to become septic and cause great harm later on. Now and then one has to clean it with pure water, apply the ointment again and put on a new bandage. In the same way in our life, there is this particular boil which has come up in our body, in the form of 'I'. If you want to really cure this boil of 'I', you will have to wash it every day with the waters of love, apply the ointment of faith and tie the bandage of humility around it. This will cure the disease that has erupted with this boil of 'I'- Sai Baba, Feb 17, 1985

Much later in the morning, Mike emerges from the Interview Room sorting out this private experience. All the Patels tell him not to discuss what Baba said with anyone. Yet upstairs in their room they are also congratulating him on his upcoming marriage to Grace Avery softly so only they hear the words. "It was good you asked Baba about Grace. We all saw your expression when you heard: 'Your wife! Yes, I will marry you two at Prashanti.' For Baba will perform the wedding ceremony, just like he did for us so many, many years ago. You both are blessed, your marriage will be blessed."

Mike, overcome, only smiles. Sushil says to his mother, "You notice Baba did not say when."

Dryly she says, "And there's the leela, Mike."

Dr. Patel says, "So we will stay tuned then. Meanwhile, may we have the mid-day meal now? It will soon be time for Darshan again."

Peace is a state of mind that is very much within one's own self. It emanates from one's heart. There is reaction, resound, and reflection for everything in the world. Only when there is hatred in you will you see hatred in others. At times, even if no one causes harm to you, you try to hurt others. Whatever you do to others, you will definitely experience the result of that action, and whatever you hear or experience is all due to the reaction, reflection, and resound of your own actions and feelings; others are not responsible for it. You forget this simple truth and lament, "so and so is accusing me or causing pain to me or hurting me" and so on. Many a times you tend to fight and hurt others. From today onwards, always help others, never hurt anyone. Follow your conscience, it will help you to manifest noble qualities – Sai Baba

Brindaven, Whitefields

When Grace wonders why Baba's ashram near Bangaluru is named Brindaven, she goes on-line as usual to check out just why that name: "Also known as Vrindavan, Varanasi, Brindavan, Brundavan, in the Vraj, Mathura district of Uttar Pradesh, India. It is the site of an ancient forest, which is the region where Lord Krishna spent his childhood days. The town hosts hundreds of temples dedicated to the worship of Radha and Krishna and considered sacred by a number of religious traditions such as Vaishnavism and Hinduism in general. It is nicknamed "City of Widows" after the large population of abandoned widows who seek refuge here. Best of karma to be born in Vrindaven. Be sure to leave the body there. Liberation from cycle of birth and death."

Satisfied, Grace clicks off the mobile and settles into a peaceful nap in Leela's guest room.

Leela's driver brings Grace back to the Ashreya Hotel in the evening as the Swamis' discourse on the Gita. Grace's plans for the night are to bathe, journal, meditate, see if the BBC has anything she can bear to watch in her newly highly sensitized state, to dream about Sathya Sai Baba. Instead she gets a continuous inner concert of Fred Astaire hits: *I Can't Give You Anything But Love, Baby.* She *dances in the dark* through the night, on a high of swing and light-hearted jazz. Her dreams are full of billowing white skirts as she dances across the stage of the cosmos, in and out of realms of golden cathedrals of towering clouds, arcs of galaxies, twirling around the mysterious masses of as yet undiscovered planets, waltzing and tap dancing with a blue-skinned partner with a peacock feather lilting on his ornate golden crown. *"Stay awhile, play awhile, I can't give you anything but Love."* It was an uplifting, lilting night of the cosmic dance of Krishna.

Grace bounds out of bed at the first rays of dawn and prays for a lovely taxi driver who will not cheat her as she has only 1500 rupees left, about 220 US dollars. It seems as if while her money decreases, the more and more riches are lavished on her. Leela spares no expense as a hostess, seemingly accustomed to waving her hand bountifully. "But I am on my own today, so I must be careful." She opens her guidebook *Saints Alive*, to a photo of a famous painted interpretation of Jesus Christ. "My Jesus," Grace says, "here in India?" *Wherever thou goest, I will go - Ruth*

It would be the first blessing of the day to come. New dawning. Now dawning. The end of her lost wandering in the desert of bitter loneliness and fear because her heart tells her so. The doorman places Grace gently in a taxi, giving the driver a one-word direction: To Brindavan. The driver flashes a gorgeous white smile over his shoulder, saying to her: "I prayed this morning to Sai Baba that I might have a customer for the ashram today. It is a special day, Bhajans and Darshan. Thank you, Miss."

Sitting in the waiting lines, a pool of luscious colored saris around her, Grace sits near the sweet European woman who held up the candy platter at her wave of invitation. Grace reads her Kabir book

And prays a contemplative prayer for today. Leela has told her repeatedly to not be shy or hold back from asking Baba for her heart's desire but to be careful what she asks for, he literally gives. "I wish men would stop calling me 'queen'", Grace says. Leela laughs, "For that you have to change."

Baba says," I give you what you desire, so that you will desire what I have to give you."

As the searing sun envelopes the waiting masses of people, all sitting quietly, content with the discipline of the Seva Dals, who know that order and calm is vital with thousands in waiting for Darshan. Grace decides the sun is intensifying the jasmine scent from the flowers in her hair, from others, as well as the garlands many hold to give to Baba. At last, she has the phrase just right: "O Baba, please heal my wounds-of-the-world that follow me around destroying relationships, career, my ability to love fully. All of the world's wounds, I ask not for me alone but for everyone." She turns to the Kabir book and opens to:

Kabir says:

Do not go into the garden of flowers!

O Friend, do not go there;

In your body is the garden of flowers.

Take your seat on the thousand petals of the lotus,

And there gaze on the Infinite Beauty.

Grace ponders, is that aroma of Jasmine internal rather than from the flowers we are wearing? Every day she buys jasmine, making friends with the Brindavan seller who shows Grace how to wrap the jasmine garland into her hair. Every day the shy woman then gives Grace a free, fresh long stemmed red rose as well. Maybe God is inside but so clearly here, outside also.

The sweet woman, who had whispered to Grace in hospitality yesterday, is again next to her. She tells softly that she came from Germany to see Baba and invited her to have lunch in the Western Canteen after morning Darshan. And when the Seva Dals call she goes into the first line to enter Darshan. "It might mean," she confides her round blue eyes sparkling, "I will get an interview with Baba. I hope you get one too." Then she disappears into the massive sanctuary.

One by one the lines of devotees pace in sedately. Grace prays, "Peace of mind, peace of mind, let me not mind which line I am in. Let me be in my right place, please. Our Jesus Christ **has** mercy on us."

Struggling with a rising sense of being deprived, Grace waits her turn. When at last, she enters the huge hall; there is a place for her, gestured to by a female Seva Dal, in the first block at the front. Next to a barely sufficient space for Grace to sit cross-legged is a Hindu mother with a rowdy girl-child in her lap. The empty space must belong to the seven-year-old girl. The Seva Dal pushes Grace in, none to gently, so she collapses and wiggles into the traditional seating posture, glad her crossed legs form a triangle for firmness with her knees and bottom on the cool floor. Grace gestures to the harried mother, "let the child sit in my lap."

Although the girl is restless, continually trying to bound up and away contrary to the decorum required of the great crowd, Grace is able to soothe her into relaxation by murmuring Dear Lord Sathya Sai Baba, Dear Lord Sathya Sai Baba, Dear Lord Sathya Sai Baba, over and over. Then by writing it on the flyleaf of the Kabir poetry booklet, they trace over and over the name with their fingers intertwined.

Pointing each English syllable, saying the words deliberately in a low, slow voice, the girl becomes placid while they wait for the dear Lord Sathya Sai Baba to appear. The girl sits in Grace's lap softly and calmly for a long time. The mother smiles, keeps patting Grace's back. Grace muses, "I'm not able to do this usually." And with that the spirit of Kripa flows mightily through her from the top of her head to the tips of her toes. "Baba does all."

After the Indian singing, silence falls on the crowd in anticipation of Baba's appearance. Then suddenly, he is there in the doorway, pausing, raising his hand in blessing. The pain in Grace's legs and back from sitting on the floor with a small girl grinding on her bones vanishes in that instant. The pain completely goes; Grace wonders what else has been removed by that blessing of divine energy.

After Darshan, Grace finds a bit of shade. She ponders what was going on in Darshan today? After holding that squirming child for hours, her mother tells me she came from England to Baba's as a last resort as the doctors are saying the daughter's diagnosis is not curable, a neurological dysfunction that keeps the child constantly agitated and destructive. Yet she sat so still in my lap. How did Baba do that? No private interview yet. What a game He plays with my hopes and fears. I am caught up in the game.

After her rest, she goes into lunch with Maria from Germany when the lines shorten. They choose pooris and chickpea curry in the Western Canteen. Baba had not selected her for an interview either. Grace is puzzled why she so desperately desires a private time with Baba and asks Maria to explain. "An interview with Baba is the most supreme blessing anyone could have in this life, but for me most important as I lost my whole family in the war – the camps. I have no one left but those were the bad days. All gone in the war." She looks at Grace, reading her thoughts:

"I know it's a long time ago, but for us Germans the whole fabric of our lives was taken away, destroyed. Do you understand?" Stubbornly, Grace didn't, they should have stopped the war, not participated in the insanity.

"Some Germans, some people, like to make war or are afraid not to participate. We were just little people." She looks intently at Grace, "We lived in a village where my father grew flowers, endive and white asparagus. He was gentle. My three older brothers were taken at gunpoint, sent to the army. Otherwise they would have been shot before our eyes. We sent them, praying, praying they would not have to kill. They all died on the Russian front anyway. Then my father sent me to Australia. Finally they took my father. My mother died in the American bombing. I was sent overseas secretly smuggled out. Pacifists did what they could; I was spared. But it was a long time ago. So now I came here to live in heaven on Earth. Pardon me, but how long are you going to hold on to your hatred? That is what makes war, cruelty, pain – not the actions of distant government. Grace, you have been called by Baba, no one comes here unless he invites. Pray you can be cleansed of the hatred that is ruining your life. Until you can be healed, are willing to be healed, you will never achieve what you want. Do it in this lifetime, or you will have to be a Gherrmann next life. I promise that's the way it works." She takes her tray, puts her hand on Grace's shoulder, a soft and very gentle touch. "I will see you again. Let go, let God."

Grace sits over the meal tray, tears coursing down her cheeks with shame, horror, embarrassment, rising like green bile in her throat. She turns to watch the German walk out of the Canteen, but no one resembling her is walking away. Half rising, perhaps she slipped into another seat? No, no. Grace stands up, begins to walk up and down the aisles, the room is packed with gesturing conversationalists. But Maria is not among them. Grace runs outside, determined to find her and bang, run right into Mike McCall's chest.

"Hey, watch it, no running in the Ashram, What??? Gracie. What are you doing here? At Baba's?"

"Mike! You, here?"

He grabs her arm. "Man, you look terrible? What's up?"

She jerks her elbow out of his arm, determined to get away. "None of your business, buster."

Mike shrugs, but something is happening neither of ken. Mike stands immobile, staring at her. Busy with her head down, she wipes her tear-stained face with the edge of her shawl, breathing deeply to steady herself, then notices he's not gone away this time.

"Mike, something just happened in that Canteen I cannot fathom. A German woman, just has been very helpful to me, kind, loving, inviting me to lunch, gave me the lecture of my life – and then vanished in thin air – to make a cliché of the most astonishing event of my life."

"German?"

"Yes, you know how I feel about German blood."

Ruefully, he rubs his jaw, "Yeah, I got that loud and clear." Silence.

"Then there's nothing to say, right?"

"Hold on, give me a moment."

"I don't think I want to . . ."

"Shut up, and listen for once, woman."

She turns to get away but Mike grabs her arm again and shakes her. "Just let's get this straight for once, Grace."

"No."

Suddenly, a Seva Dal comes up to them. "No talking like that in the ashram. No man touching woman. You go over there." She means it. Mike and Grace walk meekly to the front gate. The fumes of anger evaporating. Mike duly chastised also collecting himself.

Outside the gate, in the midst of beggars and vendors, Mike says, "Have dinner with me tonight, we must sort this out. I think you are having a miracle. I want to be part of it," his humble tone touches her, since he's suggesting a public meeting, she agrees.

"I'm staying at the Ashreya."

"Oh, the 'refuge' – ok, I will see you there after afternoon darshan, can't miss that." And he disappears into the teeming, milling, noisy village full of merchants, scampering monkeys and internationals. Grace goes back to the secluded leafy colonnade filled with Indian honeysuckle and bougainvillea's sweet strong scent on the grounds of the Boy's College next door to the ashram. Impertinent monkeys fling themselves off elsewhere. There's a light, balmy, delicious, laughing feeling of honey and honest ecstasy in the stifling hot air. She lies down on the bench to rest when a vendor from the market, not more than ten years old comes.

"Amma," he says, calling her mother. His white teeth gleaming in his wide smile, "May I rest here also, Amma?"

At Grace's nod, he lies down in the dust, plays with the hot pink trumpet flowers from the thick vine cover. In the distance Grace can hear a vina strummed lightly with true devotion. The boy daydreams, contented to rest after his long morning in the market. Grace marvels at the peace and beauty of the scene of True India siesta.

Grace can tell it is time for the prelude to Darshan as the air shifts; busyness and murmurs reach the secluded bower. The boy jumps up, flashes his dazzling smile and runs back to the village market. Grace slips back through the side gate on the Ashram grounds and waits in the back for the longest line to form then steps to its end. "Which line, Baba?" she asks internally. "Longest." She hears inside her heart.

Miraculously this longest line is given the number one token. All lines wait and wait. And wait and wait, no one is impatient and pressing. It is the protocol to wait nicely as they do their sadhana. After more waiting, Line One is led in third and to the second section. So much for playing roulette with Swamiji, he always outplays you as if just for the fun of it. For the sheer joy of life. Grace sits nowhere near the front. She is carrying Kabir and *Saints Alive* to read while waiting some more for Baba.

The aim is not self-glorification,

but to lead you to your own inner perfection

lying latent within you. . .

What else can any true teacher do except to remind you who you are?

He or she can point the way and say, 'This is your path.'

But you must walk it, you, yourself.

Nobody can walk the path for you – Pericles, Saints Alive

"May I see your book?" a strikingly beautiful Indian women queries softly as they sit together, sari brushing sari. Then everyone around wants to look at the book and know Grace's connection with it. "It was given as a very special guidebook to India. The author spent eighteen years here as she said, 'digging in with the Masters in the Orient.' I found Sai Baba through this book. And others also."

"Where have you been?"

"Quiet," hisses the Seva Dal. So Grace hands over the book. She surrenders again.

She ponders perhaps that's why I am carrying it around. So I can practice surrendering. But it eventually is handed back so Grace focuses on the cover photograph of the author. And whoosh, meditation snatches her into a sweet, light-filled, high inner place out of time and constructs.

At some point, a graceful hand nudges her wrist gently, Grace opens her eyes, Baba has already walked directly past the small group, ladies are taking padanamaskar, he was that close yet she has no regrets as Baba is the meditation.

Once out in the village she finds the driver waiting for her. He hands her a fresh pressed pineapple juice and says: Nice Darshan.

Yes. Indubitably so.

Journal
Late Afternoon Dream after Second Darshan, back at Ashreya Hotel

I am married to Baba! (I don't remember a ceremony but we are, I know definitely married). First day in his house, he leaves for his work saving the world. I need something to do, so decide to conduct a seminar on the proper use of handkerchiefs. About forty-to-fifty people attend including many I recognize from my former job, family and friends. Household staff says I can use any of the beautiful rooms, but I pick the CAVE down a spiral stone staircase where an ancient Celtic spring murmurs. The seminar goes well although some people fill out feedback forms saying they wish it had been held in the sunlight.

"When it's all over, and people are leaving, I climb up the ladder out of the cave, after a final recommendation to be sure to drink one teaspoon of cayenne in hot water as well as use tissues for overcoming grief. Then I go into my new home, Baba's home, a stone cathedral in the dream similar to Our Lady of Chartres. Although I am Swamiji's wife, his longtime devotees, servants and extended family also live with him.

"There are various degrees of acceptance of my new status and I am forced to walk a narrow plank high up in the dome of the medieval cathedral where we all live, walking carefully from one balcony towards the Rose stained glass window on the faraway other end of the nave. There are children playing in the air along the plank; they love me. (Somehow I am not surprised at this sudden anomaly since I am aware it's a dream). I give them the soft white tissues from the seminar so we can play together making life a game. As I reach the end of the high walkway, Swami comes walking on air towards me. Then we walk together down to the kitchen and out onto a broad piazza. We sit in lawn chairs to watch the glorious sun set. He asks me what I did with the day so I tell him about the seminar. He is delighted, saying he's glad I got right down to work, that although it was on a simple theme of comforting children's tears, it was well done. He says to keep doing that work. I am in awe of his words but more so that I am married to him. How did that, how could that possibly happen?

"We look out over great vistas at extensive gardens with waterfalls, rivers and snow-capped high mountains in the distance as the sky pts on her evening spectacular. A man joins us, yeek; Mike joins us at the tea table. I introduce him to Swami, they act in body language like they are at a business meeting.

"Mike: I've wanted an interview with you for a long time.
Baba: I am delighted we have the opportunity now.
Mike: Perhaps we can meet again when we have some time for real depth.
Baba: Let's take advantage of this time, as I don't know when my schedule will permit again.
Mike: But I want to be connected with you.
Baba: So you are, my dear, through your relationship with my wife.

"And Baba turns his head, full face towards me, smiles with deep, eternal Divine Love," as Grace closes the smart phone to nap.

Grace wakes up swimming in peace and love as she hears Aarthi outside the hotel window. It is sunset; a wandering sadhu waves a camphor lamp before the Krishna statue in the garden next door. Once again she treasures that most poignant time in India, the dusk falling, people changing step to adjust to the quick twilight. Orange shadows in long rays of the setting sun stream through the thick foliage. Ancient India observes her sacred ritual even in the midst of the technological skin over Bangaluru.

"Marriage, union, with the Divine in my dream. Dr. Jung please applaud. Unconscious, how wondrous, thank you, thank you, I wish you great love," then Grace stops, wondering why some call him Swamiji and Bhavagan, instead of the sweet familiar Baba. And her mind responds suggesting that perhaps Swamiji and Baba are one. One. Grace remembers her prayer of the morning, asking to have One Love towards all. But what was Mike doing in the dream? And as if he were at a business meeting? Still he had been there, is it that the Mike-role is part of me, since all players in dreams are a piece of my one inner self, according to C.G. Jung. Grace feels she has another mantra of her own now: Baba and I are one. Baba and I are one. Baba and I are one.

Now she can safely have dinner with Mike, for 'Mike and I are one.'

She happily dresses in her navy blue Punjabi with the white cashmere shawl, adding a garland of jasmine to her hair that her little boy helped her obtain in the village after darshan. He wants her to buy his rubber tubes. She gave him a rupee tip, planning to buy them all later but did not want the other vendors to see her softness and be mobbed.

Ready, she goes downstairs to the Ashreya's lobby. It is just seven o'clock and quite dark outside.

The English Restaurant is formal, white tablecloths, red roses, dark paneling, twinkling candlelight, Fred Astaire on the audio system. Mike rises as the headwaiter escorts Grace to the alcove table.

"You look marvelous, darling," he says, mocking the Governor Actor.

Grace laughs picking up a serviette for her lap, "Sounds like a new Mike."

"Seriously, Grace, this guy is amazing. We had an interview at Parthi and another one here today. Sorry if you didn't," he stops suddenly, conscious he might be bragging.

"No worries, Mike, I am glad for you. But I thought the Germans went in for the interview."

"Yes, that's right. My family here, well, some people from my grandparents' village. You know, it's really strange how I connected with them. I'm staying at Woodlands; it's an Indian hotel in another section of Bangaluru. Someone from the office made the reservation . . ." He stops, one landmine after the other. Why did he have to bring up that damn job now?

"Mike, you cheated me out of my job, that's right. But if you hadn't, I would still be that old Grace, who minded so much. No, wait." Mike stops at her gesture.

"You know Mike, I've met three other women here at Baba's who have their lives back in the US in storage, all their possessions, who just packed up after personal tragedy, not knowing what to do or where to turn, and came to Baba's. Doesn't that tell us something?"

Softly, "What, Grace, what does it tell you?"

"There's a plan. There's a plan for all of us. God knows and this time he's here, actively helping us. God has come down, or out, or up, don't make me try to explain in physical terms how it works. All I know is that what you did, you really did do a job on me, helped. Helped me get to India, to Baba, even that night of MahaShivaratri was a set-up. It made me open just the thin edge of wedge to seeing my life as it was – and what did not work for inside the pain is a blessing, if one only looks for it."

Mike looks at the white expanse of the table between them, "I'm sorry, Grace, so sorry, I am a jerk."

"Yeah. But so am I."

"Just two jerks trying to make our way in the world, huh?'

"Something like that. I want to tell you about a dream I had on the train from Trivandrum to Bangaluru, if I may?"

"You've managed very well, no pun intended, to get my attention." He catches the waiter's eye, looks at her, orders two Salty Lassi's. "No alcohol right? Yoga instead?"

She nods, takes a deep breath, begins. "In the dream, I see from way high up a young girl. I know she's me, Mike. She's starved, sick, and filthy. So thin she's almost a skeleton. Her hands are like claws, her eyes dark, dark brown. She's clearly Jewish, a big yellow star on her ruined shirt . . ."

Mike catches his breath, reaches across the table. "You don't have to say anymore, Gracie, beloved."

"I must. She's clawing at barbed wire and she cannot get out. It's a concentration camp."

"Yeah, must be." Silence. Mike takes Grace's hand without a word.

Grace looks down, "I jerked myself awake, the train was rocking, and it was dark. It must have been the slow rocking that triggered the memory – and Baba. I didn't remember it was India, traveling to Bangaluru, I just forgot but . . . I couldn't face it."

The waiter brings the tall, frosted glasses, bows and retreats. Silence.

Grace resumes, "Then, there's another piece of the puzzle. That puts the camp dream at rest. A kindly German woman at Baba's invited me to have lunch with her. She told me her story, about her village, her father's white asparagus nursery, her three brothers forced into the war, killed on the Russian front . . ."

Mike lets go of Grace's hand. He is ashen now. Finally, he sputters, "No, no, you've, your, you . . . "

Grace has never seen a man go into shock so intensely or quickly. Beads of sweat break out on his tanned forehead, his lips are trembling. "Not possible, Grace."

"But there's more, Mike. Let me tell," she pleads. "This woman was maybe seventy or eighty but so gentle like a young girl I couldn't tell. She was kind, white hair in that old fashioned buns, smooth skin with red apple cheeks . . ."

Grace stops; Mike is flipping through his mobile, searching for a photo. He places it before her on the white cloth.

"That the woman?" he whispers.

"Yes! Do you know her? How do you have her picture?"

"That's my grandmother I told you about. She's dead."

"NO! But she was the German at Darshan. She couldn't be dead, I saw her. She talked to me, she held my hand. She's alive."

"Yeah, well . . . this is my grandmother. Say, you don't know what happened to Germans who protested Hitler do you? You never read Dietrich Bonhoffer did you?"

"No, why would I, I was born hating Germans, all Germans."

"But . . . well, I guess that's right. You were born when, 1975? The war old history then. We'd been through Hiroshima, Korea and were in Vietnam before we were in elementary school. But you still hated Germans. I think now we know why. Reincarnation."

Excited, Grace puts her hand on Mike's Indian dress shirtsleeve. "Ok, I will admit that Hindus might have a handle on life after life. But, Mike, that's not all to the story. Will you listen to some more?" He nods, moving his glass out of the way.

"She made me cry, for the first time I saw that people are the same, trying their best to live a decent, peaceful life while all around them governments, or madmen whatever, are doing their best to carry out some crazy plan of destruction. People come and go, come and go, doing their best, carrying baggage that sooner or later only Divine intervention can heal. People get caught up in situations, in forces they had no part of."

Grace pauses, trying to express her thinking – radically changed so recently: "I'm just saying that I was crying, experiencing a complete change of heart and when I look up and try to follow, she is gone. No one had seen her; it was as if she'd vanished. But you know what," she sits up straight, a light of blessing on her face, "I believe it was Baba, setting me straight in the kindest, gentlest way possible. And I believe it was Baba that had you get me out of that job, and it was Baba who brought us together that magical night, and it was Baba that had you leave and it was Baba . . ."

Mike rises, takes Grace by the arm, throws some money on the table, strong-arms her out of the room. In the lobby, he punches the elevator button, whisks her inside, kissing her as the door closes. Everyone in the lobby applauds. The life-sized photo of Sai Baba keeps on smiling.

Grace punches the button and gently pushes Mike out into the Ashreya lobby. Everybody cheers and laughs again.

CHAPTER 10, Moments of being

'Moments of being,' intense sensations stand apart from the 'cotton wool of daily life'

– Virginia Woolf

Leela calls Grace after her Bold and Beautiful show is over. "How was your dinner with Mike?"

"It started out just great. I was able to tell him how Baba's holy instant cleansed me of the past, that I am walking now a free person. No voices in my head telling me awful things . . . I don't know how Swami does it, it's not magic or counseling. It's as if he knows the blocks hardwired in the mind, instantly, in a nano second, reboots so the whole system is restored to wholeness."

"Grace, can you tell me in non-electronics language. I speak English, Telegu, some Arabic, Sanskrit I understand, but this nerd talk is beyond me."

"Pardon, I guess I just cannot explain it with my logical mind except in technical talk. All I know is it's all energy, like high tech or physics. Only with the computer revolution have mystics and physicists been able to give reasonable language to holy experiences. That's why St. Theresa of Avila, who could levitate, hear the heavens, become one with her Savior, is the patron saint of Electronics. The ecstatic and spiritually powerful 16th century mystic experiencing union with the Divine in medieval Spain would understand Baba's ways of healing people, for marriage with God is a universal archetype . . . Bride of Christ. Rama, Sita. Krishna, Radha," Grace laughs ruefully and continues:

"Leela, how do you suppose you watch your show? The television waves invisibly, instantly pass through the atmosphere, around the world and outer space, to bring you a story of Santa Barbara's rich and awful. From the actors mouths to the transmitters to you. It's something like that."

"But much more you will admit? More than just entertainment?"

"O I wouldn't trivialize what Baba does for a second nor St. Theresa. No, that is never my intention. There are no words to explain, or describe, what he does. I'm just trying to twist a metaphor into a possible clarity. I really don't know how a tiny figure miles away can simply empty my life of its garbage. Without my being there, or his touching me, or even without having an interview."

"Maybe it was his wedding gift to you, Grace. You did dream you married Baba, did you not? Others have had similar dreams of being married to Baba. St. Theresa was the Bride of Christ, nuns do that even now."

"Oh? Well, yes, as I told you, a dream more vivid still tonight than – say our conversation. So real."

"Then he has given you wedding gifts more precious than gold and diamond rings," Leela said, remembering Grace writing Baba a letter asking for peace of mind, an interview and employment as well as the diamond ring she suggested. "You had your 'inner-view' in that dream. He says 'die mind better than diamond' . . . which results in this peace of mind because he erases the past life's broken record. Karma is gone. You will have a job, not to worry, Baba has granted you everything else in your letter. Even what you did not ask for, I suspect. The dream ends with Mike coming to you, does it not?"

"But I asked for an interview."

"Did you say interview with him?"

"Well, no. Just an interview, meaning of course with him. That's understood, don't you think?"

"Baba has his own agenda for you. What's ultimately best for you not just what you want or ask for."

Grace laughs ruefully, "Leela, I do see that Baba has showered more than what I asked for, answering my needs. But I think I might have thrown the Mike part away tonight. He, he was so moved when I told him how Baba healed me from hatred of some people, of Germans, of fear and unworthiness that he proposed again, grabbing me and kissing me right in open of the lobby elevator."

"So? You and Mike are to be married? Ask Baba to do it!"

"I don't think Mr. Mike McCall wants that now."

"O no, what did you do to him?"

"No so much, just pushed him out of the elevator after the kiss. And everyone in the lobby laughed. He must be blazing mad at me now. Mike McCall doesn't brook being shamed."

"Hmmm, well never mind. Baba is playing, his Krishna dance continues. Now, what about going to darshan in the morning with us?"

"I don't know, I have to go to the Mystix office first thing, and then if there's time I will take a taxi. Can I ride back to Bangaluru with you?"

"You would miss Darshan for the office?"

"I must, this is business."

"Fine, fine, you are in India once in your lifetime and can see Sathya Sai Baba. No one knows how long he will stay in this body, it is getting frail. You are a big risk taker, Grace. Get yourself to Whitefields for darshan. I will say no more."

"Yes, Leela, I hear you, thank you for your concern and guidance. But I must make that contact first. It's my job. Good night. Thank you."

On the next morning, Grace hangs up the hotel telephone, inexplicably told by the Mystix contact to come into the office the following week. "Something has come up here," the woman said clearly lying, "We will not be ready for you until the following Monday. Please excuse our disarray."

So Darshan this morning after all! Grace changes from her business wear into one of the glamorous saris she, Leela and Saraswati bought in an exclusive shop on Mahatma Gandhi Avenue. "Baba likes the ladies to dress well. He is like a rich patriarch, who showers wealth and beauty on his daughters."

"Oh Saras, that is so, so . . ."

"You think Baba is not a feminist because he likes to lavish gifts. Let God give you riches, there are no strings attached. He has done so much for women, education, advanced degrees, colleges, housing, care for widows, cures for children, water for a million people, free medical care hospitals. Let the universe lavish its richness. That is the natural state of love. To lavish goodness. Besides, we are helping the shopkeepers, tailors, jewelers, and all the middle workers. Everyone benefits from your spending money in India. There is so much more that must be done to raise all to decent living. Do get that pink sari with the blue and gold trim as well as the emerald one. Both are wonderful with your red hair."

When Grace enters the lobby in her rose-colored silk sari, the bellman rushes up to her. "Miss Grace, you going to darshan? So late? Drivers left."

"Am I too late to go there?"

"No, no, still time, but you must share the taxi. Is that alright? Australian people. Father very ill, came with the mother and daughter last night. You come now?

"That's perfectly fine, I will be happy to share," Grace says as she sees a desperately feeble man being led by a fortyish Hindu also in full sari. The mother hovers behind as they come with difficulty down the hotel steps. The brilliant blue sky foretells another red-hot day. However they all take pleasure in the just watered plants around the semi-circular driveway's the wet paving.

"Babaji, you sit in the front with the driver," cajoles the daughter who was clearly the motivating force of the family. "Mataji and I will sit with our guide." Settling tightly packed in the back seat, the taxi takes off with the driver saying, "We must hurry, time for darshan now. You will not get front seats, but I will get you there. The rest is up to Sathya Sai, ki jai."

On the thirty wild minutes ride through streets lined with Bangaluru's skyscrapers and international brand malls, the woman tells Grace their story. "Last week, my father's oncologist told us there was nothing more he could do. To our shock. You can imagine? Then he said that my father's only chance of survival is to go to India and see Sathya Sai Baba. We had heard of him, of course. As Indians living in Sydney, you hear things. But we are not followers. When I told the physician that, he said it does not matter to Baba what anyone believes. So I put the airfare and hotels on my credit cards and here we are. Still travel stained but rushing out to see this Man of Miracles. For only a miracle can save my father. And my mother has cancer also. We must have an interview. Do you think you can arrange this for us?"

Grace, totally astonished, nods 'not possible' which the Hindus took to be the wobble 'yes' with cries of joy. The New Yorker backtracks immediately, saying, "No, no, I cannot do anything, make anything happen. Sai Baba cannot be M-a-d-e to do anything. I am just a woman visitor from the United States. I cannot help you."

At their downcast faces, Grace says, "Best to talk to Baba inside, in your mind. Tell him what the situation is, ask for his help. When we are seated, use this paper to write him a note also. Writing helps to focus the mind."

Silence.

"I am sorry I cannot assist you. But practically I can tell you that purchasing some cushions for sitting on the polished floor may help. And I will speak to the Seva Dals about your father and mother. Beyond that, focus. I will also focus. But you do know that Baba arranges everything, even our riding together. It is all up to him now."

The daughter says, "Yes, I do see that we have taking the first step towards him. But will he help us? Can he? That I do not know."

Grace replied, "One thing that I do know, he will help you, what I cannot know is how he will help you. What form it might take. Pardon me for saying this, but perhaps death is welcome to some."

Shocked, the young woman burst into tears, "That's just what my father said. He said he could not stand to live this way any longer and that I must let him go. I would have nobody if my parents die."

"Please excuse me again, I believe now that you will have someone. You have Baba. He will look after you."

"I hope so – otherwise I am alone on this huge planet."

"Just one thing, where did you get the idea that you are taking one step to Baba? Did you read that in the material about him?"

"No, I just suddenly thought of it, while on the airplane out to India."

"So you do not know the rest of the saying? Sure?"

"Not at all. Is there a saying?"

"Most certainly. Baba has been saying for decades: 'if you take one step towards me, I will take ten steps towards you.' There, hold on to that assurance. One thing I know for sure is that Baba will help you. I just do not know how."

"You believe this?"

"I know it. It's not a matter of faith. It's a matter of fact. I know Baba will help you, just as I know he has helped me, changed my life, saved me from a terrible sickness of the mind."

"Please tell us, perhaps it will reassure my father, sadly he is an atheist. He just came because I wanted it so."

"Well, it's very private. But, wait, I will tell you," Grace suddenly sees her process may be of solace to others, so shares her private saga.

"For many years, since I was a child in fact, I have had terrible dreams about being in a concentration camp. Horrible, horrible dreams, so real, so vivid. The barbed wire.

Blackness. And a very ugly German woman who was a guard there saying nasty things to me – and the other Jewish children under her charge. The recurring dreams made me a fearful child and then a fearful adult. I managed my life all right, hiding the voice of fear under a surface of self-confidence. But always checking over my shoulder, always worrying about being betrayed, never able to get really close to anyone – like a girlfriend or even my husband. I was afraid he would betray me: and you know, he did just that. Then a co-worker I really liked and trusted betrayed my job away. One betrayal after another after another. Finally, from the depths of my despair, I wrote a letter to Baba when I came to Bangaluru. I told Sathya Sai the whole terrible mess I had made of my life, about the voices, the ambushes, the terror in the night from the dreams."

The taxi is pulling up to the front gate of the Ashram, vendors pressing at the car doors. "Wait, tell me the end. Did you get an interview with Baba? Did he heal you of these mere 'psychological' issues?"

Grace opens the car door, "More. Much more. He married me in a dream. Baba and I are one now. Fear cannot touch me. I belong to God. Come, let us see about those cushions before we go in."

From the ladies' section across the wide, packed auditorium later, Grace and the woman whose name she did not catch, (we are Everywoman Grace muses) watching together as Baba walks along the men's side. The father perches on a ledge, in a row of others with health issues. Baba glides slowly, gracefully down the row of up-turned faces. Some he pats, others takes their notes, but when he gets to the father with the hanging head, he stops, looks at the agony, raises his hand and sprays vibhuti on the bowed head. Baba says something to Dr. Patel over his shoulder, then moves on. The father never raises his head, seemingly unaware of the blessing.

Grace wonders: "I spoke from my experience only, I did not promise. But did I say the right thing?" It almost looked like nothing happened. Except for that lovely vibhuti shower which Baba does frequently. Inexplicably."

Outside the auditorium, having received no invitation for an interview and seeing her parents drooping with exhaustion, the woman turns to Grace. "I know Baba sent you to escort us here, to tell me what I need to know. That my parents will die soon. Both of them."

"No, do not interrupt me. You have been very kind, helpful. I now can let them go. Now I know I have done my best to be a good daughter, done my duty to them. It will take me years to pay off the credit card debt but I will do so joyfully now. With each payment, I will know that Sathya Sai Baba blessed my parents' dying and gave me a free heart. I will be sad to see them go, but that is the nature of life, to die. I have been a good daughter, now it will be my turn to live my life. Thank you."

"But I did nothing. I just told you my story."

"Yes, your truth has become my truth. I have nothing to fear, for God is here. And heard my prayers. Keep telling your story. You may put me in your book."

"But I'm not planning on writing a book."

"Send me a copy. I'll be in Sydney, Australia, waiting for it. Now please take these cushions – give them to your next assignment. Thank you and Sai Ram."

Mike falls

After the lobby scene with Grace, Mike rushes to the Bangaluru residence of the Patels, making up his mind to leave India as soon as possible. Entrench his position at Mystix; check out of Woodlands; catch a direct flight over the Gulf, maybe pause in Dubai for some gambling and get back to his city and job.

"What am I thinking? Mixed up with a crazy woman and a gaggle of true believers in a man who pulls Rolex watches out of his hair." At that, he stumbles getting out of the auto rickshaw, falls onto the curb, causing a gash in his forehead. With blood now dripping down his face onto his fancy Indian dress shirt, Mike leans wearily on the call box in order to tell Sushil he has a change of plans and would be staying in a hotel tonight.

"Yes, Mike, come up," Sharada Devi answers the ring.

"Dr. Patel, something has come up as a matter of fact, I must regretfully go into the office early tomorrow. It would be best for me to go to the hotel instead."

Wondering: "You call me Dr. Patel . . . What has happened, son? Tell me."

"Oh nothing, just some glitch at work I must take care of."

"Mike, what is wrong?"

"Really nothing. I happen to be bleeding and must go get some help."

"Nonsense, Mike. You know we are physicians . . ."

The elevator door opens, Sushil comes out, sent by his mother when she first hears Mike's voice. "Mike, for God's sake, what's happened to you? Been street fighting again, buddy?"

Mike slips to the polished floor, Sushil grabbing him under the arms before he hits the marble. Balancing Mike, now unconscious, he speaks into the open intercom, "Ma, Mike has passed out, I'm bringing him up . . ."

Sharada Devi walks serenely into the living room, telling her husband that Mike seemingly has been in an accident and is unconscious. "Sushil is bringing him up in the elevator. I'll get my bag."

The two physicians direct their son to take Mike into the hall bathroom where he is stretched out in the shower area, still bleeding profusely. In short order they have stopped the flow and revived a shaken Mike.

"Never could stand the sight of blood. Sorry, I always faint like a girl – especially if it's mine." He attempts to rise but gently is pushed back. "Stay still for awhile. Let my husband examine you. See if you need the emergency room – or just a good spanking. We will speak later about your lying to me just now." Sternly she leaves the room.

"Whoa, Bangeroo," Sushil grimaces, "Mustn't mess with Mother. That's the first Hindu law. Second law is to be sorry. Hope you are sorry, if not, you're in for it. Ever heard of Kali? Well, I think you are going to meet her in the living room shortly, right Dad?"

"Just let me finish my exam. I do not suspect any real damage has occurred. Just a flesh wound and the bleeding has stopped. Yes, he can face the terrible aspect of the Divine Mother now. If he dare . . ."

"What's this?" Mike bewildered for he thinks Sharada Devi is the most loving, gentle, mother, like his grandmother, sweet, kind, smart, gracious.

"Mother Kali drinks blood for breakfast."

"Your mom is a vampire? Get out. This is no time for jokes. I'm in big trouble with her already not to mention with Grace."

"Oh, you have had an evening of sport."

"No, I didn't do anything. I asked her to marry me – again – and she pushed me out of the elevator to the laughter of the whole hotel lobby, filled with guests."

"So hard you broke your head open? She must pack a real wallop. You're better off without her, Mikey."

"No, not at all, I left nicely, tail tucked, decided to forget this whole 'spirit-u-well' thing, finish up my assignment here and get the hell back to the US of A."

Silence.

"I tripped over the curb getting out to the riksha. In front of this building. It wasn't Grace at all."

"So you say. Not kripa. We'll see what Kali in the living room has to say about this."

"Who is this Kali? I've never heard your mother mention her friend Kali."

"She's black, has a lolling blood red tongue, wears a necklace of skulls, avenges evil and wrongdoing. MahaKali, the fierce goddess, who brooks no nonsense. You're in big trouble, Mike. My mom can be terrible when injustice appears. I advise you to be very, very careful for the next half hour." And he heads out of the bathing room, leaving Mike to stew.

There is dead silence in the large apartment. Mike pulls himself up in stages, being careful not to make any sudden movements. He looks in the mirror, turns queasy again, slips off his dress shirt. Sushil comes in with a clean shirt, says, "You cannot hide. Go in. You wouldn't want to make her even angrier by hiding out."

Sharada Devi is flipping through a glossy magazine as Mike enters. "Son, you are stronger now?"

"Ummm, yes ma'am. Don't suck my blood, please."

"Mike, whatever are you talking about? Why would I strike you? Sai Baba has taken care of you very well."

"Baba! He would do this to me? Humiliate me with my girlfriend? Knock me down, cause a concussion, blood. Now I await your punishment, Sushil has told me about how fierce you really are, Mother Kali. Spare me, I'm an ignorant fool actually. It's all an act, being big brave Mike McCall, who chews up people's jobs for my own gain."

Sharada Devi looks at him with amazement. "Mike, Sushil has been telling you about Kali? He said I will devour you? Very funny. I will speak to him later." She looks at him, then says:

"Our Goddess Kali is loved and worshipped by many millions in India and around the globe. She has a fierce aspect, yes, as she rushes to save her own from demons and wrong steps. She is avenging, snapping her followers from the jaws of the pit of error, in order to save them. But to those who understand the duality of life, she is tender love itself. She will not let her own be lost. Do you understand?"

"You mean to tell me you are not throwing me away, out in the cold?"

"Well, hardly, Bangaluru is not the Himalayas."

"Don't joke. I'm confused, miserable, broken."

"Yes, son, I know. I am glad for you."

"Now you're messing with me, like Sushil."

"Not at all, here's something I want you to understand about life on Earth, Mike. Our Swamiji wrote it in his book *Geeta Vahini*, chapter four. Read it to me:

"Happiness makes one forget one's obligations to oneself as a human being." For Mike this is new information. How can happiness not be good, a desired state?

"Isn't everyone entitled to the pursuit of happiness? Thomas Jefferson put that way in the Declaration of Independence. In the US, we believe we are entitled to happiness. Taught that in early school.""

"Perhaps that's the problem with your attitude, Mike, you do not understand that happiness is not necessarily a blessing or even a right or entitlement.

"But everyone wants to be happy. That's just natural."

"Oh, and is 'everyone' then happy? Happy all the time? Didn't you read Voltaire's *Candide*? Listen to what Baba says, "Happiness drags one into egotism leading to the committing of sins."

"I don't sin."

"No, yet you stole another's livelihood?"

"Well, business. That doesn't count, surely. Everyone does that."

"No, you are wrong, you have on dark glasses if you think robbing a person of her job is normal."

"You are Kali."

"Mike, listen, happiness draws a veil of ignoring over experiences that make one tough, hard-hearted. It also spends one's stock of merit and arouses baser passions. Is that not what happened to you in New York? Sushil tells me you were very different in college.

196

Kind. Loving. Even tempered. Now your mind is tough and you are hard-hearted, is it not so?"

"Only in business," Mike says.

Sharada looks at him over her glasses and reads on: "On the other hand, grief renders man alert and watchful. Misery makes one think and leads to self-improvement. It also endows one with new and valuable experiences, and highlights the value of happiness."

"Then some happiness is allowable? Tom Jefferson would be glad."

"Sarcasm is not becoming. Please calm your mind. You are not on trial here. We are not sparring over money or jobs or position in society. Baba is softening your heart, so you can be useful to this planet instead of helping to destroy it with greed and cruelty. Listen:

"Realize that happiness and misery are inseparable and you cannot choose only one. Treat troubles and travails, you know the word travails? (Mike nods: 'sorrows'.)

"Treat troubles and travails as your friends; at least do not see them as your enemies! It is best to regard both happiness and misery as gifts of God."

"Gifts!"

"Think about it, Mike, why would he say gifts? What in misery could be a gift? Think of how you felt when Grace pushed you away – after all the times you did that to her in one way or another."

"I felt awful, humiliated, rejected. I didn't know I could experience those feelings."

Silence.

"You are going to tell me that makes me a fuller human being? To be able to experience the whole span of feelings?"

"Well, actually no, I wasn't. But that's pretty good, Mike, to be empathetic to another's suffering is a part of being human. But since you ask me, I will tell you that it's normal, real, true to ride the waves of alternating suffering and happiness. The Buddha lays this down as one of the Four Noble Truths. One of the universal laws, that suffering comes, happiness comes – and they go."

"Grace was telling me about riding the waves at Kovalam. It made her very happy to have – say wait, is this whole talk about taking life as it comes?"

"Baba says that is the easiest path for one's own liberation. Yes."

"Not reacting to pleasure or pain?"

"Rather, say not drowning in the inevitable."

"So rushing at Grace tonight with a proposal and big romantic kiss was why she threw me out?"

"Oh, Mike, it's more than that, I'm sure, although it's not the way a mature person proposes."

"Er, a body blow! Well, what's my next step then, I do love her, I know that now."

"What is in your ability to do?"

Silence as Mike rolls options over in his mind. His face brightens, "I could get her a job."

Sharada Devi looks at him, waiting.

Mike looks out the glass wall of window to the brilliant lights in the distance of the tech skyscrapers. "I could get her job back, if I give it up."

"Don't be a martyr, Mike, don't make that mistake of becoming a pushover."

"No, wait. If I do release that job, I could spend a year at Baba's. I could really dig in with the master, see if I can take some steps towards that liberation he's talking about."

"Mike, I now advise you to sleep on this. You must not be hasty. How would you live?"

"Mataji, I have plenty of money to do this."

"But what would you do? It would be too much of a culture shock, my dear."

"Nah, I'm tougher than you think. I will wait overnight, have to anyway. Oh, the department is open all right, but the person I have to see about this only works daytime. So I have to wait for the right wave, Ma."

Mike thinks aloud, still planning rather than unfolding. "By the way, do you think I could work out at the ashram or in the hospital?".

"Of course, seva is always accepted."

"Maybe I could offer them technical computer expertise?"

"I would advise against that. You would be pushing the river again. Assigning yourself to a job. Why not ask the Big Boss? Yes, ask him tonight before sleeping, he will answer you. Now retire, let that surface scratch heal with a good night's sleep. See how you feel in the morning. And, oh, be sure to thank Kali rescuing you from disaster. Baba takes many forms to succor those he calls to him."

Kabir says:

Between the poles of the conscious and the unconscious,

there has the mind made a swing:

Thereon hang all beings and all worlds,

and that swing never ceases its sway.

Millions of beings are there: the sun and moon

in their courses are there:

Millions of ages pass, and the swing goes on.

All swing!

the sky and the earth and the air and the water;

and the Lord himself taking form:

And the sight of this has made Kabir a servant.

CHAPTER 11, The Beams of Love

We are put on Earth until we learn to bear the beams of love – William Blake

The next day, Grace, on returning to the hotel in Leela's car after Darshan, explains to her friends, "I must savor this mind-blowing experience with the Australian family. Please excuse me. India is an uncharted galaxy. I need to be alone." During the afternoon siesta, which Grace now fully appreciates, the bedside telephone rings. She ignores it; enthralled with a dream it interrupts. She turns on her mobile to catch the dream before it goes.

Cyber Journal

"Didn't see Mike at the incredible Darshan this morning. Just as well. I admit I could have been less like him, not so impulsive, and politely told him I'm not interested instead of shoving him out to the amusement of a lobby full of tourists. Of course he could have been there on the men's side and I just didn't see him. Thank you, Baba, for that also.

"Dream: Mike and I go into a Japanese house, all white with beautiful wood walls, lots of open space, elegance and beauty. Big open windows look on a central Zen Meditation garden of ferns with an ancient bonsai, blooming Winter Almond, in the center. The magenta blossoms toss in the cold spring air; leaves like mouse ears, still tiny. A teak staircase rises to a second floor, next to the picture window overlooking the garden. Along the staircase, a wall hanging of bronze sculpture of an ancient tree of life. Verdigris and golden.

"As we see some Aikido swords hanging on another wall, we grab them, bow to each other, and go at it hammer and tongs. Actually, we are rather enjoying the formal dance of Aikido, flowing long black skirts, white jackets. I notice neither of us are black belts. I say: "You make a good uke (partner), Mike," as I break skillfully through his attack. Then we both drop our guard at the laughter coming from the top of the staircase. Baba says, looking over the rail mischievously, still laughing uproariously, "Ah, Grace and Michael, practicing kata (formal sword practice). Good, good. Keep on."

"It takes no Jungian to dissect this dream: So Baba sees we are playing at fighting. It takes a harmonious partner to do kata well. Hmmm."

As she finishes tapping in the entry, Grace notices the voice mail light blinking and the time. She dashes into the shower room, towel dries her hair, twists it up on top of her head, chooses at random from her new saris, emerald, and hurries out of the hotel for her ride to afternoon darshan.

"What was that call? I'll check when I get back."

Leela, Saras and Grace squeezing and swaying together in the back of the Toyota, urge the driver on as he races through the traffic. 'He acts as if his life is at stake,' Grace murmurs to Saras who whispers back "it might be" rolling her eyes at Leela's persistence.

They pull up to the front gates at Brindaven, the Whitefields ashram, in time to get tokens for the afternoon Darshan. Leela leaves them, to sit on the side in her usual privileged place. When the other two are seated they are halfway back in the massive hall but on the front row at the back of their section. A wider than usual clear aisle leads from the men's section directly across to the women's side. Leela is nodding at them pleased.

"Wonder why she's so happy about this position, it seems so far back to me," Saras says as they settle in to wait in the blazing late afternoon heat. "Remind me, again, there's a rainy season in Bangaluru." Saras pulls out some handwork; she has finished three embroideries in their days of Darshan waiting. Grace reads a chapter in *Saints Alive* on Joan of Arc, buoyed by the courage and strength the author urges her readers to call upon.

"Hold the banner of your truth high, as did Joan. Your victory will come if you hold your banner high." Hilda Charlton.

The doors from Baba's Mandir open, showing a tantalizing glimpse of an Indian rose garden as he comes through, pauses, raises his hand in blessing and begins the stately dance called Darshan around the blocks of seated people. Starting in the front of the women's side, he moves smoothly, a small dot of sacred orange flame, the enormous halo of hair, bowing as he pauses, listens to one, asks a question of another, makes and sprinkles the sacred ash vibhuti on others. He pauses and takes the chalk tablet of a young child, Grace now knows he is inscribing an OM symbol on it to bless her schooling. Then he crosses the invisible gender barrier to the men's side instead of coming section by section into the women's areas as he sometimes would.

Grace feels a drop of confidence, a plunge into despair, another Darshan without an invitation to come for a private, or even a group interview. She looks down, tears starting. She's caught in the crowd's craziness of longing for more, for intimate moments with this incalculable holy person. But her eyes fall onto the open page of *Saints Alive*, a photocopy of a French card of Joan of Arc. Something of Joan goes into Grace like a flash. She raises her head, straightens her back, curls her hand around an invisible staff, waving her own inner banner of Life and Courage, the Christian ascension, the Holy Spirit, the white dove symbol.

Baba, by now, is walking directly towards her on the wide shining path of light from the lowering sun. He is backlit with the stream of light, dazzling Grace's eyes. "He's coming to me," she thinks, "straight towards me. He hears my call. He sees my banner." But five feet away, across the aisle three darling pre-adolescent Indian children, freshly coiffed in the Indian hairstyle, their saris sherbet rainbows, lean out and so catch Baba's eyes. They hold up letters, pleading silently to him with their eyes to bless them, "take our letters."

He veers away from his trajectory towards Grace Avery and pauses, as the girls, giggling, take padanamascar, touching and worshipping his feet, so reminiscent of the Christian story of the woman with the Alabaster Jar anointing Jesus' feet with her tears of repentance.

Grace starts to slump, then remembers with a flash Joan of Arc's courage and determination to overcome the inner negative force. She raises her head, against all protocol, calls, albeit despairingly, hopefully, prayerfully, "Baba, Baba, Baba!" Loud enough that a Seva Dal starts pounding on her, loud enough that Baba with his back to her, straightens seemingly in surprise at the yearning call.

"O, O, you are in for it now," whispers Saras, putting a hand on Grace's knee for support. But something has gone into the former victim. She looks directly at Baba, regaining her dignity as he heads across the wide aisle. To her. Straight to her. She holds her ground. Strong.

For the moment.

All five foot three inches tower over her. His eyes gazing directly into hers. Grace looks back, holding firm, an inner crackle on the top of her head and whoosh she's no longer in the Darshan Hall, sitting on the hard floor but they are out in the universe, among the stars, passing the sun, planets. Galaxies swoop past in a blur, Earth far behind them. And then the locked gazes reach a place of absolute nothingness. No feeling, no thought, no visions, no experience. Absolute.

Nothing.

Time probably passes. Baba's eyes change subtly, crinkle a bit. He's smiles at her. He breaks the interlocking union of the sight of blessing and says, "Wat have here?" Grace becomes aware of the book she's clutching, with Joan of Arc's photo, face up. "*Saints Alive*, Baba, a book."

"I bless your book."

"Not my book, Baba."

"I bless your book." And he saunters on, taking their letters from Saras with a sweet smile and working his way on to others waiting for him.

Grace, stunned by the light blazing in her, feels tears of joy running down her face. As smooth as rose petals.

Then the afternoon Darshan is over Baba returns to his global work, and the crowd disperses. Leela hovers over Grace, who is sitting inside a whirlwind of people. "Get back, give her some air. Get back, I say, give her some space."

Grace, still sitting in a daze of all encompassing love, starts to feel appalled at breaking protocol by calling to him Is it possible she argued with Baba? Saras takes her arm, assisting Grace to rise, and the trio makes their way out of the ashram and into the blue car. "Breathe, Grace, breathe, don't lose it. You have been given your inner-view as you asked for," says Saras gently. "Just hold the power inside, don't try to talk," Leela adds, "Back to her hotel."

By the time rush hour traffic allows the car to reach the Ashreya, Grace collects herself, thankful for their tactful silence in the face of the enormity of her inner experience.

"I told you he is unpredictable," says Leela.

"And I said everything is his play," says Saras.

"But what you didn't say was that I could call him up and tell him what I want," laughs Grace somewhat giddily. The Hindu mothers look at each other. "Dinner, she needs to eat. But something light."

When they arrive at the hotel, Mike waits in the lobby with a dignified woman he introduces as Dr. Sharada Devi Patel. "You met her son on the plane from Mumbai to Trivandrum."

"Oh? – well, how nice to meet you, Mrs. Patel."

Mike: "Don't mind us coming, I left a voicemail and texted you but when I didn't hear, I persuaded Dr. Patel to come meet you."

"Oh, sorry, I didn't know it was from you. I haven't checked it yet."

Mike and Sharada Devi exchange glances, realizing Grace does not know the news. Mike starts again:

"We saw your Darshan today."

"Along with thousands of others who saw it," Leela is protective, she knows about Mike.

Sharada Devi says, "I also saw the title of your book. Hilda Charlton is a friend of mine. I knew her at Baba's ashram in the early days. Would you three be my guests for dinner tonight at my home? Mike will be there on good behavior I promise, as well as my son and husband. At 9, shall we say? Give you a chance to journal and rest and listen to that phone message."

Grace, startled that Mrs. Patel knows her routine, nods, glances at a quiet Mike, turns to her companions, who are smiling affirmatively. Everyone is amused except Grace who is still reeling.

"Umm . . ."

"We accept," breaks in Leela. "Now please excuse us, I think tea, strong Chai and some chocolate cake, are in order for our Grace."

Entering the physicians' high-rise flat, exchanging their outer shoes for decorative velvet slippers for guests, feeling honored, Leela, Saras and Grace flow smoothly into the gracious home. Beyond, open doors lead out to a garden terrace overlooking the dancing lights of Bangaluru yet high above the traffic whirlpool. Their hostess Sharada Devi, presents delicate blue jasmine garlands, waving cordially they sit on the terrace's low couches. Sushil between Grace and Leela, while the two Australians, Mike and Saras, share another across. The physicians anchor either end in a deftly managed seating plan. As frosted glasses of fresh mango juice rise echoing Sharada's gesture, she toasts: "*Om Sri Sathya Sai Baba*," more a prayer and benediction than a toast.

Immediately an easy, harmonious air brings the separate-seeming persons into unity. "We shall forget and forgive our differences, shall we not, as we acknowledge the driving force that has so fortuitously brought us together this holy night," as she takes the first sip of the saffron drink.

"O, this is a holy night?" Grace says, "I did not know. Which one?"

"Shivarathri," says Dr. Patel smilingly, looking at his wife, amused by her phrasing of the toast.

"But I thought we celebrated Shivarathri already, all India celebrated. I was at Kovalam .
. ." Grace's pause trickles away at kind smiles, Mike's quick glance over his glass.

Sharada Devi leans over to take Grace's hand, softly forestalling her gathering confusion
as memories of that night suffuse Mike and Grace. Mrs. Patel smiles, "We are both
correct, MahaShivaratri was one cycle of the moon ago, yet here it is another dark night,
the moon is once again waning, see?" And they look up at the carpet of stars overhead
to the white sliver on the horizon. "Each month we also celebrate Shiva, as the heavens
dance overhead, as we remember that all here on Earth belong to the Cosmic Dance."

She turns to Saras, "You know our calendar supports us, is a touchstone to remind us of
the rhythms of our lives."

"Yes, even in Australia, I feel my connection with my traditions. No matter where I am, I
keep track of the moon; it grounds me. And helps me remember who I am."

Sushil, "And for me, the lunar calendar, forewarn me when the air traffic and the
passengers are more volatile. All the uproar happens around full moon."

His mother laughs, "Well, not to generalize, of course, son. But the tides of the moon do
rise and fall in us as well as the oceans. We are such watery creatures."

"Watery," Mike, speaking for the first time. "Emotional you mean. But bound by the sea,
the moon."

"No, no, we are not luna-tics, Mike, if you will pardon my pun. I am speaking of the
inner-connection of all living beings, the elements that we share within creation: water,
fire, air, earth and to the spiritually-aware the element of akosh, space. Most certainly
we are made of these elements, you do not deny that? And for Hindus the calendar
reminds us of our roots, who we are, and is an outlet for our energies. Much better to
chant, perform sacred dance, pray and meditate to handle the vagaries of life, than to
take these normal energies as nuisances to be ignored, stuffed down, boxed. So we
celebrate. Then we go back to our work."

"Makes sense, the way you say it, Mataji," he winks at Grace, who stares at him open-
mouthed, wondering at his graceful shift. What happened to argumentative, skeptical
Mike?

"Thank you, Mike, there's hope for you; I've known it from the start. But Grace,"
Sharada Devi turns to the young woman, "You had a big day today, did you not? At
afternoon darshan?"

Grace breathes in, at a loss how to reply. Her private transformative moment viewed by thousands, a topic of light conversation at a dinner party? In front of Mike? How could she politely reply? "Baba . . ." and tears spill gently down her cheeks.

Smoothly Sharada Devi continues, "Would you like a tour of our home? Have you been in an Indian dwelling before? Or has it all been resorts and hotels, temples and ashrams? Asia is important above all for its people!"

"My friend Leela has been very gracious with her home and car and love," Grace manages through more tears, overcome with gratitude.

Sharada rises, takes Grace's hand, leading her away from the balcony, "I have been waiting to talk with you about my friend Hilda. What a trip she is. Have you not felt her around you in India?"

Mike only hears a fragment of Grace's reply, "Ahh, that explains some things but I thought she had passed in 1988?" and Sharada's response, "Saints Alive, dear," as they move into the drawing room and exit.

The simple furnishings of their apartment nonplus Grace, knowing that both of Sushil's parents are physicians working as volunteers at Sai Super Specialty Hospital, after sitting on the lavish bower overlooking the city. Everywhere, except the flowering garden, utilitarian, plain low tables, no-nonsense cabinets and bookshelves, chests instead of dressers, cushions instead of chairs. There were antiques, carpets, vases, statues and wall hangings of the myriad gods and goddesses but few in number which Sharada Devi indicates with a gesture: family pieces. The apartment serene, while exquisite with peace and beauty in the classic-less-is-more school.

"At some point in our marriage and partnership, we looked around, saw generations of family collections and thought why not give all to Baba?"

"Ah, you both agreed to financially support the guru?"

Sharada Devi laughs, amusement lighting her dark brown eyes. "No. We do not donate to Sai Baba: he does not accept donations. No, we gave our skills to him. Our things to our children if they wanted them. Sushil did not. But yes, we changed the items into money to support Sai programs, like the water project, the hospitals, the colleges and universities. And we give our time and experience. We give all."

"I don't know if I could do that: I have to take care of myself. I have to find a job, support myself."

"Yet, you came to India following what you call your 'guide book.'"

"Really, I had no choice, someone stole my job. I came here to get it back."

"Making any progress? (pause as Grace shakes her head in the negative). Still you trust in this guidebook?"

"There's something about the author. You said you knew her."

"In the sixties, she came to Swami's as we called him then, after many years in Asia as a wandering renunciate. She was such fun, so completely gung ho for God. Rail thin after so many austerities in the Himalayas, Sri Lanka, many ashrams. I was there when Baba said to her: 'You have yogic heat' and gave her some warm halvah from the air, 'That's heat, you eat.' And she danced with great glee causing Baba to laugh and laugh. But other times she would sit in meditation day and night, completely gone in God awareness."

"What does 'yogic heat' mean?"

"Energy of God or Kundalini rises in the spine, pours throughout physical, mental, emotional and spiritual body and then out to others through prayer as healing power. That's why when you read her words, listen to her CD's, and for those who went to her classes in New York, healed, up lifted, transformed."

"You mean she was oceanic. I think I felt some of that in Kovalam. I changed there; I learned how to ride the waves instead of letting them knock me down. I felt the ocean was like a great mother."

"Our poets and holy souls have had many metaphors for God. The ocean is an excellent one, but still a metaphor."

Grace responds: "But I love water metaphors, I was reading Baba's words today: 'The sea scatters on the shore only shells and foam. But if one dares to dive into the depths they will be rewarded with coral and pearls. This should be your real mission.'"

"Yes, just as our real mission was not to be the caretakers of our families' treasures, the inherited jewels, art and furnishing, but to transform them into service for those who desperately need medical care, water, shelter. Sri Ramakrishna said be 'as the salt doll who goes down to the sea and dissolves, becomes one with it.'"

"So you are saying that could be my life too. To throw away getting a job and move to the ashram. I don't know if I could do it."

"No, do not get the idea that you may walk my, or Hilda's path. But do not delay in choosing the goal of life and deciding on the best method of achieving it. You must find your own service. Accepting service as a way of life is the grand step. Ask yourself how can I serve? Then listen to what the world is asking of you."

"I don't know . . ."

"Be alert, listen to your inner self. Your dreams, your inward journey, don't just keep a journal, explore it. Dive into the depths of yourself in meditation. Look for opportunities to 'help ever, hurt never.' Hilda was invited by Baba to stay in the ashram, 'don't go back, only troubles, only sorrow there' but she listened to her inner being, she went back to the US. She had to help ever. Yet she just began living there in New York. People found her, at first a few than many hundreds came to hear her talks. And now that she has passed on, so many new people find her through the books and through the ones who loved her. Sometimes people don't even know what guides them, they just trust themselves. 'Listen to the air' as she would say. Listen to yourself."

"I was thinking Baba might be telling me to write, since he tapped Hilda's book."

"You will know. Be alert."

Sharada Devi links her arm to Grace's as they walk back to the group still on the terrace. "But for now, let us enjoy Shivarathri. We have a feast to celebrate tonight."

After thanking Baba and the Patels for a memorable evening of conversation, dinner, beauty, Grace, Leela and Saras prepare to leave the apartment. At no point in the evening has Mike approached her directly merely as one of a group of deeply simpatico friends. But in the midst of saying goodnight, after intercepting a look between him and Sharada Devi, Grace notices she and Mike are as if alone, in a circle of light from a recessed ceiling fixture.

"Would you be willing to stay behind for a small conversation?" He raises his hands as if an outlaw surrendering to Gary Cooper. "I promise to behave. I need to talk to you about Mystix, just take a moment. Better here than in the office . . . neutral ground, friendly ground, all that kinda thing."

"And I almost got away free," Grace shrugs. "I cannot. I won't leave Saras and Leela to go home alone."

Mike turns to the group at the front door. "Mataji, mind if Grace and I conduct some business on the terrace – just for a few minutes."

"Really, Mike," Grace begins.

"Sushil, would you escort Saras back to the hotel please, and Leela home?"

"If they both wish this, of course, no problem."

O.O.O!

So once again, stage managing, Mike walks to the garden door, Grace gravely following: "You've got your job back – if you want it."

"What?" distressed, Grace backs away from Mike, blocked by night blooming jasmine in a deep terra-cotta planter.

"Don't make me say anymore, Gracie."

"Michael McCall, what is this? You really mean it? How do I have my job back? I demand to know."

He turns his back on her, lifts his hands up to the sky, then pivots as she guesses.

"You!"

"Now don't make a scene, it was nothing."

"Nothing. A position you were willing to scheme and lie for, this job is not nothing to you and you know it."

Mike does not say anything. He looks at her, completely at peace. Grace turns and walks back to the door, turns again, walks to the far end of the garden, scans him. Sits down.

"You got me my job back?"

He comes over to the sofa, she nods – he can sit. Still he says nothing. Below them the faraway traffic swarms and flashes. Overhead, above the pollution, traditional bouquets of stars in their southern constellations. Nataraja dancing horizon to horizon, into the universes.

Grace sitting silently, reviewing the stunning news, her job back. As easily as that, like a string had been pulled and her life comes spiraling back. What had changed Mike? Or who?

"Did they find out what a rascal you really are, Mike, is that it?"

"Nope."

"I'll bet I have to work with you, then. I won't do that, no matter what."

"Nope."

"Look, something must have changed your mind. At least you could tell me that. Is the company merging?" It dawns on her, "You got a better deal elsewhere!"

"Yes, you could say that. (Long pause) If you won't rest easy, which is what I want for you, I'll have to tell you: I'm going to . . ." he pauses, "Ah, Gracie, you're spoiling my thing, can't you just accept it? No strings."

"Tell me what you are moving on to, now," she demands.

"I have hopes that I will be . . .

peeling carrots and potatoes."

Grace laughs. "Carrots and potatoes? Nothing fancy like eggplant, huh?"

Mike, who had been sitting with his arms on his knees, hands clasped, head down, almost like a shy boy, snorts with laughter. This will power thing is hilarious somehow.

"Gracie, this is for real. I am not supposed to say this but since either I've said it so badly or you are the densest broad I've ever met . . . "

"That's more like the Mike I know and despise."

Once again, the Mike she loves, grabs her by the shoulders as if to shake her, then drops his hands. "I see I have tons more peeling ahead of me," he mumbles.

Sharada Devi, at this point, looks out into the night, inquiringly. "How are you doing, you two?" In unison:

"Mataji, she won't believe me."

"Mrs. Patel, Mike has lost his mind."

"I will then have to step in, like Mata Kali, let me sweep away the delusions that are smothering you. Good job, Mike, I am glad to hear you have lost your mind. But perhaps there is still more to be done? And Grace, you asked for clear direction in what you should do. Has it not been presented on a golden platter, free for the taking?"

"But it's my job."

"Yes. It is your job again."

"I cannot comprehend this. That job is the most important thing in his world."

Mike raises a hand, "May I say, job not the most important thing, anymore?"

Sharada Devi looks at them. "You are doing so well, Mike, Grace. Why don't you two meditate now. Very auspicious time for meditation. Look, the moon is directly overhead. The traffic sounds like surf. Shiva is beckoning you. Sit. Now. It's *Some Enchanted Evening*." And with a laugh that goes into their bloodstream like champagne, they straighten their spines into each into meditation posture, closing two sets of eyes: one pair so blue, the other hazel-bronze.
And it's as if they are in deep South India again, sweet breezes riffle the calm ocean sending skipping surf, sussurupting sounds of water and sand twirling and retreating, the singing stars of Shivarathri gradually calling, responding; calling, responding.

Mike and Grace settle still as the planters on the garden terrace high above Bangaluru's twenty-four hour agitation as tech capital. Each breathing into their own hearts, knowing now the heart is the doorway to divine love within. After the intense practice sitting in darshan at Baba's, and so filled with the energy poured freely upon them, their bodies have learned to hold still without aches, itches or squirming.

Heads are erect, shoulders relaxed down, spines straight, as they watch the process of breath coming in and going out, flowing in, flowing out like the majestic sea. Time passes without counting as they sit unmoving, blessed by deepness.

Breathing stops,

no longer necessary to support the stilled body,

Light becomes the lifeline now.
The sacred Kundalini completes its circuit,

the energy of Light flow up the spine over the head,
enlightening the pathway within,
so full are they with the darshan energy.

Meditation runs its path.
Neither aware of the background: the place, the sounds,
the very air they sit embracing them,

Activity stops as they enter eternity –
without moving a foot.

A few pollution clouds race above as if at play with the waves of energy.
The moon inexorably pulling liquid of their souls
drop by drop into the Ineffable.

At the peak of the meditation, God-energy comes to the crown.
Like molten gold, brighter, blazing, shining.

Millions and millions of lights, soft:

The Kiss of God.

CHAPTER 12, After Words

If you discover the inner spring of joy, you will be – happy, content, peaceful and loving.
Sathya Sai Baba

With the sunrise, Grace stirs slightly, then memory awakens within from deep meditation: breathing returns. She comes back into her body, inhaling and firming her boundaries so merged in meditation with the air, garden and fountain flowing fresh water. Gratitude fills every pore, an overwhelming notion of gratefulness, the highest emotion humans can perceive of the angelic emotions. She breaths in thankfulness, wills herself jelling into Grace, happy, peaceful, loving.

Taking time now as if existed, to anchor herself to this body, Grace watches a inner smile play on her face. She opens her eyes to find Mike breathing regularly a few paces away. They turn as one to focus out to the sea of Bangaluru's monumental buildings, then to each other, careful the first thing they look at after meditation not be another person. Too many beings have been caught in time and relationship when filled with love from the spirit. Thinking the other person causes such enormous well being instead only the first thing their eyes lit upon after communion with the Whole.

She and Mike surrender deeply to the Love Divine, a love in the fourth dimension. Their human bodies now fueled by this communion with the Eternal, plugging into cosmic energy, their atoms recharged. It was the way they want it to be from now on. Deeply loving but not attached.

"As always, we have been tenderly watched over. No drowning in bliss this time."

Mike smiles, stretches. "You are right, Gracie, we remember it's the inner life for us, we are part of the new normal. I am glad we made our way to India together. Otherwise I would still be a jerk and you would be – what? Your adorable self, my dear. But do you have any idea where I can get a decent breakfast? Do you think Mataji will let us come inside now that we have made up? We have made up, right?"

"So you say Mike. Made up but everything's changed. Thanks to you." The light in her eyes radiates with peace.

"Hold on, you know as well as I do, this whole Indian saga has all the earmarks of the

Divine Play of the Author of Creation. The only author-ity."

"Let's be clear, Mike, I'm still going back home. By myself. To the job. New York, my life. I have things to do, a life to live now that I am not burdened by my past. All the kripa I've been given. . . It's inside me now. If I've learned one thing it's that everything is within – God, the past, my mind, you. I have to find out if you are a projection or we really have something together. I know I have to integrate this grace into my life – which has to mean, return to the city. Plant a garden. Help others. Be active at church. I have to live inside out now."

"Good! And I'm staying to peel and chop vegetables at my new job in the Western Canteen if they will have me, for the same reasons, even if I would not say it your way. OK? I have this golden opportunity to recover and extend my soul, I'm staying."

Grace exhales slowly, "So we are friends then?"

Mike rises from his cushion, comes over to the couch, taking Grace's hand. "At the least, friends. A good place for us. At this moment, let's just say, what? Spiritual companions, partners in glory. But I don't think the story's quite over, do you?" He raises her now well-tanned hand to kiss.

Then, he's laughing with sweetness, "didn't you tell me you are married to Baba, but I come in there somehow."

Grace nods, "Yes, you do. Yet I am going back home."

"Cara, my own, my heart, go back to New York but remember this, please, the heart knows no distance."

Sharada Devi opens the terrace French window, they scramble up just ahead of the incoming tide of her force. "Breakfast. How about some Chai as you leave the mountaintop. It will take you down the other side of the mountain, on to doing your work. Otherwise why explore the inner Himalayas?"

Grace muses as she and Mike walk along companionably into the apartment, how they learned to adjust and integrate the changes that define their relationship from the early seemingly sexual pull to the intensity of God-passion. They've been through a rock tumbler. Yet she knows she's not what's called 'realized' still just Grace walking her path one step at a time. Now meditation in Union with all that is created, having merged

214

with creation and the glory of that big love, draws them beyond the seeming hungers of the flesh. Correspondingly as their love intensifies, the desire for physical passion changes, transforming into perfected love. She's not enlightened but hopefully now she can love Mike, and others, trusting herself. Grace says to Mike as they stroll onto the silken carpet inside, "It's possible to deeply love people and still not be fed as we are during meditation," then practical, "Besides, we will text."

"Yes, always in touch. We've seen a lot of short-term pairing, perhaps the time has come at last when men and women can become one. Leaving conquest and the battle sexual behind for realized love. Still, woman, I like my food, what about eating breakfast together? India is a feast of life."

Sushil looks up from his idlis, "Did you see the garudas circling overhead? Auspicious!"

"They are like us," Grace muses to Mike as they gaze awed at the circling golden birds. "Our hearts are our homes, we carry India where ever we are, go. What a gift, to have a gypsy heart. Allowing memories to range back and forth, and be at peace with those memories in this life. Even the ones we weave now, pulsing with the richness of design. Like that mandala we saw on MahaShivaratri, one hundred thousand lights of prayers. "

Mike turns his face into the wind, listening attentively, watching the free flight. Grace calls to the birds. "Feast on your life. Jai Prema Sai."

Whether one believes in a religion or not, and whether one believes in rebirth or not, there isn't anyone who doesn't appreciate kindness and compassion - The Dalai Lama

ACKNOWLEDGMENTS

Dear Readers, Thank you. The author of this novel believes she has written it, but we know better. She did type, research and spell check it and all errors are her own. But, we played our parts, enjoying the process especially when she was thinking she came up with our story. We wish you very well. Love, Mike and Kripa McCall, Sydney, Australia

Besides the fictional Mike and Grace, I wish to thank and acknowledge the help, encouragement and patience of the following: Hilda Charlton, who mentored me into writing and for her permission always to quote her. The Rabindranath Tagore people who sent a gracious letter confirming use of extensive quotes from the *Poems of Kabir*, as the copyright has long ago expired. The kindness and patience of the staff at Ramana Maharshi and Sri Aurobindo ashrams and Yogi Ram Surat Kumar. For the life and blessing of Sri Sathya Sai Baba and Prema Sai. For Meg Lundstrom, who twice now has given titles for my books, the ticket to India for research for this book well as permission to use her photograph of One Hundred Thousand Butter Lights. For early reader Becky Nielson, who suggested more Mike; for Rick Jarow for the Manifestation Café and Choosing the Work You Love workshops, for reading a draft and looking over the Sanskrit terms. For Lyn Burnstine for her love of Shrunk & White. For those who helped with the blurb and kindness: Georganna Dillon, Valerie Meluskey, Deborah Medenbach, James Judge, Steve Drago and Elizabeth Hepburn. For my son Andrei, and his sister, for Lilly and Alex. For Allen Verter. For Alison Quin. For the wikies even though they are as flawed as I am. For the writers group Wild Plums; for writing companions Phylliss Rosen, Kate Weston and Nancy Owen for hours and hours of listening to the novel and encouragement. For the New Paltz Monday Writing group for sustaining the inspiration. None of them are responsible for the content, but I do blame Mike and Gracie. With love, Garnette

ABOUT THE AUTHOR

Garnette Arledge received a Bachelor of Science degree, in journalism, from the University of Maryland, and a Master of Divinity degree from Drew Theological Seminary. A spiritual director, award-winning journalist and author Garnette Arledge teaches writing to groups and individuals in the mid-Hudson River Valley, New York. Recently published non-fiction books include: *Wise Secrets of Aloha* on Lomilomi; *On Angel's Eve,* supporting friends and families based on her work as a Hospice Chaplain, and her first book, *Blessings Hilda* as well as Creativity & Spirituality interviews in *Sacred Journey* magazine. Pending publication are two novels: *Night of the Mothers* and *Medieval Cloister* plus a three-act play, *Butterfly Women: Spiritual Guides.* Her roots are originally from Western North Carolina

Books available by Garnette Arledge

Wise Secrets of Aloha, Learn and Live the Sacred Art of Lomilomi, 2007, Weiser Books.

Kahuna Harry Jim, Keeper of the Deep Mysteries, shares to Garnette Arledge, author, for the first time ever in print, the healing secrets of Lomilomi. He teaches the techniques that open us to healing in body and spirit. Lomilomi is an esoteric healing tradition with four basic techniques.

"This is a lovely book that raises the vibration of the reader and imparts both knowledge and wisdom about the traditional Hawaiian practice of Lomilomi, and about Hawaiian thought and spirituality in general. It will appeal to all seekers who look to the ancients for current day techniques and inspiration to realize goals of health and happiness – Charlotte Berney, author of Fundamentals of Hawaiian Mysticism.

On Angel's Eve, meaningful things you can do to provide comfort, support and cceptance, 2004, Square One Publishers.

On Angel's Eve begins by exploring your understanding of dying and death, addressing the importance of building a support team, and providing the tools you need to improve your communication skills. The author then offers spiritual support by showing how four major religions and philosophies – Christianity, Judaism, Buddhism and Hinduism – provide healing perspectives on dying with grace. Finally, the author suggests activities that help make the most of your shared time together. Whether you create a video or recording of your loved one, fill the room with much loved music, or use the calming power of touch therapy, you'll find that you can both dispel the fear of death and create lasting memories of love, laughter and forgiveness. Throughout the book, inspirational true-life stories, timeless poetry, and invaluable personal insights highlight the meaning of your Angel's Eve while providing comfort and support. When you realize you can be one of the angels, this precious time becomes blessed by meaning, purpose, and peace.

Blessings Hilda, a private interview on spirituality and creativity, available soon in e-book, second printing, 1985, Singing Stars.

14883022R00119

Made in the USA
Charleston, SC
06 October 2012